PENGUIN BOOKS
WIND FLOWERS

V. Abdulla was born in 1921 in Tikkodi near Kozhikode. His father, B. Poker Sahib, was a distinguished lawyer and Member of the Constituent Assembly and of the Lok Sabha. After graduating MA and BL, Abdulla joined Orient Longman, from where he retired as divisional director in charge of publication. For a time he was an Executive Member of the Kerala Sangit Natak Akademi. Both before and after retirement he used to write regularly in English for the *Hindu* and *Frontline* and in Malayalam for *Mathrubhumi*. He published many books of translations from Malayalam into English, mainly in the area of prose fiction and including novels and stories by M.T. Vasudevan Nair, S.K. Pottekkat, Malayattoor Ramakrishnan, N.P. Mohamed and Vaikom Muhammad Basheer. In 1998 he received the Yatra Award. He produced two films in Malayalam, *Ammaye Kaanaan* and *Adyakiranangal*. For many years he lived in Chennai. He passed away on 16 May 2003 at Kannur, Kerala, after a brief illness.

R.E. Asher is Professor Emeritus of Linguistics at the University of Edinburgh, where in addition to his teaching and research appointment he also held senior administrative posts. He has published books on the literature of the French Renaissance (the field of the first of his two doctorates), on the history of linguistics, and on contemporary Malayalam literature, grammars of Tamil and Malayalam, and translations of five Malayalam novels. He is editor-in-chief of the prestigious ten-volume *Encyclopedia of Language and Linguistics* (1994) and of the *Atlas of the World's Languages* (1994). In 1983 he was elected Fellow of the Kerala Sahitya Akademi and in 2000 was appointed member of the General Council of the Tamil Sahitya Academy, Chennai. In Kerala he is particularly associated with the work of Vaikom Muhammad Basheer and Thakazhi Sivasankara Pillai, both of whom became close personal friends. Asher was born in 1926 in the small village of Gringley-on-the-Hill, Nottinghamshire, England.

Wind Flowers
Contemporary Malayalam Short Fiction

Edited by V. Abdulla and R.E. Asher

PENGUIN BOOKS

PENGUIN BOOKS
Published by the Penguin Group
Penguin Books India Pvt. Ltd, 11 Community Centre, Panchsheel Park, New Delhi 110 017, India
Penguin Group (USA) Inc., 375 Hudson Street, New York, New York 10014, USA
Penguin Group (Canada), 10 Alcorn Avenue, Toronto, Ontario, Canada M4V 3B2 (a division of Pearson Penguin Canada Inc.)
Penguin Books Ltd, 80 Strand, London WC2R 0RL, England
Penguin Ireland, 25 St Stephen's Green, Dublin 2, Ireland (a division of Penguin Books Ltd)
Penguin Group (Australia), 250 Camberwell Road, Camberwell, Victoria 3124, Australia (a division of Pearson Australia Group Pty Ltd)
Penguin Group (NZ), cnr Airborne and Rosedale Roads, Albany, Auckland 1310, New Zealand (a division of Pearson New Zealand Ltd)
Penguin Group (South Africa) (Pty) Ltd, 24 Sturdee Avenue, Rosebank, Johannesburg 2196, South Africa

Penguin Books Ltd, Registered Offices: 80 Strand, London WC2R 0RL, England

First published by Penguin Books India 2004

10 9 8 7 6 5 4 3 2 1

Typeset by R. Ajith Kumar, New Delhi

Printed at Saurabh Printers Pvt. Ltd, Noida

Dedicated to
the memory of V. Abdulla,
the principal architect of this volume

Copyright Acknowledgements

The editors and the publishers gratefully acknowledge the following for permission to reprint copyright material:

B. Saraswathy for 'The Packet of Rice' by Karoor Neelakanta Pillai;

Anees Basheer for 'Mother' from *Poovan Banana and Other Stories* by Vaikom Muhammad Basheer, translated by V. Abdulla, Disha Books, and for 'Anal Haq' by Vaikom Muhammad Basheer, translated by R.E. Asher;

Stree for 'The Goddess of Revenge' from *Cast Me Out if You Will: Stories and Memoirs* by Lalithambika Antherjanam, translated by Gita Krishnankutty. Original Malayalam text © Saritha Varma, this English translation © Gita Krishnankutty, published by Stree, Kolkata, 1998;

P. Kamalakshy Amma for 'In the Floods' by Thakazhi Sivasankara Pillai;

Sumitra Jayaprakash for 'The Night Queen' by S.K. Pottekkat;

N.P. Mohamed for 'The Bull' by N.P. Mohamed;

T. Padmanabhan and A.J. Thomas for 'The Death of Makhan Singh' by T. Padmanabhan, translated by A.J. Thomas;

C.V. Sreeraman for 'The Razor's Edge' by C.V. Sreeraman;

O.V. Vijayan for 'After the Hanging' and 'Wind Flowers' from *Selected Fiction* by O.V. Vijayan, Penguin Books India, 1998;

Kamala Das for 'A Colony of Hermaphrodites' by Kamala Das from *Kalakaumudi*, 1983;

M.T. Vasudevan Nair for 'Oppol' and 'Sherlock' by M.T. Vasudevan Nair;

The Centers for South and Southeast Asian Studies Publications, University of Michigan for 'The Bathroom' by M. Mukundan, translated by Donald R. Davis, Jr;

Anand for 'The Sixth Finger' by Anand;

Affiliated East-West Press Pvt. Ltd for 'Bhaskara Pattelar and My Life' from *Bhaskara Pattelar and Other Stories* by Paul Zacharia, 1994;

Sarah Joseph for 'The Scooter' by Sarah Joseph, published by Current Books, Trissur, 1989;

N.S. Madhavan for 'Fear of Pulayas' by N.S. Madhavan from *Mathrubhumi Weekly*, 1999.

Contents

Introduction

In distant parts of the world, Kerala is known as a region of great natural beauty, and as the home of the unique combination of poetry, drama, music, dance and mime that is Kathakali. There is less awareness of its thousand-year-old literature or of the extraordinarily flourishing state of its literature in the modern age. Though the number of speakers of the language of 96 per cent of Kerala's population is not large by today's standards, the potential readership for any book is considerable by virtue of the fact that Kerala has long enjoyed by some margin the highest level of literacy in South Asia, among members of both sexes and in rural and urban parts alike—a possible factor in the success of authors of the present and preceding century.

Prose fiction in Malayalam began, as in the case of most of the major modern languages of India, in the last quarter of the nineteenth century. The earliest significant work was the social novel *Indulekha* (1889) of O. Chandu Menon (1847–99). This was followed soon after by *Marthanda Varma* (1891), the first of a series of historical novels by C.V. Raman Pillai (1858–1922). Short stories began to appear at approximately the same time, from the pen of a number of writers born in the 1860s and 1870s, who aimed to add variety to the material contained in the growing number of periodicals that followed the widespread use of printing and developments in education. None of these earliest short stories is remembered outside scholarly circles. Their importance lay in developing an appetite for short fiction, rather than in the display of any marked aesthetic sense.

The century that followed these earlier efforts was to see many important developments, including a move away from a simple temporally organized sequencing of events, and increase in psychological complexity in the depicting of both character and emotions, a more subtle presentation of background and setting, and a more sophisticated theory of the nature and purpose of fiction. Theorists and practitioners—with the two occasionally being combined in one person—argued vigorously about the legitimate aims of a novelist or short story writer.

In the theorizing there were inevitably changes of fashion, with the result that Malayalam literary historians have been able to see the twentieth century as being divided into a number of periods as far as prose fiction is concerned. The first of these periods is one in which there was a minimum of influence from outside the Malayalam literary world—though clearly, in spite of the age-old tradition of storytelling, both oral and written, in all parts of India, there was some outside impact in the very establishment of the novel as an art form. Indeed, the introduction to Chandu Menon's *Indulekha* explains that one of his objectives in writing it was 'a desire . . . to try whether I should be able to create a taste amongst my Malayalee readers, not conversant with English, for that class of literature represented in the English language by novels.' We can be sure that the same motivation applied in the case of some of the first authors of shorter fiction.

However, it was not until the 1930s that there was a widespread acknowledgement in literary circles of lessons that might be learnt from external models. A major influence here was Balakrishnan Pillai, the radical editor of the journal *Kesari*, who encouraged younger writers to become acquainted with the work of the great European novelists and short story writers, in particular those of the French realist and naturalist schools and their Russian contemporaries, whose works were available in English translation. Along with ideas on creative technique, these young writers imbibed notions, from Zola among others, of the need for a writer to display social commitment. Such notions were strengthened by an acquaintance with political and scientific writings from abroad, notably those produced by Karl Marx, Charles Darwin and Sigmund Freud. No less important were ideas and ideals from nearer home, as contained in the writings of Gandhi and Tagore.

This was the generation of Kesava Dev (1904–83), Thakazhi

Sivasankara Pillai (1912–99) and Vaikom Muhammad Basheer (1908–94) with Dev being the most committed to the espousal of left-wing views in his fictional writings, and Basheer the least. Indeed, it is virtually impossible to point to a piece of overt political or social commentary in Basheer's creative work, though there can be no doubt of his interest in social reform. In the same age group was S.K. Pottekkat (1913–82) who, though a very different writer from Basheer, was like him in displaying little by way of explicit ideological commitment.

Coinciding with the early post-Independence period, there was a general fading of the belief that prose fiction should have as one of its goals the promulgation of ideas on the reform and restructuring of society. It is easier, however, to characterize what the modern novel and short story in Malayalam are not than what they are. New elements manifesting themselves in prose fiction may be identified in the work of a given writer, such as the lyricism that is evident in the novels of M.T. Vasudevan Nair (b. 1933) and others, but it is impossible to point to this or any other element as being generalized across the whole spectrum of prose. If it is difficult to define in any simplistic terms the modern short story in Malayalam, then identifying what is postmodern is bound to be no less problematic. What can be said, however, is that among the best writers there is a great willingness to experiment, in matters of choice of subject, treatment of selected theme, psychological examination of character, style and language. It is this willingness to avoid the slavish following of the elements of success in the great writers of the past that gives one confidence in the future of the Malayalam short story.

Generalizations that might be proposed in respect of the century-old history of the Malayalam short story can thus indicate no more than tendencies at a given moment in time. This is firstly because not all gifted writers necessarily followed what in retrospect may appear to have been a dominant trend, but also because in the work of a given writer there will be developments over time. In addition to this simple fact, it is also the case that some writers are very versatile, while others occasionally produce a story that is strikingly different from what is commonly deemed to be representative of their work.

Our aim in putting together this collection has therefore not been that of illustrating a view of the history and progress of the short story in Malayalam. Nor have we attempted to select the story most representative of a given author. Nor, because of limitations of space, do we claim to have provided an example of the work of every short story writer who has made a lasting impact. The selection is a personal one intended to give an idea of the enormous range of themes, settings, treatments and styles that are to be found in the best of the short fiction written in the language. Of the writers selected, some have made their reputation primarily in the realm of the short story, some are known above all as novelists, while others have shown themselves to be equally at home in the shorter and the longer forms.

Our writers can be seen as falling into two distinct groups, the first being those who were active both before and after the dawn of political independence, and the second those whose careers are confined to the post-Independence period. Of the latter group, members of one set were born within a short period of four years, from 1929 to 1933. In spite of the enormous variety of theme and style that is to be found in Malayalam short fiction over its century-old history—often within the work of a single writer—it may be possible to detect certain similarities within each of the three sets, and for this reason we have arranged the stories chronologically.

Only one was born in the nineteenth century—Karoor Neelakanta Pillai (1898–1975), the first major figure in the history of the short story in Malayalam and a prolific writer of stories marked by a careful observation of human nature and a keen sense of the frequent presence of pathos in human interactions. Like Vaikom Muhammad Basheer, his junior by ten years, he is known for his delicate touch. Humour, too, is a frequent element in the narratives of both, though it is with

Basheer that this characteristic is particularly associated, even in stories where the prevailing atmosphere is one of gloom. Yet no one sentence can sum up Basheer, so great is his range. One of the stories by which he is represented here is in its central characteristic unique in his output, while the other belongs to a group of several, mainly autobiographical, stories based on his experiences as an active participant in the harsh world of the freedom movement. Almost his exact contemporary is Lalithambika Antherjanam (1909–87), the first of many truly great women writers of Kerala. Author of one fine novel, *Agnisaakshi* (Fire for witness, 1976), she produced many short stories that, in common with those of many writers of her time, were often concerned with implied criticism of aspects of social structure and behaviour, particularly those that disadvantaged women of her own community of Namboodiri Brahmins. She was also a poet and writer of books for children. Thakazhi Sivasankara Pillai was one of the firmest adherents of the socially committed approach to the writing of fiction, but there is much more to his many novels and numerous short stories than this. His best-known novel outside India, *Chemmiin* (Shrimps, 1956), is a love story set among the fishing community of the coastline near his home. His longest and, for many critics, his greatest work, *Kayar* (Coir, 1978), is a saga recounting the life of a village over many generations. This, like many of his stories, including the one in this volume, is located in Kuttanad, where he lived most of his life. The last of this group, S.K. Pottekkat, though very much a man of the left and for some time a Communist Member of Parliament, was, as we have already noted, somewhat less concerned in his creative writing with issues of social reform. Successful in a number of different genres, he showed in his novels and shorter fictional pieces a strong concern for local colour, a tendency that one might wish to relate to the fact that he remains Kerala's most accomplished writers of travelogues.

N.P. Mohamed (b. 1929), too, the first of our chronologically central group, has a travelogue to his credit and has an even wider range, having published novels, short story collections, books of critical studies and children's literature. As with Basheer, his stories are often peopled by members of Kerala's Muslim community, and like Basheer he shows a special understanding of human mental processes. T. Padmanabhan (b. 1931), who, like Thakazhi Sivasankara Pillai, began his professional life as a lawyer, is more of a specialist in the short story. A leading member of the generation that moved clearly away from a concentration on social or political issues, he nevertheless is far from lacking concern for human suffering and unhappiness. He is a master of the lyrical style and his work is full of penetrating observation of the inner motivation of human actions. C.V. Sreeraman (b. 1931), too, has devoted his energies to the shorter fictional genre. Using what is, superficially at least, the simplest of prose styles, he has a special gift for portraying the sadness of life. O.V. Vijayan (b. 1931), in some ways the most inventive of living Malayalam writers, made an enormous impact with his imaginative *Khasaakkinte itihaasam* (The legends of Khasak, 1969), whose success has been repeated by two later novels. In these, as in his many short stories, he shows himself a master of prose style. This is paralleled by his subtle use of English, and he has translated a number of his own works. In addition to enjoying an enviable reputation in the English-speaking world for her poetry, Kamala Das (b. 1932) has published several novels and many short stories in Malayalam under the name of Madhavikutty and is known as a strongly feminist writer. For much of her earlier years she lived in the metropolitan centres of Calcutta and Bombay, but is very well acquainted with both urban and rural life in Kerala. In more than 200 stories she has portrayed all aspects and conditions of the life of girls and women in her home state as well as other parts of India. M.T. Vasudevan Nair, very successful as a novelist, shows himself in both novel and short story a master of creating atmosphere, whether his chosen setting is Kerala or farther afield—say in Kashmir. Most usually his stories are placed in the region he knows best, and one of his achievements has been the skilful depiction of the effect of social developments on family life, especially among the Nair community. Anand, the name under which P. Sachidanandan (b. 1936) writes, has turned Malayalam prose fiction in new directions, both in his treatment of current social topics and in his development of an individual style which has the effect of seeming to extend the range of Malayalam syntax.

Our last group of writers were all born in the 1940s, and all their experience of life has therefore been that of citizens of an independent India. M. Mukundan (b. 1942) has among his fictional compositions a novel about the independence struggle as it related to the movement to free the French enclaves in the subcontinent, in this case Mahé. Some of his stories seem to enquire into the very nature of human existence. Paul Zacharia (b. 1945) is well known both as a creative writer and as a political commentator. His fictional output includes not only short stories but also longer pieces of the novella type—illustrated here by 'Bhaskara Pattelar and My Life', which has been turned into a film under the title *Vidheyan* (The servile) by one of India's great directors, Adoor Gopalakrishnan. Often his characters are from Kerala's Christian communities, but seen from a very personal point of view. An academic who is also a political activist, Sarah Joseph (b. 1946) is even more vigorous a campaigner in her stories for the liberation of the oppressed members of society than were, say, Kesava Dev and Thakazhi, but where the downtrodden for them were poorly paid and cruelly exploited manual workers from the lowest castes, for her they are made up by the female half. Like them, she avoids making her stories into political tracts, in her case partly through her understanding of the subconscious mind. N.S. Madhavan (b. 1948) shares with T. Padmanabhan a reputation for significant innovations in narrative technique, a reputation that began with the publication of his first story in 1970. His themes may be relatively commonplace, but their treatment is far from this, with the unexpected being what his readers have learnt to anticipate.

*

The prime mover in this project was V. Abdulla, widely known for his skilful translations of many of the greatest pieces of fiction that have been written in Malayalam and for his sensitive evaluation of the work of his favourite authors. Sadly he passed away while work on the volume was in progress. I should like to express my feelings of deep appreciation and indebtedness to him for his kindness in inviting me to participate in this venture. Corresponding with him about it and eventually discussing it with him at his home in Chennai have been a privilege and a source of real pleasure.

Our grateful thanks are due to the translators who have contributed to this volume, including those who have translated their own stories. We are especially indebted to Gita Krishnankutty, one of the most accomplished of modern translators from the Malayalam into English. Contact with members of the editorial staff of Penguin (India), mainly by electronic correspondence but on one occasion in person in London, have been wholly pleasurable throughout the project. My own personal sense of gratitude to those writers, almost half of those included in the book, who have given time to discuss both literature and life with me, is immeasurable, especially to those who over forty years of visits to western India granted me the privilege of their friendship.

23 July 2004   R.E. Asher

The Packet of Rice

Pothiccooru

Karoor Neelakanta Pillai

'Sir, the rice this child had kept here is not to be found,' said the teacher of the second standard to the head teacher.

The head teacher stopped writing, raised his head and looked up. He saw fresh tears rolling down the channels they had already made on the child's cheeks. He sat for a minute, gazing at the tender, famished face.

'Where had you kept the rice?' asked the manager of the school. The child said, amid his tears, 'In that room.'

The class teacher explained, 'He kept it where he always leaves it. Another child in his group had kept his in the same place and that packet was there.'

'Did you search everywhere? Isn't it anywhere?'

The child: 'I looked all over. It wasn't anywhere.'

The teacher: 'Didn't you look for it as soon as class was over?' 'I did.'

The teacher: 'This is really shameful! It's very distressing if children come to school just to steal food!'

The head teacher comforted the child. 'Let all the children come. I'll question them. I'll find out who it is. And make sure no one does such a thing again. Don't cry, child. If you're hungry, take your books and go home.'

The teacher: 'Will you go alone?'

The child: 'I don't want to go now.'

'Then go and sit down in class,' said the head teacher. The child obeyed.

The class teacher discussed the incident for quite a while

longer and requested the head teacher to take it up seriously.

The head teacher agreed to everything.

The bell announcing the end of the afternoon recess rang. The mentors who, to get over their tiredness, had stretched out and gone to sleep on the benches that had emptied when the children went out got up, rubbed their eyes and sat down in their places. The children who had been running around playing in the schoolyard, ignoring their hunger and the hot sun, came back to the classrooms, perspiring profusely. The benches filled with the fortunate ones who had come back after partaking of their kanji or rice and the unfortunate ones who had come to school knowing full well that nothing had been cooked at home that day. The satisfied children who had eaten their packets of rice and the little ones who had drawn and drunk water from the neighbouring well to take the edge off their severe hunger sat down in their places. Among them was the child who had lost his packet of rice.

The story of the stolen rice spread through all the four classrooms in the school, filling them. Each child sent his guessing powers racing towards a number of other children.

'Sir, Balakrishnan says it was I who took the rice and ate it,' complained a child. He turned to the child who had accused him and said in the same breath, 'Thief, it's you who stole the rice and ate it! Thief!'

Gopalan said to Joseph, 'It must be Pappu who ate it up.'

Mathai said, 'I won't keep my rice here any more.'

This matter remained the topic of discussion among the children for a long time.

The teachers looked closely at the faces of the little ones seated before them to find out the thief.

The head teacher, who was in charge of the affairs of the school, began to walk around, stick in hand, pursuing the investigation. He tried all the levels of persuasion—kind words first, then serious questioning and finally force—but to no avail. He then counselled the children, 'Theft is a sin. You might be able to hide it from human eyes. But you can't hide anything from God. Stealing is an evil habit. If you do it without meaning to, you must confess and ask for forgiveness. Then I will forgive you. And God will forgive you as well. If you do something wrong and are able to hide it one time, you will want to do the same thing again. And you will thus become bad children. In the end, you will become thieves. Haven't you seen policemen catch thieves and take them away? You there, haven't you seen that? Is there anyone who hasn't seen that happen?'

The children: 'Yes, Sir.' 'No.' 'Yes.'

'Ah! That's what I said. Tell the truth.'

No one confessed to having done anything wrong.

The child who had lost his rice turned around to see whether anyone had confessed.

But no one had.

The head teacher then asked each of the children, 'Did you take it? Or you, or you? The next child. You?'

'No.'

'No.'

'No.'

'I went home for lunch.'

'I brought my food.'

'N . . . no.'

All the children denied having done such a thing.

The teacher asked around a hundred and eighty children individually. Then he gave up. He felt ashamed. His colleagues respected him. The children worshipped 'Fourth Class Sir', the teacher of the fourth standard; they feared him. The villagers were proud of him. The manager thought highly of him. The school inspector was satisfied with him.

The head teacher, who had been unsuccessful in his mission, sat down in his broken chair, his face dull and pale. He had no enthusiasm for anything. He made a mistake in a sum he did on the blackboard. When he taught geography, he refused to accept the right answers the children gave him. It was only when a colleague came and told him that it was past time—it was already ten minutes late—that he remembered to ring the bell announcing that school had ended for the day.

Everyone left. The man who swept the place waited to lock the building. The head teacher was writing and he kept writing until it was past dusk!

He finished writing and came out.

That night, as the manager was enjoying listening to the radio after dinner, he received this letter:

Respected Manager,

A theft took place in our school today. Someone took a packet of rice that a child had kept aside for his lunch and ate it up. It was shameful. Such a thing has never been heard to happen before. After all, it is thirty years since I came here. Today is the first time such a thing has taken place. If it was to steal, there are so many things in school that are more valuable than a packet of rice.

Someone who was hungry must have taken it. But there were so many more packets that had more rice in them than this one. If it were not a very small child who took it, his hunger would not have been satisfied. But would a little child do such a thing? Even if it was an older child, how unbearable his hunger must have been for him to eat up someone else's food! Children who had eaten something in the morning would never risk doing a thing like this. If a child had eaten nothing in the morning, his mother would have provided some food at least for his lunch. He would not have had to steal. If they had to starve morning and noon, mothers would not send the children to school—what if they collapsed on the way! A child might steal a slate or a pencil or a book. He might steal a mango or an orange. But to steal rice—and that too, without even knowing to whom the packet belonged— no, it is impossible to imagine that a child would do that. It is a terrible insult to look a child in the face and ask whether he stole rice. Among our teachers, there are some who eat nothing at noon. How could we imagine that they would do this? It was not the children. Or the teachers. And no strangers came here. Then who was it? I?

Yes, it was I.

It was I, who am in charge of running this school, who did this.

I, who am responsible for the intellectual welfare of around a hundred and eighty future citizens, for showing them the right and good way to live.

I, who control and direct five teachers who work with me.

I, who punish all the misdemeanours in this school, who must be a model to everyone.

It is I who have to shape the next generation and make them good people who stole the food meant for a child's lunch and ate it—a mean thing that only a dog would do.

You may feel not only contempt for me but anger as well. I might have brought disrepute to your school. You might be thinking that you will have to dismiss me from my post. None of these things seem very important to me. The face of that six-year-old child, pinched with hunger, his tears flowing because his rice was stolen, gives me pain.

Just try and imagine why I did this, the act of a dog. I would have done it earlier. It was not that I did not have reason to. I just did not, that's all. If my companions do not do what I did, it is not because they do not need to; it is because they are afraid of an evil reputation. I have gone beyond that. I happen to have been born; should I not somehow live? I have worked for thirty years and do you know how many people have to be cared for with the twelve rupees you give me? Why should you know, isn't it? No one need know.

But even if you do not want to know, all of you will one day.

Twelve rupees that have to last for thirty days for a family of eight—and in these times when everything is so expensive!

I have to be a model to the children. I have to govern a school. I have to work all the time on tasks that never end. I have to live a decent and respectable life.

I too have a mother and a father—who are old and incapable of working. I too have a wife and children—who are dependent on me. I too have desires and emotions—like you.

I took a child's rice and ate it up. Was I stealing? Perhaps I was. I tell you now frankly—after I had some kanji yesterday morning, I ate no food at all for twenty-eight hours. Exhausted with work, I thought I would collapse and fall down and I took the three or four mouthfuls of rice belonging to a child—never mind who it was—who must have had some food of some kind three hours earlier. Maybe it was wrong. Maybe it was a sin. When I go to the next world, maybe I will be forced to answer for it. Maybe I will have to answer for it in this world as well. I will do so.

But tell me this too: What else could I have done?

[*Translated by Gita Krishnankutty*]

Mother

Amma

Vaikom Muhammad Basheer

The mother writes to the son eking out his living amid the miseries of a distant city. She writes with pain in her heart.

'Son, I just want to see you.'

It didn't stop there. Many more words were strung together into sentences with no grammar and put down in a scrawling hand. And yet the sorrow in her heart is clear beyond doubt. It is a long time since they have seen each other.

The son knows that his mother is expecting him every day. But what can he do? He has no money to undertake the journey. Each day's living is a problem. Somehow I must leave tomorrow; I must go and see mother, so he consoles himself. But the days become weeks, the weeks turn into months and the months run into years.

The mother waits for the son every day.

I am saying this about my mother. Whatever I intend saying hereafter is about my mother. Every son would have similar things to say about his own mother in this India where we live. I am going to talk of the freedom struggle. It has no direct relationship with my mother. Except that I am the son of my mother. All over India there are mothers who have given birth to children like me. What did they do when their children were locked up in prison in the cause of the freedom of their motherland? The young women and men of India were persecuted and beaten up and had their bones broken by the lackeys of the foreign government. They were herded into prisons. What did their mothers in the thousands of homes outside do? I cannot say for certain. But I know well what my mother did.

I am jotting down what happened without any aim. When I read mother's letter some old memories come back to me. The story of how I went from Vaikom to Kozhikode to take part in the salt satyagraha.

I have to say something before I record that event. I am not revealing a secret when I say that I am writing this in 1938 or that India is still not free. I have however to reveal the secret that I received blows and was persecuted because of Gandhiji. Anyhow, if my mother had not given birth to me none of this would have happened. My mother would not have suffered any mental agony because of me. Why did my mother bring me into this land of slavery and poverty and untold misery? Perhaps this question is being asked of all mothers in India by their sons and daughters. Or else this question must be lying unasked in the minds of men and women. Why is India so poor? I cannot say with pride, 'I am an Indian.' I am but a slave. I detest the enslaved country that is India. But . . . is not India also my mother? Just as the mother who gave birth to me has expectations of me, does not India also expect something from me? The earth of India expects to receive my dead body just as my mother expects to see my living one.

Expectations!

I remember.

My mother gave birth to me. She fed me at her breast and brought me up. She made a man of me. Mother says I was born out of her longing. 'You were born to me after fond expectation and yearning.' Every mother says this to her offspring. I cannot record here the feelings that fill my heart. Like the chains that bind my hands, I see before me police lock-up rooms, prisons, gallows and in front of them policemen, soldiers, jailors!

'India is a vast prison with high walls that confine the mind and body!' Gandhiji said this. I do not know when. I remember well the beating I received because of Gandhiji. I was beaten by a Brahmin called Venkateshwara Iyer. He was the headmaster of the Vaikom English High School. Seven sharp blows with a cane. That was during the days of the Vaikom satyagraha.

There was much excitement and commotion in the town because Gandhiji was coming.

There were large crowds on the banks of the canal and at the boat jetty. I pushed through the crowds with other students and reached the front line. We saw Gandhiji in the boat at a distance. A roar as if from the sea rose from a thousand throats. It rose like a challenge to foreign rule, 'Mahatma . . . Gandhi . . . *ki* . . . *jai!*'

The half-naked fakir bared his gums from where two teeth were missing and smiled as he landed at the jetty with hands folded in salutation. There was a great deal of noise all round. He got into an open car. The car moved forward slowly through the crowd, heading for the Satyagraha Ashram. A number of students hung on to the side of the car. I was among them. In all that confusion I had one wish! To touch the Mahatma, beloved of the world! I felt I would drop dead unless I touched him. Suppose someone among the hundreds of thousands of people there saw me? I was frightened and anxious. I shut out everything and lightly touched Gandhiji on the left shoulder!

No one knew of that.

That evening when I went home I told my mother with pride, 'Umma, I touched Gandhi.'

My mother, who had no idea of the nature of this thing called Gandhi, trembled in fright and consternation. 'Oh . . . my son . . .!' said mother, looking at me open-mouthed.

I remember.

Our headmaster was against satyagraha. He was against Gandhiji also. So he had prohibited the students from wearing rough homespun khadi. He had also ordered that they should not visit the ashram.

I wore khadi those days, and went to the ashram. One day, as I entered the class, the headmaster called me. He said with cruel laughter, 'My! Look at his clothes!'

I said nothing. Again he asked me, 'You rascal, has your father ever worn this?'

I said, 'No.'

One day I went into the class some three minutes after the bell had rung. He was standing on the veranda with a cane. When he asked why I was late, I replied that I had gone to the ashram.

'Who have you got there?' He stood erect and gave me six blows on my palm with the cane.

'Don't go there again! Understand, you rascal?' He gave me one more blow on the back.

But I went again.

I remember.

In those days I owned one khadi shirt and one khadi dhoti. Just one shirt and one dhoti. At that time khadi was a symbol of protest. I swore that I would not wear foreign cloth. I would say that if I died I should be buried wrapped in khadi cloth.

Mother would ask, 'Where did you get this coarse cloth which itches?' She believed that khadi next to the skin would make you itch!

I would say, 'This cloth is made in our own land, in India.'

And so—Gandhiji, the Ali brothers, self-government, British domination—these were the topics of conversation.

The old men in our town had only two youngsters whom they could ask to clear their doubts about England or China. One was Mr K.R. Narayanan. The indefatigable Mr Narayanan was the special correspondent of most of the newspapers. And if anyone asked me any question on any topic I hardly ever said, 'I don't know.' But once I was stumped for an answer.

Mother asked, 'Well, will this Kanthi put an end to our starvation?'

It was a big problem. It affected the entire country. I knew nothing about it. But I said, 'When India becomes free, our starvation will end!'

The year was 1930. I think it was that year that Gandhiji sent from the Sabarmati Ashram his letter containing his famous eleven-point programme to the Viceroy, Lord Irwin. I think it was a young Englishman named Reynolds who took the letter.

But no satisfactory reply was received. As mentioned in the letter, Gandhiji started his programme of satyagraha. Gandhiji set out with seventy followers to the sea near Dandi to break the salt laws. The British government had levied a tax even on salt used by the millions of poor in the country. Before starting on the Dandi march, which shook the entire country, Gandhiji announced, 'Either I shall return to the ashram after having succeeded in achieving our demands or my body will be found floating on the Arabian Sea.'

Gandhiji to die? The question echoed from the Himalaya to Kanyakumari and the whole country was in seething turmoil. The British government used all its power to oppose the unarmed Indians. The military, the police, jails—the government was only these. Gandhiji and his followers were arrested on the seashore near Dandi.

Like other parts of the country, Kerala was also agitated. The people who broke the salt laws on the seashore at Kozhikode were treated brutally under instructions from the police superintendent. They were kicked by heavy booted feet and beaten with lathis. And that too at the hands of Indian soldiers and policemen!

Kelappan, Muhammed Abdur Rahiman and other leaders were arrested. More people flouted the laws and there were more arrests. And police violence. The most heart-rending, however, was the treatment meted out to the students on Kozhikode beach. Students so young! The future citizens of Kerala. They were beaten and felled to the ground by the policemen. Hundreds of students lay on the beach at Kozhikode bleeding, with heads broken. This is a statement made by one of the leaders, published in the *Mathrubhumi:*

That policemen should have raised their hands and beaten up the poor students who had gathered on Kozhikode beach to do their duty by their motherland! They were mere boys, unarmed and innocent. Their heads and their arms and legs were broken by policemen who claim to be born of Malayalee women! When I find that the so-called men of status and wealth in this town remain silent about such goings-on, why should I blame the ignorant policemen who blindly obey the orders of their superior officers?

Those were days when men of status kept silent. But the common man was not silent. Men and women marched in protest, singing songs of defiance.

I went too. Without asking anyone. I gave up my studies and went to Kozhikode with a companion named Bavo. Bavo took a gold ornament from his house. We sold it at Vaikom. That evening my mother was cooking in the kitchen. Mother knew nothing. I asked for a glass of water from my mother as a kind of farewell. I drank it, looked at her and left.

We were afraid someone would follow us. We got off at Ernakulam and walked to the Edapalli railway station. It was dark, well past sunset. The train was very late. Then some policemen came in. We were trembling in fear. They called each person and questioned him. We pretended to be asleep. One of them jabbed me in the belly with a lathi and called me. He shone a light in my face and asked, 'Where are you going, you rascal?'

What was I to say? I was afraid to tell him that I was going to Kozhikode to join the Congress. I lied, 'I'm going to Shoranur.'

'Why?'

One more lie. 'My uncle has a tea shop there.'

Luckily he did not ask any more questions. They were in search of a thief. We bought tickets to Shoranur, got off there, walked up to Pattambi and again took the train to Kozhikode. There we stayed at the Al-Ameen Lodge. The first thing I did was write to a person who had come from near my village: Syed Mohamed, who was then in Bellary Jail. I wrote to him saying that I had made up my mind to dedicate myself to the service of the motherland. I would use all my powers to break the chain of slavery which bound her. I would court arrest immediately.

He replied, 'I have just a few more days left. Then I will be released. You may join the Congress only after we meet and talk.' He was at that time the joint editor of the newspaper *Al-Ameen* and an important leader. He, along with E. Moidu Moulavi and others, had received a severe beating from the superintendent of police, Amu. I did not have the patience to wait till his return. India was going to be free the next day; I must also have a part in fighting for that freedom! Many who belonged to my religion had not joined the freedom struggle. I had to redress that imbalance.

But my companion did not wish to join the Congress. He tried in many ways to dissuade me. His father came down and abused me a great deal for inducing his son to run away from home. I gathered that the incident had caused a great commotion back home. I felt despondent. It was not I who had run away from home with his son. But no one would believe me, for I was older. I was in a sad plight. At that time my father also came. Again I lied. 'I'm not joining the Congress. Nor am I going back to school. I'm looking for a job. I'll get it soon.' I managed to soothe my father's feelings and send him back. I then went straight to the Congress office. There again I was to be disappointed. They suspected I was in the pay of the CID! Their doubts were strengthened by my diary. I had jotted down things in it in different languages—English, Malayalam, Tamil, Hindi and Arabic. I had left it on a bench while I went to the toilet. When I returned I found that the secretary had picked it up and was reading it. He could not have understood much of it. But it gave him reason to doubt me. I showed him Syed Mohamed's letter. Even then his doubts were not cleared. They tried to assess me from my appearance and my general demeanour. Photographs of national leaders hung on the walls of the office. I saw the picture of a man with a thin moustache on his upper lip and a look of quiet dignity. He wore a felt hat at a rakish angle and a white shirt with broad collars. I felt contemptuous of this leader dressed in foreign clothes and I asked who it was.

The secretary said, 'Bhagat Singh.'

My heart missed a beat when I heard that. The great

adventurous Bhagat Singh! He had not been hanged then. I had read in the papers about the three revolutionaries involved in the Punjab Conspiracy case—Bhagat Singh, Rajguru and Sukhdev. I had heard of their attempts to throw a bomb in the Assembly and to blow up the Viceroy's train. I looked at the photograph intently. The secretary said, 'You have Bhagat Singh's features. Your moustache and shirt collar are identical. All you need is a felt hat!'

I said nothing. I too was thinking of the similarity of features between Bhagat Singh and myself. The secretary again asked me, 'Are you really a Muslim?'

I said, 'Why do you doubt that?' I told him my life story until then. Finally he asked me, 'Are you ready to go to the beach tomorrow and make salt?'

'Ready!' I agreed.

And so we got up early the next morning. We were getting ready to start with the mud pots and flags and other things when we heard a thud–thud on the stairs. We were surprised to see some six or seven policemen walking in with an inspector in charge. All eleven of us were arrested and taken away.

That was a Sunday morning. None of us had eaten anything. I was weak with loss of sleep. A crowd followed us. When we reached the police station all my courage evaporated. It was my first visit to such a place. Swords, bayonets and handcuffs hung from the wall and gleamed balefully at me. I was thoroughly intimidated by the shining weapons and the cruel faces of the policemen. The place reminded me of my conception of hell.

We were lined up on the veranda. The inspector with the narrow grey eyes went in. A hefty policeman with long arms marched up and down in front of us. His bulging red eyes looked at each of us in turn. His number was 270. He caught hold of our volunteer captain by the neck and pushed him into the office room. We heard the sounds of blows and kicks and loud cries. I trembled. I was standing fourth in row. Ten minutes later the second man was taken in.

I shivered as I heard his heart-rending cries. I decided I would ask for pardon. But only for a minute. For again I thought to myself, why ask for pardon? I have done no wrong. How many young men and women have courted death in the cause of freedom. I thought of Bhagat Singh and his comrades. Let me die. It is my duty!

Constable No. 270 was asking each one of us where we came from. The others replied, 'Kannur. Talassery. Ponnani.'

He asked me, 'Yours?'

I said, 'Vaikom!'

Vaikom. He looked at me with surprise. 'Name?'

I gave my name. No. 270 raised his head and asked me, 'Does Thiruvithancoor have self-government?'

I replied, 'No. Gandhiji has said there need not be any struggle in the Indian states.'

'Hmm,' he grunted fiercely. Phut–phut! Two violent blows fell on the nape of my neck! Then he caught me by the shoulders and made me bend down. He began beating me. It sounded as if he were beating upon a copper pot. I counted up to seventeen, or perhaps it was twenty-seven. After this, I stopped counting. Why keep count?

Badly beaten up, I was finally escorted inside with the help of two policemen. Seeing the state I was in, the inspector asked, 'Hmm?'

A policeman said, 'Nambiar had a small go—'

The inspector grunted as if it was nothing, 'Hmm.'

Another policeman took off my shirt and other clothing and called out my height, girth and identifying marks.

Finally the eleven of us were sent to the lock-up.

It was a small cemented room. In the corner was a pot full of urine giving out a powerful stench. We did not get any food that day. The night was extremely chilly. There were no mats to lie on. In the morning all our faces were bloated. We could hardly walk. We were handcuffed and made to walk through the bazaar to the court with a police escort carrying bayonets.

We were remanded for fourteen days and sent to the Kozhikode Sub-jail. There, my companions later told me, when

No. 270 got tired of hitting me with his closed fist he used his folded elbows on me. One volunteer massaged me with oil. He told me that there were nine places, each the size of a rupee coin, where blood had congealed and where the oil had no effect.

I received nine months' rigorous imprisonment. I was taken to Kannur Central Jail. There were six hundred political prisoners there, including T. Prakasam and Batliwala.

The food in the jail was very bad. In the rice gruel they served us, there would appear a floating layer of worms. We removed these before eating it. We had news of the outside world only when new prisoners came in. When we learnt that Bhagat Singh and his comrades had been hanged, we went on a three-day hunger strike.

There were prisoners there from all parts of India. There were people of different ideologies—revolutionaries, anarchists, socialists and communists. However, all of them had one objective in common: freedom for India. After some months we were released as a result of the Gandhi–Irwin Pact. I did not know where to go. There were many volunteers like me. Most of us did not even have a railway pass.

I had two wishes. One was to possess a shawl. Mr Achuthan bought me a khadi shawl with a grapevine border. However, my very first wish was to kill No. 270! But I had no weapons. If only I could get a revolver! I longed for one. I saw him standing on traffic duty at Palayam junction. A demon of a man six foot tall. If I hit him with bare hands he would hardly feel it. I must stab him in the chest with a knife! I stole a pen-knife from Al-Ameen Lodge. As I was taking it away, I saw Mr Achuthan. He was surprised to see me.

'Haven't you gone yet?'

I said, 'No.'

'Don't you want to go home and see your father and mother?'

I said, 'I have something to do before that.' I told him everything. He led me to a place near Mananchira tank, speaking to me very gently. 'Are you a satyagrahi?' He told me the story of how Gandhiji lost his two front teeth. 'And if you want to kill, remember there is not a single policeman who deserves to live. The policeman is an indispensable part of the government. The poor creatures are mere instruments. What is the use of blaming them? Have patience. Go and see your father and mother.'

Mr Achuthan put me on the train. At Ernakulam I stayed for a month at the Muslim Hostel. I was filled with disappointment, sorrow and unwillingness! Finally one night I reached Vaikom. From there I walked to Thalayolaparambu. It was past midnight, about three in the morning. At home, when I entered the yard my mother asked, 'Who is it?' I stepped on to the veranda. Mother lit a lamp, and asked as if nothing had happened, 'Son, have you eaten anything?'

I said nothing. I was shaken, unable to breathe. The whole world was asleep! My mother alone was awake! Mother brought a vessel of water and asked me to wash my hands and feet. Then she placed a plate of rice before me.

She asked me nothing.

I was amazed. 'How did you know, Umma, that I was coming today?'

Mother replied, 'Oh . . . I cook rice and wait every night.'

It was a simple statement. Every night I did not turn up, but mother had kept awake waiting for me.

The years have passed. Many things have happened.

But mothers still wait for their sons.

'Son, I just want to see you . . .'

[*Translated by V. Abdulla*]

Anal Haq

Analhakh

Vaikom Muhammad Basheer

According to legend, when the government and the religious leaders who went along with it murdered Mansur al-Hallaj, dismembered and burnt his body and threw the remains into the Euphrates, then, like a raging ocean, the river with a mighty roar produced the words 'Anal haq! Anal haq!'—words that Mansur had been in the habit of using. The story of Mansur's life is one that arouses terrifying fear. In the history of the world thousands of such incidents are recorded in the name of every religion. Mansur's principal fault was his habit of uttering these words. The sense of the expression is the same as 'aham brahmasmi', or 'I am the Truth'. It was as if Mansur had been saying that he was God. Had Mansur really made such a claim? Even if he had, what wrong did he do? It could have been dismissed as the ravings of a madman. Yet Mansur was not a madman. He was a Sufi who believed in the divine spirit of man. What he said was on a par with a drop of water in an ocean claiming to be the ocean or a grain of sand on a mountain claiming to be the mountain. He may have meant that there is a touch of the divine in everything; nevertheless, what he said had this fearful and bloody consequence.

It was in an age that was hostile to the development of ideas—some time after Hijra, at the beginning of the fourth century. Men of science, religious leaders, poets and artists prostrated themselves before dissolute rulers and were no more than sycophants. The Persian kingdom was immersed in the intoxication of wine, the fragrance of roses and the embraces of courtesans. It was at such a time that Mansur al-Hallaj was born. He grew up in the tranquil environment of the small village of Baida, far from the royal palace and its empty show. Thoughtful and enquiring as a boy, Mansur al-Hallaj, having passed over the threshold of youth, succeeded in gaining entry into a renowned centre of learning in Tushtar, a nearby town. He became exceptionally proficient in metaphysics, religion, politics, literature and the like, and yet when he left, Mansur was a very dissatisfied scholar. He felt that he was ignorant—that he had learnt nothing. He had an insatiable thirst for enlightenment, a burning desire to know and to understand. Yet in his ignorance he was groping in the dark. Dejected, he wandered around despairingly as a fakir in search of a ray of light. It was while in this state that he met Umar ibn Usman. His ashram seemed to Mansur like an oasis in the middle of a desert. The guru pointed out to him a new way—Sufism.

The blazing glory of spiritual knowledge! Filled with a primeval longing, Mansur plunged with the speed of a tempest into this source of enlightenment. Like a speck of cloud he merged with the boundless and eternal light. Deep in meditation and filled with passion, he called out, 'Anal haq! Anal haq!'

I am eternal Truth! I am Creation and the Creator!

Eternal Truth! The ashram shook. Thunderstruck, the guru and his disciples stared in terror at Mansur. What a pronouncement! The fearful utterance 'Anal haq' had demolished the whole edifice of centuries-old human belief. They consoled themselves with the notion that Mansur had lost his mind. But in the end the guru advised him, 'Mansur, it is sinful to regard the Creator and the created in this way as one and the same. It is a violation of social and religious law. Do you not know that the penalty for transgressing the Sharia is death?'

The penalty of death!

Mansur forgot all that and returned with zeal to what had preoccupied him. Fearing that the ashram would be destroyed, the guru expelled him. Mansur was abused and chased by a mob that stoned him as if he was suffering from a contagious disease. Knowing that without a refuge he could not remain in Basra, Mansur resumed his wanderings. He sought sanctuary in many hermitages. Finally he reached Baghdad. There the renowned and distinguished Sufi scholar Hazrat Junayd welcomed the fugitive Mansur with a smile and gave him shelter. However, he also gently advised him to keep his opinions to himself. Mansur was stunned by the thought that there was not a single place on earth where one could breathe the refreshing air of freedom. Nevertheless, he established himself there. Feeling inspired in their company, he involved himself in philosophical debates with the great man's disciples. Everything developed in the usual manner. With sorrow in his voice, Hazrat Junayd warned him, 'Mansur! Beware! A fateful day is approaching. Beware of that final day when the white sand on the banks of the Euphrates is tinged red with your blood . . .'

'That final day!' Mansur gave his reply. 'I do not fear it. But you, dear master, will have to step down from your position of eminence, throw off the dervish's attire and stoop to being simply an executor of the law. You too should beware. Anal haq!'

So the story continued.

With myriad events many pages of history were turned. Mansur came out into the open. Temples, marketplaces, open grounds—all reverberated with his inspired preaching. People were captivated by his new vision of the divine. It represented a violent storm in the world of ideas. In it were heard the drumbeats of a revolution. Religious leaders were filled with consternation. The number of eyes secretly watching the now very famous Mansur increased. Rumours were spread around that he was an apostate, an atheist. There were plots to kill Mansur. It was in these circumstances that he travelled all over the country and wrote books. With all his suffering, in those five years he composed forty-seven treatises. Because of the government ban on the circulation of these works, they became very widely disseminated. Some poets and intellectuals did not fail to praise Mansur, spreading his renown through the whole kingdom by calling him a great poet and supreme philosopher.

Powerless, the sultan's government was alarmed at these developments. The opposition of the theologians intensified. Thus it was that Mansur found himself having to contend with two powerful enemies—authority and tradition. To weaken his position they promised him high offices of state. Religious bodies invited Mansur to participate in a debate on the issues. Confronting a large assembly of religious leaders in Baghdad, Mansur said, 'Man's ideas are not to be confined within a fortress. They will break free of the bonds binding them to the earth and spread heavenwards in countless directions. My ideals and beliefs cannot fall in with your commands. It is better therefore not to think of me as belonging to your flock.'

The blazing eyes of thousands of priests turned towards Mansur. Moved by uncontrollable wrath, one of them rose from the assembly, grabbed Mansur, threw him to the floor and gave him a severe beating. The rest of the priests gathered round Mansur like a flock of vultures and formulated a fatwa against him: 'Mansur, having violated the Sharia, has become a kafir. As a result he merits the penalty of death . . .'

Without a word of opposition, a thousand ulemas put their name to the fatwa. The minister in Baghdad, Hamid ibn Abbas, too, added his support to the charge. Only Sultan Muktadirbillah refused. He was adamant that he would not add his signature to any chargesheet that had not been agreed by Hazrat Junayd. So a delegation of the religious leaders went to Hazrat Junayd's sanctuary. Six times they returned disappointed. Finally, the caliph himself ordered him to send an answer saying unambiguously 'yes' or 'no'. Filled with anguish, he tore off his ascetic's robes, donned those of a lawmaker and signed the fatwa. His eyes filled with tears, Hazrat Junayd wrote on it with a trembling hand, 'In terms of the laws of society, Mansur is liable to be sentenced to death. However, if it is on the basis of truth, only God can decide.'

But it is with the laws of society that power rests!

Wooden fetters were put on Mansur's wrists and he was taken to the banks of the Euphrates. There he was tied to a wooden cross and subjected to all kinds of torture. When finally he was incarcerated, he preached from behind the bars of the prison. Large crowds gathered there every day. Statements proclaiming Mansur's innocence began to circulate. The ulemas visited him in prison. When the news of this reached the sultan, he reacted in this way: 'If we continue to hold Mansur in prison, it will cause problems for the state. For the sake of public well-being it is a matter of urgent necessity that he be executed. If he causes unrest by saying "Anal haq", beat it out of him. Mansur must be put to death this very day . . .'

The twenty-ninth day of Dhulkada, Hijra 304, is a day that history shudders to remember.

On that day they brought Mansur from jail. Before a multitudinous throng, the death sentence was read out for all to hear. Mansur smiled and let out the joyful cry, 'Anal haq! Anal haq!'

Then more than three hundred blows fell on his back. They stripped him and made him stand in the blazing sun. Little by little his back swelled up, cracked and bled. Frenzied shouts came from the crowd. Mansur was led to the scaffold.

'Taking a brave man to the gallows is like opening to him the gates of heaven.' Mansur embraced the scaffold. His executioners made ready. Mansur was saying his last prayer. Then stones whizzed through the air and struck his body. The frenzied mob roared.

'Chop off all his limbs!'

The executioners carried out the command.

Mansur smiled as he said, 'It is easy to destroy my arms which are but flesh.'

Next they chopped off both his legs. He fell face down into the pool of blood. His executioners lifted him up.

'Let not my pale face look upon the world.'

His two fearless eyes shone brightly. Immediately they took a dagger and gouged out both of them.

The mob roared, 'Tear out the kafir's tongue and cut it in pieces.'

Mansur begged them to hold off a little. 'I have one last thing to say.'

Raising his unseeing eyes heavenward, Mansur uttered this dying prayer, 'O ultimate object of my innermost desire, let not my tormentors be deprived of their happy outcome! Anal haq!'

At once an old woman came forward and, having pulled out his tongue and sliced it off, spat into his face before cutting the tongue into pieces.

Finally, Mansur's proud head, severed from his body, fell on to the sand that was seeped with his blood. Even then the fury of the mob was unsatiated.

According to legend, they hacked Mansur's body into thousands of pieces, gathered them all together, threw them on a huge funeral pyre they had built and set fire to it. Watching the flames, they laughed boisterously. Finally, they pulverized the ashes and cast them in the river.

And then—!

The hitherto peacefully flowing waters of the Euphrates suddenly became violent and bloody. The natural order of things was suspended, as thundering mountainous waves rolled by like a tempestuous and mighty ocean. As if to bring terror to the whole of creation, the Euphrates let out a dreadful and terrifying roar, 'Anal haq! Anal haq!'

*

Author's note

I wrote this forty years ago. We are now in the year 1982. I believe that it is presumptuous for man, who is only one of God's creations, to say 'Anal haq!' or 'Aham brahmasmi'. The story of Mansur is not based on historical fact. The whole thing can be treated as mere fantasy: anal haq.

[*Translated by R.E. Asher*]

The Goddess of Revenge

Praticaradevatha

Lalithambika Antherjanam

It was nearly midnight. I was alone in the room where I usually did all my writing. The compassionate Goddess of Sleep stood by me, waiting to enfold in her caress the wounds that my spirit had accumulated in the course of the day's hard work. But I knew that if I threw down the pen and paper I had taken up to write my story, I would not be able to touch them again till the same time tomorrow, when the usual obstacles would again present themselves. I sat there wrapped in thought. Silence lay deep around me, interrupted now and then by the sounds of two rats engaged in love talk in the attic above or the snores of the children sleeping in the next room. The light from the lamp on the table crept out through the window and cast fearful shadows on to the thick darkness outside. The hooting of the many owl families that were my neighbours sounded like a warning in my ears. I must confess: I am a coward by nature. Especially at this deceptive hour of the night.

I closed and bolted the window and raised the wick of the lamp. I checked whether any of the children were awake or whimpering, then came back to my usual place. I had to finish writing today, come what may, but what was I going to write about? How was I to begin? Now that I had sat down to write, all the attendant problems rose up to confront me. Writing stories is not a pleasant task especially for a woman like me, for whom status and prestige and a sense of being high-born are all-important. When fictional characters come to life and argue heatedly about contemporary issues, the author has to face opposition from many quarters. If an opponent were to use the weapon of obscene language against me, would I be able to defend myself with a like weapon? And then, the subject of caste distinctions was taboo, and religious controversies were to be avoided at all costs. Indeed, we have arrived at a point when writers have perforce to consider well in advance which particular literary theorist's recriminations they would have to face. It was all very distressing. I suddenly wanted to give it all up.

Filled with an obscure sense of anger, I threw my pen on to the table, and closed my eyes. Innumerable characters passed through my mind as I sat there: people I had seen and not seen, people who were alive and who were dead. Women and men. Creatures tormented by pain, those who had lost their voices, though their throbbing hearts thudded like thunderclouds, flashed like lightning. Were they demanding to be transcribed? I was afraid, but also inspired. Suddenly, I heard the sound of footsteps coming towards me from the next room.

What could it mean? I sat up, startled. I had closed the door, bolted it securely and locked it. And I had not even heard it being pushed open. It was midnight. Although I did not believe in ghosts, I trembled in fear. My head began to spin. My eyes closed tight. The footsteps grew firmer and firmer. Someone came and actually stood next to me, but I could not move.

The seconds ticked by. Did five minutes pass, or a whole hour? I couldn't say. Time stopped for a long while. Then I heard a woman's voice, just in front of me, a firm yet fine and delicately modulated voice. 'Are you asleep? Or afraid?' she asked.

I remained very still. I did not have the strength to move anyway. Her voice went on, its sweetness tinged with a shade of mockery, 'When I heard that you wrote stories, I did not imagine that you would be such a coward. After all, a good writer usually has to witness so many scenes of agony and terror.'

The eagerness to know the identity of this person, who knew so much about me, drove my fear away. I opened my eyes. In front of me, the figure of a woman took shape from the surrounding texture of a dream. A woman . . . not a young girl. Not bold or proud. Not old either. All I can say is that she seemed a wonderful manifestation of meaning itself. Sorrow, a certain austerity, disgust, disappointment, all struggled to find expression in her face. The sparks of an intense fire burned fearfully in her eyes—I recognized the emotion as from the leaves of some forgotten book from the distant past. She went on in a voice powerful yet tender, 'I've come with a purpose. I know you are looking for a story to write, but cannot find one. I have a first-class story, which is going to waste for want of someone to use it. If you agree . . . if you can listen to it without being terrified . . .'

I had mustered my courage by now. 'It's true that I panicked. But that's because of the time and the circumstance. Please, for heaven's sake, tell me who you are and how you got here at this time of the night through a locked door.'

'Who am I?' She burst out laughing. 'So you want to know who I am, do you? Whether I'm a human being or an evil spirit, a ghost or a witch. What amazing courage!'

She laughed out loud again, sounding like a forest stream that breaks its banks and overflows. Her laughter thudded against the walls of the room. But this time I did not wince.

'I confess that I am a coward,' I said. 'But how can I have anything to do with you unless I know who you are? Human beings come to know the very stars in the sky by giving them names and positions of their own.'

'Human beings? For heaven's sake, don't count me among them, sister,' she interrupted, looking displeased. 'There was a time when I loved to be known as a human being, when I expended my greatest efforts on staying as one. But I have learnt—and taught others—that I never want to be called a human again, and particularly not a woman. To be human, how deceitful it is, how cruel, what an experience of agony!'

'Maybe you are right,' I admitted. 'But pain and agony are gifts that are granted only to human beings. They are links in a divine chain of gold.'

She shook her head and prevented me from going on. 'Stop this foolish raving: "divine", "gold". What melodious descriptions! A "chain of gold" indeed! Let me ask you what advantage gold chains have over iron ones if they are meant to be fetters? Only this: that iron shows its true colours. And gold? What a glitter! A mere coating. God! What does it prove but the difference between a human being and a demon?'

Her face, which was full of hatred for her fellow beings, seemed transformed into something non-human. I could not be certain whether her expression signified sorrow, hatred, pride or revenge, but I found it a singularly attractive mixture of all these emotions, and my eyes were riveted on her. What deep despair, what grief this life must have borne!

'So you're waiting to hear my story,' she continued, after a short silence. 'All right, I've come for that anyway. It's an old story. It happened more than fifty years ago, and it is a true story, one that shook the world to its foundations when it happened. You had not been born then, neither had your social organizations, with their penchant for debate, nor their leaders. And yet the turmoil that this story created over a great part of Kerala still continues. Some of the characters who figured in it may still be alive. Have you heard of Tatri?'

Oh, oh, so this was she. I drew back sharply in fear. This was the woman whose name our mothers had forbidden us even to utter, the very memory of whose name awakened horror. This was—oh, what could I say?

She smiled with evident delight at my distress. 'Yes, yes, you're thinking, which Namboodiri woman has not heard of that unfortunate creature, aren't you? No one says so in so many words. But everyone knows. But, look, child! Do you know for whom, for what that ill-fated person sacrificed her life? She too was a pure and untainted young woman once, like all of you. She wove chains of sacred karuka grass. She recited her prayers with a holy thread in her hands. She performed all the ritual fasts. She was as meek as a doll; after the age of ten she never looked at a man's face or spoke to him. Grandmothers advised young girls who had reached puberty to learn from Tatri's shining example. But you and I know that all this is part of an outward show. By the time we are seventeen or eighteen, we acquire an amazing capacity to keep our feelings under control. As we sit in the veranda by the light of the new moon, chanting our prayers, we hold the sighs that rise in our hearts in ourselves; no one ever hears them. Singing the *Parvathi swayamvaram*, the *Mangalayathira* and other auspicious wedding songs, moving our feet in time to their rhythm, we learn to control the trembling in our throats. Yet, do we not listen to the sound of men's footsteps from the living room? Even while struggling with the prickly, exasperating kuvalam flowers, our hearts are full of the fragrance of mango blossoms. And we wait. Not just days and months, but years. Till at last one day our mothers come to us with henna and a silver ring. Whether our hands are placed in those of an old man or a young one, a sick man or a libertine is all a matter of destiny. We can do nothing but endure.

'People told me that I had been singled out for a very special destiny. I was his first wife. And he was not an old man either. He had enough to live on at home. So I started married life with a boundless sense of happiness. He was a passionate man. I nurtured my desires to suit his. I did my utmost to satisfy him in bed, with the same attention with which I prepared food to please his palate. After all, a husband is considered a god. It was to give pleasure to this god that I learnt a harlot's ways, those talents that were to become so notorious later. It was he who taught them to me. If only it had been otherwise, my sister! If I too had become a meek wife, ignored by her husband, like countless women in our society, I wonder whether this cursed incident would have been blown so out of proportion. I don't know. Maybe the intoxication of physical pleasure crept insidiously into my mind and lingered there as a fragrance. But he was the only person enclosed within that fragrance, I swear it. That is why I was so upset when we began to drift apart gradually. He began to stay away from home for many nights in succession. Occasionally, it was to perform a religious rite or to attend a temple festival. He would stay in rich princely homes then. When we met, more and more rarely, I would weep before him, find fault with him. To whom could I unburden my sorrows, except to him?

'He would laugh, indifferent to the pleas of a broken heart. Man is free. He lives for pleasure. Just because he was married— to an uninteresting Namboodiri woman—it did not mean that he had to waste his youth on her.

'Anger and fury sharpened within me. I wanted to batter myself; I wanted to die. I even cursed myself for having been born. Why had I been born a Namboodiri woman? Couldn't I have been born into some other caste in Kerala, some caste that would have given me the right to pay this arrogant man back in his own coin?

'And yet, on every birthday of his, I bathed and prayed for a long and happy married life. I offered ghee lamps and garlands of thumba flowers in the temple. All I wanted now was to see him sometimes so that I could fill my eyes with his presence. Just as when I had reached puberty I had begun to pray for a husband, I longed now for my husband's love.

'Thanks to the generosity of our karyasthan we did not starve. But emotions and sensations have their own hunger, don't they? Greed. Thirst. Once brought to life, they cannot be quelled. They creep into the bloodstream, into the veins; they melt in them and simmer there. That was what happened to him too. But then, he was a man and I a woman, a woman born into a cursed society.

'Like all antharjanams, I too endured, kept my feelings in check, and carried on. It happened, without any warning: one evening, he came home with his new wife. They slept in the very room where I had slept with him. I did not mind serving food to that harlot. But though I had read Shilavathi's story a hundred times, making their bed was—Although I was a Namboodiri woman, I was a human being too. Maybe I had accused her of being a prostitute. Maybe I had cursed her for being a slut and harlot. This was the first time I thought of men as monsters, the first time my husband became a murderer in my eyes. I could have borne the torture for myself. But when he, my husband, used the same words—"I brought her home deliberately, knowing she's a harlot. I like harlots. Why don't you become one yourself?"—what a cruel blow that was.

'Even to think of it petrifies me. Imagine a husband telling his chaste, high-born wife, a woman who worships him, "If you want me to love you, you must become a prostitute." An irrational, uncontrollable desire for revenge took hold of me. But only for an instant. My faith stood in the way. "No, I can't remain here, even for a single day."

'After that I never spoke to him again. I never spoke to anyone. The days went by somehow, empty of events, empty of love. If only something would move in this hell of darkness! I went back to the house where I was born, my heart full of limitless grief, a burden of sorrow that it could hardly bear. I thought I would find comfort and relief at home but I was wrong. In truth, are not all Namboodiri households a kind of prison? There is little to choose between them. My father was dead, but all his five wives were still alive. My elder brother was looking for a wife to replace his fourth one, who had just died. Two of my elder sisters, both widowed, were living at home. The third one had gone mad because her Namboodiri husband had tortured her, and she wandered about here and there. Two unmarried younger sisters had become a burden on the house, a continual source of worry to their mother. I joined them, going from the frying pan into the fire. Amid such grief, who would not long for whatever comfort society permitted? I was still young. My body bloomed with health. I knew I could afford the arrogance of being certain that I was more beautiful than the prostitutes who kept my husband company. And yet, when I combed my hair, placed the bright red sinduram between my eyebrows and peered out through the barred door, all I felt was a desire to see the world, or, at most, an innocent longing that someone should notice how beautiful I was. There were men who met my eyes, returned my smile. After all, people tend to smile if you smile at them. It soon became a habit. Were not those high-born Brahmins susceptible precisely because they knew I was a Namboodiri woman? They were aware of the consequences. But as long as nobody was aware of what they did, they indulged in the basest actions.

'Scandalous reports began to spread. And meaningful looks. I heard murmurs. The women's quarters turned into a fifth column. Amma cursed whenever she caught sight of me. "You sinner, born to ruin the family's honour! Why were you ever born in my womb?"

'My brother's wife said one day, "Tatri, don't come into the kitchen any more. I'd rather you didn't touch anything there."

'I did not understand the nature of the crime for which I was being punished. I had touched no man except my husband. I had not even dared to think of another man in that way. If I peered out of the window, if someone saw me and was attracted to me, how could that be my fault? But the world does not concern itself with such questions. My heart hardened as stones of mockery were hurled at me. My mind whirled with the fear of disgrace. Then suddenly I knew that I could take anything that came to me. I had reached a point where I could bear anything. Darkness surrounded me on all sides. My enemies hissed at me like poisonous serpents in a smoke-filled darkness. They stung me, bit me. To defend myself in this battle unto death, I had to become a poisonous serpent too. The desire for revenge and the hatred that had lain dormant within me blazed high. If I tell you about the decision they forced me into, you will draw back in fear. You will tremble and drive me out of here. Oh, my sister, what I did was as much for your sake as for mine. For the sake of all Namboodiri women who endure agonies. So that the world would realize that we too have our pride. I wanted to prove that we have strength and desire and life in us too. I delighted in the sorrow each man had to bear, for not a single tear shed by a Namboodiri woman has value. But alas, all of you, for whom I did this, despised me. My very name was uttered with disgust in my lifetime. I was feared more than a demon. Even in the fashionable world of today, Tatri remains despicable; even you look upon me as a fallen and disgraced woman.'

Her voice trembled at this point. Her eyes filled. Weighed down by an unbearable sadness, she put her head down on the table. Silently, without moving, I watched that personalization of hopelessness. The destiny of a woman like her, placed in such a situation, could take so many directions. If that broken life were to disintegrate completely, if its shattered remnants were to be scattered on the roadside like fragments of broken glass, surely it could not be her fault. Only the base tenets that had made her what she was could be blamed. For a Namboodiri woman who feels the heat of emotion, who feels proud to be alive, there is only one of two ways possible: she must go mad or fall from grace. Both ways are hard.

Maybe she had no tears left to shed. She sat up. A flame that would have burned up even the fires of hell blazed in her eyes.

'No, child! I will not cry any more. This is my last moment of weakness. I knew I would never be terrified again, not even if the seas swept over me or the skies fell down. Fear ceases to exist when life and death seem no different from each other. I had made my decision. If this was to be my ultimate destiny, I would transform it into an act of revenge. I would avenge my mothers, my sisters, countless women who had been weak and helpless. I laid my life, my soul, everything I possessed, at this sacrificial altar of revenge and sought the blessings of the gods. Let everyone see—and learn—that not only man but also woman could bring herself down to the lowest level. My capacity to err would have to be strong enough: if I were to be cast out of society, if I were going to be pushed aside, others who were mean and cruel were going to fall with me. I wanted people to learn a lesson. If there was true justice, would it not be necessary to cast out more Namboodiri men than woman?

'From that night onward, a new face was seen at all the temple festivals, the face of a fascinating courtesan. She was passionate and beautiful. But more than her loveliness, it was a bewitching air of shyness, a gentleness of nature, that attracted men to her. Princes, titled chiefs and many other well-known men crowded round her. I told them all that I was a married woman and not a prostitute. I told them I had a husband; I told them everything, offering them a chance to break free. The only thing I hid from them was that I was a Namboodiri woman. But the answer that they gave never varied: that bondage to a husband was not stipulated in this land of Parasurama, and that all women, except the Namboodiris, were free here. They could do what they liked. This was the pattern of their comforting excuses. Oh, the minds of these men, who pretended to be self-respecting, pure and saintly, even ascetic. If only men who insisted that their wives remain chaste did not deliberately seduce other men's wives.

'Would not a woman who was aware that so many were attracted to her succumb, finally, in spite of herself? Particularly one condemned to the inner rooms of a Namboodiri household, whom other women spat on and kicked? It was an age when the greed for flesh knew no bounds. The fame of this new harlot spread far and wide. Those who came to her went away gladdened. And she did not forget to persuade them to express their satisfaction through gifts. Thus the reputation of many who swaggered as honourable men of society came into the keeping of this prostitute.

'Only one man was left to come to me. The man I had waited for unceasingly. Surely, he would not fail to come when he heard of this beautiful, strong-willed woman, for he loved passionate encounters. It was five years since we had met. Although I recognized him when we met at the trysting place in the temple courtyard, he did not make me out. How could he have? How could anyone have guessed that this proud and confident woman, this jewel among prostitutes, was that humble Namboodiri wife of long ago?

'That was an unforgettable night. It was the night I had lived for, for so long, the night for which I had let myself be degraded. At least I was able to delight him for once. Ever since he had said to me, "Go and learn to be a prostitute", his command had lain simmering in my consciousness. If a woman who learns the ways of a prostitute in order to delight her husband can be considered chaste, I was another Shilavathi. I think it was a blissful night for him too. For, a little while before we parted, he said to me, "I have never been with anyone as intelligent and as beautiful as you. I wish I could always stay with you."

'He had trapped himself. As he slipped his ring on my finger, I asked, "Are you certain that you've never met anyone like me?"

'He lifted his sacred thread, held it high in his hand, and swore, "By this wealth I possess as a Brahmin, this symbol of caste, I have never seen a woman as passionate and as intelligent as you in all my life."

'A triumphant smile was on my lips. I raised my voice a little and said, "That's a lie. Remember your wife? Was she not as pleasing as I am?"

'Light dawned on him. Suddenly, he looked at my face and screamed, "Ayyo, my Vadakkunnathan! It is Tatri! Tatri!" Then he fled; I do not know where he went or when he stopped.

'The story is nearly over. You know what happened after that. The affair provoked a smartavicharam[1] that rocked Kerala to its very foundations. From great prince to high-born Brahmin, men trembled, terrified because they did not know whose names this harlot was going to betray. Some men ran away to escape. Others performed propitiatory rites, praying that she would forget their names during the cross-examination.

'One man's ring with his name engraved on it. Another's gold waist chain. Yet another's gold-bordered angavastram. The incriminating pieces of evidence were used to prove the guilt of sixty-five men, including vaidikans. I could have caused not just these sixty-five but sixty thousand men to be cast out of the community. And not I alone. In those days, any lovely and intelligent woman who practised this profession could have

---

[1] Trial convened to try an antharjanam who had, or was suspected of having, broken out of her isolation and formed a relationship with a man.

brought ruin upon entire families of landlords and wealthy aristocrats. And yet I did not go that far, even though I knew the power of a Namboodiri woman's curse. That historic trial had to end there. A long-standing grievance was assuaged. Was it simply an act of revenge performed by a prostitute? Or was it also the expression of the desire for revenge experienced by all Namboodiri women who are caught in the meshes of evil customs, who are tortured and made to suffer agonies? Tell me, sister! Who is more culpable, the man who seduces a woman in order to satisfy his lust or the woman who transgresses the dictates of society in an attempt to oppose him? Whom would you hate more? Whom would you cast out? Give me an answer at least now, after so many years have gone by.'

I had sat dazed, unable to utter a single word, while she recounted this extraordinary story. I was frozen, helpless. Remarking on my silence, she continued with an air of profound hopelessness, 'Perhaps I've made a mistake. Why did I come here today? Why did I try to talk to yet another of those antharjanams who were without shame or self-respect, another slave among slaves? They will never learn to improve their lot. Never.' Her voice trembled with anger and grief.

But I felt no anger towards her. I said to her softly, 'My poor sister! I am not trying to find fault with you. On the contrary, I have deep sympathy for you. Truly, you are not an individual any more; you are society itself. You are timidity and weakness weeping before strength, helpless womanhood screaming for justice, bloodstained humanity whose desires and talents have been ground into dust.

'How can the expression of irremediable hopelessness and helplessness be identified with your own? Consider, there is another side to all this. I have been thinking about it. Fired as you were with the intoxication of revenge, why did you not try to inspire all the other weak and slavish antharjanams? Why did you shoulder the burden of revenge all alone? In such matters, sister, individuals cannot triumph. On the other hand, they can bring disaster upon themselves. Consider, now, what good did that hurricane you set in motion do to society? Men began to torture antharjanams all the more, using that incident as a weapon. We are close now to bowing our heads once again under the same yoke. Not even the women in the families of the sixty-five who were cast out have been released from their agony.'

I too was shaken. I continued, my voice trembling, 'So, forgive me, Tatri sacrificed her very soul, but in the eyes of the world her sacrifice is remembered only as a legal affair involving a prostitute—an affair that certainly created a turmoil but did not succeed in pointing the way to anything positive. The end cannot justify the means, sister. Even while I recognize your courage and self-respect, I disagree with you. But Namboodiri society can never forget Tatri. From the heart of a great silence you managed to throw out an explosive, a brightly burning spark. It was a brave warning, a cry of victory. In the minds of the generations to come, this cry ignited a torch that still burns high and threatening. In its radiance, all the sins of that praticaradevatha, that Goddess of Revenge, are forgiven.'

I held out my hands to that woman's form in affection and sympathy. Its face paled. Its eyes grew lifeless. 'Oh, I am a sinner. A fallen woman. An evil spirit. Even my shadow must never fall over society.'

Continuing to talk, her form faded slowly, dissolving like the morning mist. The crowing of the cock woke me from my dream.

[*Translated by Gita Krishnankutty*]

In the Floods

Vellapokkathil

Thakazhi Sivasankara Pillai

The tallest building in the village is the temple. God stands there with water up to his neck. Water! Water everywhere! All the villagers have gone in search of dry land. Leaving one person to guard the house and the boat, if there is one. In the three rooms on the first floor of the two-storeyed building in the temple are sixty-seven children, three hundred and fifty-six adults and domestic animals like dogs, cats, goats and cows. All living in amity; no quarrels at all.

Chenna Parayan has been standing in the water a whole night and day. He does not have a boat. It's been three days since his master escaped with his life and reached dry land. When the water had begun to seep into the hut, he had fashioned a roof and a loft with twigs and palm branches. He had spent two days crouched in there, thinking the water would soon recede. Moreover there were four or five clusters of branches lying around and haystacks as well. If he went away, some able-bodied man would come and carry them off.

This makeshift roof and loft was now under knee-deep water. The two layers of thatch on the roof were submerged. Chennan called out from inside but who was there to hear? Who was there nearby? A pregnant Paraya woman, four children, a cat, a dog: all these creatures were dependent on him. He was sure it wouldn't even take fifteen hours for the hut to be entirely under water. He and his family were nearing their end. It was three days since the heavy rains had stopped. By dismantling the thatched roof, Chennan somehow managed to get out. He looked around. A boat made of planks fastened together with ropes was moving northwards. Chenna Parayan hooted as loud as he could to attract the boatmen's attention. Luckily the boatmen heard him. They turned the boat towards the hut. Chennan dragged out the children, the woman, the dog and the cat one after the other through the doorway of the hut. The boat had reached there by then.

Just as the children were getting into the boat, someone called, 'Chennacha phoo!' from the west. Chennan turned. 'Come here!' It was Madiyathara Kunheppan, calling from the top of his hut. Chennan pushed his woman into the boat hurriedly. The cat saw its chance and jumped in as well. No one remembered the dog. It kept walking along the slope of the roof on the western side, sniffing every now and then.

The boat moved; it went farther and farther away.

The dog came back to the top of the roof. Chennan's boat had moved into the distance; it was flying. The animal began to moan as if it were in death throes; waves of sound that resembled a helpless human voice emerged from it. Who was there to hear? It ran along all four sides of the roof, moaning, sniffing certain spots.

A frog seated peacefully on the roof was frightened by this unexpected commotion. It moved in front of the dog and jumped, dhudeem, into the water. The dog sprang back, terrified, and stood staring for a long time at the swirling water.

The animal kept sniffing here and there, perhaps in search of food. A frog jumped into the water, spraying urine into the dog's nostrils. The dog growled sharply, then sneezed, feeling intensely uncomfortable. It tossed its head and growled again and wiped its face with a fore leg.

Once again, a terrible storm began to rage. The dog endured it huddled up. By then, its master had reached Ambalapuzha.

It was night. An enormous crocodile floated along slowly, dragging the half-submerged hut along with it. Overwhelmed with fear, the dog lowered its tail and barked. The crocodile floated on as if it knew nothing of what was happening.

Crouched on top of the roof, the famished animal stared into the fearful darkness, blackened by rain-clouds, and moaned. Its pitiful cries reached out into the distance. The god of wind, stricken with compassion, rushed along bearing them. A handful of kind-hearted beings, aware of the responsibility of guarding a house, might have murmured, 'Ayyo, there's a dog moaning on top of that hut! Its master will be eating his evening meal now, on the seashore. He is sure to roll a ball of rice, as usual, and set it aside for the dog.'

The dog howled unceasingly at the top of its voice for a long time. Then its voice grew softer and died down. Somewhere in the north, a man watching over a house was seated inside it, reading the Ramayanam. The dog stood quietly, looking in that direction, as if listening to him. Then it moaned again for some time, its throat ready to break.

Once again the sweet voice reading the Ramayanam rose and spread through the total silence of that dark night. Our dog stood motionless for quite some time, listening attentively to that human voice. The sweet, serene voice dissolved into a cold gust of wind. Nothing could be heard after that except the roar of the wind and the babble of the waves.

Chennan's dog climbed on top of the roof, breathing heavily. From time to time it barked hopelessly. A fish darted through the water; the dog sprang up and barked at it. At another spot, a frog leaped and the dog growled uneasily.

Dawn came; the dog began to moan softly; it began to elaborate on a raga that would have easily melted any heart. The frogs stared at him; he watched them expressionlessly as they leaped through the water, slipping and sliding on its surface, plunging down sideways.

He looked longingly at the thatched huts visible above the water. They were all deserted. No fires burned in any of them. The dog snapped at the flies that were happily pecking at his body. Every now and then he scratched his chin with his hind legs to drive them away.

The sun appeared for a short while. He dozed in the mellow

sunshine. In the gentle breeze, the shadows of the banana leaves fluttered over the hut. He sprang up once and barked.

The cloud climbed up and the sun was hidden. The countryside turned dark. Carcasses floated on the water, bouncing on the waves. They wandered everywhere of their own free will and went ahead fearlessly. Our dog growled, looking greedily at them.

A small boat moved rapidly in the distance. He got up and wagged his tail, watching its movement carefully. It disappeared into the reeds.

It began to drizzle. Folding its hind legs, the dog dug in its fore legs and crouched low, gazing around. Its eyes reflected a look of utter helplessness that would have made anyone weep.

The rain stopped. A small boat came out of Vadakkeveetil and approached a coconut palm. Our dog wagged its tail, yawned and growled. The boatman climbed the palm, plucked a tender coconut and came down. Seated in the boat, he bored a hole in the coconut, drank the water, picked up the oars and started to row away.

A crow flew down from a branch and fell on the putrefying, dripping carcass of a buffalo. Chennan's dog barked greedily while the crow gnawed at the flesh, paying no attention to anyone. Satisfied, it flew away.

A parrot flew on to a banana palm neat the hut, perched on a leaf and screeched. The dog barked, full of distress. The bird also flew away.

An anthill that had come floating down on the floodwaters dashed against the hut. The ants escaped. It must be because he thought they were edible that our dog gave them a kiss. He hissed and sneezed as the soft flesh of his face reddened and swelled up.

In the afternoon, two men came that way in a boat. The dog barked gratefully and wagged its tail. It said all sorts of things in a language that resembled the human tongue. It got down into the water and made ready to jump into the boat. One of the men said, 'Look, there's a dog!' As if acknowledging the man's sympathy, the dog moaned thankfully. 'Let it stay there,' said the other man. The dog opened its mouth and closed it, making a noise as if sucking something to swallow; it prayed. It lunged forward twice to jump.

The boat had gone quite a distance. The dog moaned again. One of the boatmen turned to look at it.

'Ayyo!'

That was not the boatman. It was the dog's voice.

'Ayyo!'

The pitiful, heart-rending wail dissolved in the wind. There was only the ceaseless sound of the waves. No one turned back after that. The dog stood in the same position until the boat disappeared from view. Growling as if saying its last farewell to the world, it climbed to the top of the hut. It must have been telling itself that it would never care for a human being again.

It lapped up a lot of cold water. The poor animal gazed at the birds flying above. A water snake darted up, weaving its way through the water. The dog jumped up to the top of the roof. The snake glided in through the gap through which Chennan and his family had got out. The dog peered in through the crevice. Cruel creature that it had become, it began to bark. Then it muttered something. It was filled with fear for its life and with hunger. Anyone speaking any language, any visitor from Mars, would have understood its intention, so clearly did it speak.

It was night. A great cyclone set in, and rain. The roof swayed when the waves dashed against it. The dog stumbled twice and nearly fell. A long neck rose above the water. A crocodile. The dog began to bark in agony. A flock of hens could be heard, cackling in unison.

'Where's the dog that's barking? Haven't all the people here left?' A boat loaded with straw, coconuts and clusters of bananas appeared under the banana palm.

The dog turned towards the boatmen and barked. Furious, it raised it tail, stood by the water and barked. One of the boatmen climbed the banana palm.

'Ho, there! I think the dog's going to jump.'

The dog sprang forward. The man who had climbed the banana palm slipped and fell. The other man caught him and helped him into the boat. By this time, the dog swam to the top of the hut, and was standing there, shaking the water off its body, still barking angrily.

The thieves cut down all the bananas. 'We'll show you,' they said to the dog that was barking so hard that its throat was in danger of bursting. They loaded all the straw on to the boat. Finally, one of them climbed up to the roof. The dog bit his leg and tore out a mouthful of flesh. The man screamed, 'Ayyo!' and jumped into the boat. He gave the dog a thwack with the oar. 'Mew, mew, mew!' The dog's voice grew gradually softer and ended in a weak whimper. The man who had been bitten lay in the boat, crying. 'Shut up! If someone . . .' They drifted away.

After a long time, the dog looked at the place where the boat had disappeared and barked fiercely.

It was nearing midnight. A huge dead cow floated down and dashed against the hut. The dog watched it from above. It did not come down. The carcass moved forward slowly. The dog growled, tore at the thatch, wagged its tail. As the carcass began to move out of its reach, the dog crept down cautiously, pulled at it with its teeth and began to eat it with relish. Enough food to satisfy his fierce hunger!

Dhoom! A blow! The dog was no longer to be seen. The cow bounced up, went down again and floated away.

From that moment nothing could be heard except the roar of the cyclone, the splashing of the frogs and the sound of the waves. Everything was silent. The moans that had voiced the helplessness of that tender-hearted watchdog were heard no more. Rotting carcasses floated here and there on the water. A crow pecked at some of them. No sound disturbed its peace. No obstacles confronted the robbers in their job. Emptiness everywhere!

In a little while, the hut collapsed and was submerged. Nothing could be seen above the endless expanse of water. The devoted dog had watched over its master's house until it was dead. He went, and the hut held itself above the water as if to serve him until the crocodile caught him. Then it too sank deep into the water.

The water began to recede. Chennan came swimming back to the hut, splashing through the water, in search of the dog. Its body lay under a coconut palm. The waves moved it gently. Chennan turned it this way and that with his foot. He had a suspicion it was his dog. One ear was torn. Since its skin had putrefied, the colour was indistinct.

[*Translated by Gita Krishnankutty*]

The Night Queen

Nishaagandhi

S.K. Pottekkat

One of the fragrances I like best is that of the nishaagandhi. There is nothing I find more attractive than the scent that emanates from the small flowers that bloom on this plant, called the night queen in English. Its fresh fragrance, wafting through the darkness from a bush by a fence or the corner of a garden or from behind the screen of a wall, always fills my mind with intoxicating delight. The night queen is a prostitute among flowers: after sleeping all day, she creeps through the darkess at nightfall, embraces people without their being aware of it and seduces them! Yes, that fragrance that intoxicates the mind is well suited to a prostitute.

But I will never allow a nishaagandhi to be planted in my own garden. In my beautiful garden, decorated with many varieties of flowers, you will never see a single nishaagandhi. There is a special reason for this and an old tale behind it.

I will narrate it to you. I was a seventeen-year-old college student at the time. The seventeenth year is quite a dangerous one in the life of a young man. Although the English call this age 'sweet seventeen', I have christened it 'calamitous seventeen'. Many ideas that seem intoxicatingly novel occur to a seventeen-year-old. A dreamer who does no one any harm, he intervenes in unnecessary love affairs and complicates them; runs behind every new ideal he hears about only to stumble and fall face down; imagines all the reasonably good-looking girls he sees to be goddesses, nurtures secret desires about them and encounters disappointment. Editors find these seventeen-year-olds great problems. This is because it is a period of life when even a youth with an idiot's mentality wants to write poetry. Disliking to be materialistic, he will prefer to be a vedantin with spiritual inclinations. And his love will follow the same direction. He will favour the love in *Nalini* or in *Leela* rather than in *Vilasatilakam*. His ideal lover will be an Italian dandy.

After I had conducted research on the beauty and character of many young girls without their knowledge or permission, it was Malathi who had the good fortune to finally become my ideal girl. She was a high school student. She was fair-skinned and quite stout with a short, stocky body and rounded breasts. A face as beautiful as the full moon. The first thing that attracted me were her intoxicating eyes.

Somehow, beauty flowed through every part of her. She was a serious little person who never smiled. I liked her seriousness very much. Girls ought to be like that, I thought. At that time, I hated girls who walked around laughing all the time. I would stand on the veranda of the topmost floor of my house every evening to eagerly watch the wonderful spectacle of her walking like a female swan at the edge of the road with her eyes downcast, wearing a coarse green skirt of khadi and a white khadi blouse with red dots, a huge bundle of books pressed tightly to her chest and a small umbrella with a handle shaped like a cashew fruit from which the seed has fallen off hanging from her left hand. She did not know I worshipped her. Pushing our mathematics professor Ramanatha Iyer's homework sums filled with logarithms, co-tangents and such rubbish to one side, I began to compose poems about Malathikutty, her gait and her bundle of books:

Seeing her breasts grow like mushrooms,
My heart burns . . .

Bravo! I appreciated those lines myself. But although I wrote poems like this, I was determined not to think about her in sexual terms. A divine love, faultless and ideal. And it had to hold within it a sorrow, a feeling of disappointment. I prayed I would find an occasion to wander around singing spiritual songs touched with the disappointment of love like Madanan. I visualized the scene where Malu would fall on to my shoulder 'like a flag flapping down on a flagpole'.

Malathi lived in a two-storeyed house set in a huge compound about two furlongs to the west of our place. There was nothing more than a casual acquaintance between her father and me, confined to the formal exchanges of 'How are you?', 'Fine, thank you.' It was doubtful whether Malathi, who always walked with her eyes on the ground, had ever seen my face.

I used to go for a walk after dinner at night. The path that cut across the fields started from the road and ended at the huge gate on the west of Malathi's house. In the corner of the compound, four yards from the gate, someone had planted a thick bush of nishaagandhi that had grown dense and high. I once discovered that if I sat right inside that bush, I could see Malathi seated in her room, reading, through the shutters.

The glow of the table lamp revealed the expressions on her face clearly. She wore a blouse that lay partially open, exposing her breasts. Since her unbound hair hung down over her shoulders on to her breasts, covering the blouse, only part of a fair breast was visible, bursting out like a waterfall. Her English reader open in front of her, her forehead supported on her left hand, she would sit leaning downwards slightly over the table and begin to read—no, to recite. The girl was not in the habit of reading aloud. 'And Sita wanted to go with Rama,' she would murmur carelessly. The poor girl would sometimes read so much that she would feel sleepy; as the weight of sleep grew heavier, her face would droop lower and lower like the pan of a weighing scale and when it finally swung gently against the table, she would put a stop to that journey to Vaikuntam, open her eyes, raise her head and examine her surroundings. After that, she would sit for a long time gazing out of the window into the darkness. As I watched all this from the bush, an impulse of love would make me feel like calling out, 'Enough darling, now go and sleep.' But after rubbing her eyes for a while, she would begin to read again. Holding my breath, I would stare steadily at this sleep-dazed goddess of my heart. And the intense, exciting fragrance of the nishaagandhi would fill my nostrils and flow into my heart. Every second I spent in that cave conferred the bliss of nirvana upon me. That jewel of beauty would float before me like a heavenly dream glimpsed in a gentle and fragrant slumber . . . I felt as if the perfume of the nishaagandhi permeated all my thoughts and dreams.

Sometimes she read Malayalam poems. She recited verse in the manjari metre beautifully:

. . . not only a mother but anyone at all
would feel like picking her up and kissing her . . .

Ah! You had to listen to her sing those lines . . . I would want to kiss her lips then.

And so I silently worshipped that beauty, hidden inside the cave of that nishaagandhi for an hour every night for three whole months without missing a single day. The scent of the nishaagandhi and Malathi's lotus-like face imprinted themselves on my heart. I savoured that beauty every day.

The rainy season began. The rains of mid-Edavam poured down, and then the Thiruvathira season, when the rains were at their heaviest, began.

Storms were no hindrance to my expeditions. But sometimes, when the rains were very heavy, she would close the window. Ayyo! The doors of my heart would slam shut as well then. Disappointed, drenched in the rain, I would return home, my heart dark and heavy.

One day, as I sat in my cave, I happened to overhear her father tell her brother, 'Tomorrow we must cut down and bury all the plants in the garden. Parts of the compound are overgrown with bushes as well—we must clear all that.'

A fire ignited in my heart. In their attempt to cut down all the branches and twigs, clear their garden and compound and graft anew, it was certain they would cut down the nishaagandhi bush. It had grown very dense and high and spread over a large area. If my love-refuge was going to be destroyed what would my condition be? All my pleasures and dreams were gathered there. I would become like a bird whose nest had broken. Where would I go? How would I be able to sit gazing at that face all by myself again?

There was no other alternative: I decided I would send Malathi a letter appealing to her to spare the bush.

I sat up till three that night, thinking, and composed this letter:

Queen of my heart,

It has been three months since I began to crouch inside the nishaagandhi bush near your room every night and worship you. It was my desire to spend years like that as a silent devotee, not letting anyone, even you, know. But can 'anyone break fate's decree?' Ah, I cannot even think of it—tomorrow morning that cave is going to be destroyed by your father! My penance will have to end. Respected lady, I appeal to you: save that bush and, through it, this person, me. If a routine as pure and unselfish as the one I follow is to be safeguarded, only your mercy can help me. Om Shanthi. Rest later.

Your slave in love, (Signature)

I set out early morning for Malathi's house with the intention of getting the letter to her as quickly as possible. I entered the compound on the pretext of asking for the branch of a white Prince of Wales plant. A commotion of some sort seemed to be taking place there. A handful of people who lived in the neighbourhood were gathered in the yard. I pushed my way in through them to peer in.

An enormous serpent had been beaten to death and flung on the ground. It must have been about three feet long.

A poisonous snake of the most vicious kind!

'Look at that—the fellow was inside that bush that "gives off a scent at night". When we cut down the bush, we saw a huge hole. We dug into it and the fellow jumped out! The incredible thing is that this serpent was so close to us all this time and none of us knew!' said Velu Ashari, who had beaten the creature to death, looking at me, his finger laid on his nose in a gesture of astonishment. 'Look at it lying there with its stripes and spots!'

Seeing its tail twitch slightly like a telegraph wire, the carpenter said eagerly, 'What? The rascal isn't dead yet?' He started to hit its head again with the big palm branch he had in his hand. Blood sprayed out from the snake's crushed head.

I did not stay there any longer. I have no idea how I got home. The more I thought about it, the more I felt that someone was pouring fire over my heart. I thought I was growing insane with fear when I realized that while I had sat in the darkness of that bush savouring Malathi's divine beauty, a fearful serpent had been next to me, its mouth wide open to breathe in the fragrance of the nishaagandhi. However hard I tried, I could not erase from my mind the image of a poisonous snake poised behind me with its hood unfurled.

That very night, I began to run a temperature. It grew steadily higher. I had terrible nightmares and became delirious. I felt there were serpents everywhere I looked. A snake on the canopy of my bed; innumerable snakes crawling in through the bars of the window; a poisonous snake poised on a box with its hood raised; a snake hanging upside down next to me. 'Ayyo! A snake, a snake!' I screamed. Those who were in the house came running with sticks and searched the whole room. Imagining that a snake was trying to rest its hood on my shoulder from behind, I scrambled up, startled.

In these nightmares, I saw Malathi as a nagakanyaka with a serpent's body and a woman's face. While looking at her face gave me pleasure, her body frightened me.

I lay in bed a month with fever. Then I grew better. When I went out for a walk, I saw a board saying 'For rent' hanging outside Malathi's house. I made inquiries and found out that her father had been transferred to Kannur and that all of them had moved there a week earlier.

I never saw Malathi again. I heard recently that she is married and the mother of two. It was just a week ago that I took out the letter I wrote her from among copies of my old letters and destroyed it.

Whenever the fragrance of the nishaagandhi wafts out to me from anywhere the old, pleasant memories of my mad seventeen-year-old passion arise in my mind. Through that fragrance, I see simultaneously the images of a schoolgirl sleepily learning her lessons and of a poisonous snake poised with its hood unfurled . . . It is because of this unreasonable fear that I never allow the nishaagandhi to enter my garden.

[*Translated by Gita Krishnankutty*]

The Bull

Kaala

N.P. Mohamed

He felt a pull at his silk shirt as he stepped over the wicket gate. He looked back. His shirt tail has caught in the fencing. Lucky! It didn't tear.

Within the fencing one could see a caved-in hole where the wild jack had been. Farther on lay the court compound. Pigeons sat cooing on the window sills of the courthouse, their wings aflame with the rays of the sinking sun. The lush cashew orchard had locked in the night.

He walked on. There remained only a crumbling mud platform where his tarward had stood. A painful sight. A compound can hide its nudity only if there is a house with a courtyard and kitchen and a lean-to. When had he last come to the tarward? How well he knew the ancestral home and compound with its boundaries! He had been born there, but how unfamiliar everything looked after the lapse of years.

He walked on. He had heard about the house his Moothappa, great-uncle, was building. He was building the house as a single unit. No courtyard or lean-to. No one wanted a large house these days. There were no members of the family in the tarward. The different branches of the family had flowed from the summit of the gabled roof like so many little streams in different directions.

There were only three people now in the house. The head of the tarward was Moothappa, unmarried. The housewife was Ammayi, his aunt, who had been divorced by her husband. Then there was Ammayi's daughter Pathook.

He stroked his upper lip with his hand. Below his nose lay a thin adolescent strip of hair which had been blackened by a burnt matchstick. Some of the black came off on his fingers. Pathook would be filled with wonder when she saw his moustache. Would she not laugh when she saw it? When she laughed, the dimples on her round face would deepen. Pathook would still be getting up with the crows at dawn and roaming the compound to gather the cashew nuts bitten by the squirrels. He must get them from her tomorrow, roast and eat them. There was no one about. He stepped into the yard. The unfinished house stood there gaunt in the darkening twilight. The doors had not yet been fixed. Nor the window panes. The unplastered walls looked like a pock-marked face.

The mango tree still stood there. With its gilt scarf of branches it was telling him, Mohamed, have you forgotten me? How could he forget? The mango tree and he had been good friends. When he climbed to the top of the tree, when his sweat fell down in large drops on the ground, Pathook, who could not climb, would shout, 'Umma, the boy is shaking down the tender mangoes.'

Now Pathook would be stunned at the sight of his moustache. He had grown up. Was he not coming from college! Now he could curl up and sleep till the sunlight got into his eyes. Now Moothappa would not beat him with the bamboo strip for not going to the mosque at the crack of dawn. Now he would study hard and become a munsif—

'The boy?'

He was startled. What cheek! He touched his moustache. He stared. Was it Pathook who was standing before him?

Pathook stood bending, her right leg on the step. She looked at him unblinking as she tried to capture between her legs the kachi fluttering in the breeze. The long, thin eyes in the round face were full of life. The lids that stood sentry over them fluttered in a rhythm of their own. The unknotted hair blew in the wind and hugged her waist and raised its tail like a little squirrel.

'Umma, the boy, the boy!'

He felt like going up to her and giving her a couple of slaps. How could she still see him as a young boy? She had taught him the magic art of blowing bubbles into the air with a papaya stem dipped in soapy water. In the light, the coloured bubbles would float around pathlessly and then burst. Granted. Still she ought to have remembered the fleet-footed years that had passed them.

Does Pathook still wear the round kasturi flowers strung on brass and pierced through her ear lobes? He was very curious to know. He stared hard. In the reddening twilight her ears lay bowed with gold rings from top to bottom.

Tearing through the veil of those past years, he could hardly believe his eyes. Was it really Pathook?

She must be made aware that he was no longer a stripling. What if he pinched her on her long nose? Or tweaked her ears?

He stepped on to the veranda. A gaping doorway. Pathook who stood leaning against the door post. He stretched out his hand towards her nose. She wriggled aside. His hands brushed against—a streak of lightning went past. His hands lay in mid air. He felt weak all over. A quivering in his heart. A song in his head. He felt dwarfed.

The mango tree in the yard still shed its perfume. He felt a burning, felt limp. His throat was parched. He wanted water. He wanted to gulp and gulp hugely. He did not ask for any.

He stepped into the house. In the middle room on the high, broad chest, covered from head to foot in a loose white dress, Ammayi had gone down in Sujood, genuflecting with head bowed down. With head bowed down before Allah, she had not seen him. Ammayi would not finish her prayers for some time. She took a long time doing her prayers.

His body felt weak and giddy, as if he had eaten raw areca nut which had gone to his head. He took off his shirt and hung it on a chair.

'Pathook, a glass of water.' There was no movement.

'Pathook!—'

He could hear Pathook through the sound of her suppressed laughter. He peeped into the kitchen. Dry leaves burnt in the hearth. The fire greedily licked the bottom of the burnt mud pot with its little tongues of flame. Pathook took aside the pot, holding it with a piece of cloth. She did not see him.

The years that had passed. Years which had broken up like cotton pods. Near the fence the tall silk cotton tree had gone right up to the sky. The ripe pods of cotton had burst and scattered. Then it had been a thing of wonder. The scattered silk cotton flowers had been caught in the beaks of the bamboo brambles in the fence. It was fun to watch them glittering in the sun like so many pieces of broken glass. Those flaming days had died out sadly.

When he next stepped into that house Pathook would not be there. She would be in her husband's house. She would blossom in the new surroundings. He had once gone as a guest to that house beyond the town, across the country paths and the green fields. He had fallen ill there. How long he had to lie there! As he lay on his back near the window he could see the peaks of the Uroth range stretched out like so many washed white garments hung out to dry. Perhaps he would go there again. Then Pathook would be the lady of the house. Pathook would get ready a gruel of rice flour and a curry of pumpkin leaves and yam. She would stand behind the kitchen door. He would hear the tinkle of the bangles on her hand.

The Uroth mountain of family ties would stand between the two of them. When he bid farewell he would hear the voice from behind the door: 'When will you come again?'

Meaningless words. The camaraderie of two ships anchored at port. Two ships come to port. Then they depart, each going its separate way.

Have the flames in the heart died down? Before his eyes the future appeared in faded colours. The lines were blurred, the colours dim.

'The boy stands as if he has swallowed a spear!' He was startled.

How long had Pathook been standing before him with a glass of black tea held aloft? He saw her only then. Had she also stood there like him?

He took the glass. His hand trembled a little. Drops of tea fell on Pathook's fair, plump arms. 'Ay, ay!' Then he saw the gold bangles which kept her arms prisoner.

'Have you satisfied your thirst?'

'This isn't enough for me.'

'How much more do you want?'

'One glass, two glasses, plenty.'

Pathook was laughing.

'Has the boy become Dhajjal?'

'Who knows? Go and find out.'

'Don't you know of Dhajjal's thirst?'

He knew. But by that time Ammayi came, lifting up the trailing end of her prayer dress. He drank the tea when he saw Ammayi.

Ammayi unstrung the pouch of family welfare. Was Mayi well? Is Kunhoya also studying? What is the good of girls studying? Answers struggled as the questions streamed out.

'When will the house be finished?'

Ammayi was saying something. Beyond the wide open window was the compound bathed in moonlight. His mind was somersaulting into childhood days. He picked up a spade for the first time when he was in the fourth standard. He was digging trenches with Pathook to plant country-bean seedlings. When kurutholanattan bloomed they did not look like flowers. They looked like butterflies with white wings bordered with blue, sitting on the shrubs. As he thought of it and lowered the spade, the toes of his feet were red with blood. He didn't go to school for a week. When he went to school after that, Mary Teacher pinched him on the chin and called him 'lazy fellow'. Then Mary Teacher herself became the lazy one. Not for one but for many days. Mary Teacher did not come to school. Pathook told him the secret. Mary Teacher had been married and taken away . . .

He looked into the yard. The bamboo clusters were crying out loud. Was the dim moonlight quietly sobbing? The last bus to Kottakkal sounded its horn.

'When is Pathook's wedding?'

'On the twenty-eighth of Rajab.'

'Plenty of time.'

'Where's the time, son? When she also goes!' Ammayi brought out the words sorrowfully and then became silent. Poor thing! That empty house would then have just two souls.

Moothappa who had never married.

Ammayi whose husband had deserted her.

They would be waiting for death.

From inside, the sound of Pathook speaking: 'If the boy wants rice, let him wash—'

'Girl, why do you call him—'

'I'll cut off her tongue.'

She ran away. Ammayi laughed. Pathook returned quickly. She stretched out a kitchen knife held in her hand.

'Here, cut off my tongue.'

He jumped up.

'You, you!' She put out her tongue and grimaced at him. 'Nha-nha!'

'Get along!'

As she stepped out of the kitchen door, lantern in hand, he could hear Pathook say, 'Look down. There may be crawling creatures there.'

He felt pins and needles all over his body. The first thing he saw as he stepped out was the well with the half-broken barrier wall. There had been a snake beside it. Moothappa stared at the snake. The snake crawled on the ground like spilt paint. What did Moothappa do? By the time he opened his tight shut eyes, all that he could see was Moothappa waving his arm in a circle. One could hear the crackle of the snake's bones breaking as he held it like a silk thread in his finger. He was sick. Moothappa threw it off into the distance. He felt too disgusted to go to school that day. But fearing Moothappa, he went to school. When he went, Eddy Master was taking the Bible class. In the Garden of Eden, with its tail wound round the tree of knowledge and head swinging down, was the snake. Satan. Who saw Satan first? Eve or Adam?

As he walked across the ground sown with chama seeds he felt as if his legs were being brushed by kitten fur. He walked up to the edge of the little pond. In doubt, he looked back. No, there was no one.

He discarded his mundu. He put the dry towel on it. He stood staring at the shimmering water throwing gleams in the dim moonlight. He must have a good swim. It was chilly. He must run and jump into the water. If Pathook was there he could have splashed water on her.

He shivered. He wanted to warm himself at the fire in the hearth. One doesn't get what one desires. He went in. In the middle room the circular rush mat (which did duty as a table) had been spread and rice and curry were already served. Ammayi and Pathook were sitting guard over it.

Only one plate was there. Earlier, Pathook too would sit and eat with him. Hereafter that would not be allowed. He didn't look at Ammayi's face.

'Come on, Pathook.'

In reply he only heard Ammayi's empty laughter.

Dry rice, tailless young fish, dead and bloated in coloured water, fried pappadam full of boils. He disliked it all. How could one eat alone? He drank up the water in one gulp.

'Girl, he couldn't have liked your curry.'

'Umma, he didn't touch the rice.'

He washed his hands. He felt a sadness. He went and sat on the veranda. He lit a cigarette. He could at least do that freely here. As the cigarette smoke merged into the moonlight, he looked out at the yard. He felt sorry for the mango tree standing there with a gilt umbrella. A solitary figure, how long it had stood there! Would not the mango tree have felt like a walk in the compound? Was he mad? The question that had leapt up from his mind stood trembling on the tip of his tongue.

A wind was blowing. The doors and windows without panes welcomed the wind. The chill kept creeping in. He must lie down all covered up in a blanket.

'Ammayi, let me lie down. I feel very tired.'

'Child, have you made the bed in the eastern room?'

'I have.'

She did everything required without being asked to.

'Have a glass of water by you too.'

'The thirst of Dhajjal!'

He lay on his back. He felt shame in his breast. He was beaten down by weariness.

A purple mist hooded over his eyes. Light yellow needles pierced them. He shut his eyes. Flecks of gilt before his eyes. Black circles. Slow hesitant darkness. The darkness moves. The darkness becomes thinner. Before his eyes, colours, forms.

The picture of Pathook holding aloft a glass of black tea, the colour of blood, and staring. Thin eyes gleaming and glowing, black eyelids beating. Small dimples. Half-open lips.

'Don't you know of Dhajjal's thirst?'

He knew. What did she mean by it? Dhajjal did all the evil things. God became angry. Now Dhajjal is in captivity: God had placed a huge mountain on his belly. Dhajjal licks through it and eats it up. The mountain melts and looks like a swollen cake. It becomes smaller and smaller till it could disappear with the next lick. Every Friday noon Dhajjal hopes to escape. He lifts his hand and legs. Then God places another huge mountain on the belly of Dhajjal. On Doomsday Dhajjal escapes before a mountain is placed on him.

Then he comes into his own. He walks with strides that reach from milestone to milestone. He flies across the skies with his huge wings. He knocks buildings together. He uses the water reservoirs in railway junctions as cups and takes tea from them in one massive gulp. He drinks the oceans dry. He rules the earth by terror. He becomes God on earth.

Men and women would flee in fear. Suckling babies would be split into two and fall from their mothers' breasts.

When Dhajjal ruled, the sun would darken. The moon would be extinguished. The stars would burn out and fall from the sky. The powers of the sky would be shaken. The one who sits in the skies would issue his command. Then the sign of the son of man would glow in the sky. Intoning the names of all the tribes of mankind, the son of man would come riding on the clouds, resplendent, mighty. He would send his messengers amid great blasts of the trumpet.

The Messiah would slay Dhajjal. Peace would come on the earth and happiness to mankind. Again, when cotton flowers smile on the land and red-beaked parrots dance on the trees . . . There was nothing in front of his eyes. A black, dark world.

Icy fingers played hide-and-seek amid his hair. A light warmth crept up from his feet. A smell of musk and dried fish pushed into his nose. Above him a soft mountain.

His mind lay slumbering on the thin borderline between dream and wakefulness.

In his mind, strangled sighs. Intertwined legs in warm scissor holds. In his ears the sigh of soft songs that sought distant horizons. He did not know.

Pathook, you should not have done it.

Sharp knives that cut good sense into little shreds. Beyond that, desire that beats its frustrated head, and beyond, fiery arrows that were aimed at the heart. He did not know.

On the head of the snake with its hood spread out, where lumps of snow fell and scattered, when one desired to be man as well as woman.

Or in the midst of it all light, unmindful of everything, wanted for everything. Darkness wipes out everything, to bring things together. The world of light, the world of darkness, when they flower in the little room.

When the searing streak of lightning from her face struck his chest, when sharp nail tips jabbed the pearly drop of softness, he heard the roar that pierced his ears and stunned him.

He had to look.

Beyond the yellowing moonlight, beyond the gaping doorless

frame, stood a gigantic bull with curving twisted horns.

The bull, it struck left and right with its arch-like, rounded, spiralling horns. Through the doorway it came.

His body turned cold; his hands and legs shook. His lips were parched. Sparks flew from the palms of his hand which were pouring water on the burning hearth on his chest.

The roaring, running bull entered the inner doorway.

Eyes that spit fire. Whiskers that stand out like tridents. Breathing out smoke, the huge, big bull comes running and bellowing, beating with its head, butting with its horns.

His eyes closed shut. His eyes opened wide. His body was dripping with water as if he had come out of the pond.

The bull was covered over with hair that had the appearance of red-hot wire rods standing out like spikes. Hair ablaze. The bull as big as an elephant came roaring and bellowing towards the bed.

Fiery smoke came out of the bull's nostrils. His whole body was on fire.

The bull came near, aiming at him with its horns. He closed his eyes. The gates of hell were opening. It would toss him now; he would die!

Pathook.

The words died in the throat. The earth was opening up. Out of step, out of depth, he would fall down. Did the bull's horns touch his face?

—I am being gored! I am being killed! . . .

[*Translated by V. Abdulla*]

The Death of Makhan Singh

Makhansinghinte maranam

T. Padmanabhan

Night had fallen when the bus reached Banihal. Makhan Singh stopped the bus in front of Panditji's restaurant as usual. As the passengers hastily got out, he leaned his face on the steering wheel and shut his eyes. He was overcome by an indescribable fatigue and discomfort.

In fact there was no special reason for him to be late with the bus. Usually, there would be several military trucks on the way and he would slow down, letting them pass. But that day, there had been no trucks, yet he was late with the bus.

He had been late before, too. But nothing of this sort had ever happened.

When he remembered the reason, he felt his head would split. He had resolved not to think about anything, ever. But could he keep that resolution even once? Makhan Singh said to himself, death is better than this. Why didn't I die that day?

So much had happened. Weren't they uprooted from the land of their birth? Still he lived. Not because he wished to. But it was destined that way. He had calmed down by telling himself, never mind; the roots may sprout again in fresh soil.

He had been searching. Where was that fresh soil?

He wasn't certain where it was. Sometimes he had the feeling that it was Delhi. In any case, he was sure it would be in India. All that he feels now is that it is enough if he can somehow go on living somewhere.

He must forget the past if he has to live. But, however much he tries, he cannot help brooding over the past again and again.

When he met Bachan Singh recently, he had said, 'I am going to the Andamans; there's fifteen acres of land for me.'

Fifteen acres! Can't believe it! Why have so much land? Bachan Singh cannot cultivate it by himself. He needs someone to help him. So . . .

Will wheat grow there? Maybe. The soil is very fertile, it is heard.

If only he could get one acre!

Yet, he would never go to the Andamans. Even if he died here! Even death holds forth a solace! Man prizes his pride the greatest. To go away from this soil where his father and grandfather are laid to rest . . .

In Makhan Singh's choking heart, the smoke of memories billowed.

He heard as if from a great distance the noise of the tarpaulin being removed and the luggage unloaded from the top of the bus. He thought, it is very late. Everyone must have had their supper. Only I am late. The very thought of eating nauseated Makhan Singh. He decided against eating.

Getting off the bus, he walked up to the restaurant's veranda. It was as if there was a heavy chain on his legs. It grew heavier as he put each step forward.

When he reached the front of the veranda, he stopped in his tracks. The two of them were standing there. The old woman and the young lady. Their hollow eyes seemed to be searching for something. Like a blade of grass in the hands of one drowning.

Those fragile forms of misery moved over to the lighted patch from darkness.

Makhan Singh was unable to face them. He turned round. He was aching all over.

His lips trembled, eyes shut by themselves.

If only the earth would open and swallow me!

I am a disgrace even to my father!

Coward!

'Sardarji!' Someone thumped his shoulders.

It was Panditji.

'Panditji.'

'What happened?'

He couldn't say anything.

Panditji put his palm on Makhan Singh's brow.

'You have fever.'

'Let it be.'

'Come. Let us go inside.'

He didn't budge.

Why go inside? To avoid seeing them?

'It is snowing.'

'Let it snow.'

Makhan Singh wanted to lie face-down on that bare earth and weep. He wished to stand before them, his head erect. Wishing thus, he recollected several painful things. He saw his mother, father and wife in his mind's eye. He pressed his chest hard. Memories were breaking out of his heart in the form of blood. He said to himself, I will help them; certainly I will.

He went in with Panditji.

Moonlight spread in the Banihal pass. A cold wind began to blow from the pass.

He was still sitting in front of the fireplace. There was no fire in the fireplace. But there was fire in his mind. It was not blazing. And so, no one saw it. Yet, he was aware of that all-consuming heat.

All this while, he was brooding. Panditji gave food to everyone.

(They did not have any money on them. I had guessed it all along. If only I had some money with me! They didn't ask for anything. Only stood in the far corner. Like me, they also must have a lot to ponder over.

Can't human beings keep away from thinking about anything?

Then I said to Panditji, give them something.

He asked for money. I am not angry; I am only amazed. Does one keep an account of feeding one's own mother and sisters,

and demand money from them? To think that he is a Brahmin!
He is a dog!)

Everyone retired for the night, and they too lay down. He
alone sat up, thinking.

When the midnight-cock crowed, he got up and walked out.
Ramlal was snoring away inside the bus. He said to himself,
'He must be sleeping all wrapped up in blankets. It is really
cold. Let him sleep! Isn't he young! But I cannot sleep tonight!'

In that cold, he recalled his childhood when he would keep
vigil in the fields.

Wheat lay ripe in the fields!

It was before the harvest. Who would be there now?

Makhan Singh sighed. He strolled along Banihal's streets.
There was total silence everywhere. The road that crept into
the pass shone like a black snake in the moonlight. He took that
road every day. And would take it tomorrow too. But . . .

This moonlight seems to have a peculiar sheen. The colour
of blood!

The smell of burning human flesh.

He thrust his hands into the pockets of the old corduroy
trousers and walked on.

He was recalling something.

The moonlight, road and hillsides faded from Makhan
Singh's vision. He was aware only of the comforting touch of
the old corduroy.

Makhan Singh felt the cloth again.

He couldn't bear the thought.

He had bought it in Lahore.

She was also with him that day.

My first . . .

Lahore!

Lahore is now in Delhi!

How contented life was then!

He sighed. If only the past were a mere dream!

But how could it be? Lahore is gone. Rawalpindi is gone.
Punjab's . . .

Where were they coming from? He should have asked. The next morning he would ask them everything. He went back to the restaurant. He was dead tired. But couldn't sleep. The forms of that mother and daughter would not fade from his mind. They seemed to be asking for something from far away, weeping. It was for help. He felt infinitely sad.

He should help them. It was his duty.

If he doesn't help them out in this condition, what is the use of his staying alive?

To think that he didn't have any money at all with him.

He would ask Panditji. If he got it, well and good.

God would find a way.

He comforted himself.

Towards morning he dozed off a little. Even in that reverie, a vague memory of them filled his mind like a mist.

Where did he spot them first? Must be at Pathankot. But his attention turned towards them only at Madhopur. There was a special reason for that. It took almost an hour for the search in the bus to finish. Even beddings and boxes were not spared. Standing under the tree in front of the tea-bunk, Makhan Singh enjoyed watching the fun.

The proceedings that day were very strict. It was not just a cursory affair, as usual: each person was individually subjected to the search. People were impatient to have it over and done with. Makhan Singh thought, maybe some high-ranking official is visiting the area.

Munshiji took the register from Ramlal's hands and went through it.

'There are two persons in excess,' Munshiji said, raising his still-damp pen towards the sky.

Munshiji is always impatient.

'Where are they?'

They were there.

Munshiji lost his temper. He doesn't talk, once he is angry. He roars.

Munshiji asked, 'Don't you have ears? Where are your things?'

It was Ramlal who said, 'Munshiji, they do not have any baggage.'

'Is that so?'

Advancing two steps, he asked them, 'Where are you going?'

'Srinagar.'

It was the old woman who spoke up. Makhan Singh thought that her voice faltered.

He got up from under the tree. Something was wrong somewhere. Why does that woman weep? Why does she weep standing at that roadside in Madhopur, in front of soldiers, passengers and shopkeepers?

He saw the old woman producing the tickets from the bundle in her hands.

'Isn't this to Jammu?'

No one spoke.

Munshiji drew something in the air with his pen.

At last a soldier said, 'Never mind, Munshiji, this is not your headache! Let them go anywhere. Why do you bother?'

Munshiji flared up. 'Oh, is that so?' As he was leaving, he said, 'It is also you who did away with Punjab.'

Hearing that, Makhan Singh turned pale. He had not forgotten the fate of Punjab. He hailed from Punjab. He had never wished to go anywhere else. His father was a farmer. His grandfather was a farmer too. They had at home swords that were old, but not rusting. But he had never seen anyone striking someone else with them.

It was when things were thus . . . Makhan Singh could not contain himself. Whom did that scarecrow-thin Munshiji have in mind when he said that? Was it aimed at him? If it was so . . . True, he was never vengeful. But whether he could have retaliated then was another question. He could have, if he wished. But he didn't. That is why Munshiji spoke thus.

Why didn't he retaliate?

Makhan Singh gnashed his teeth. He should have struck back.

But he had been away. Later Bachan Singh had said, 'They hacked your father to pieces.' He himself had not witnessed the scene. Then, who did?

It is a son's sacred duty to avenge his father's death. But upon whom should he take revenge?

Thank God Mother was long dead by then. Otherwise, what they would have done to Mother . . .

When I went away that day, my Preetham was with Father.

Nothing was heard of her.

All the places I searched!

Who knows what has become of her?

She might not be dead.

Makhan Singh felt his heart break.

Her name must have been changed. She must be thinking about me and sighing at this very minute as I sit wondering what might have happened to her. We shall never meet again.

Oh my Preetham!

Where are you?

In Karachi?

The bus was waiting for him.

Ramlal said, 'Let us go, Sardarji.'

With a sigh, Makhan Singh started the bus.

As the bus hurtled towards Jammu, leaving behind the landscape of a wild expanse of bare land strewn with gigantic rocks, and cornfields irrigated by camel-drawn Persian wheels, he thought, whatever the provocation, I am incapable of harming anyone. Why should I then rack my brains thinking about revenge? What is past is past.

Makhan Singh thought about many other things. It was a few days since he had got the letter from his aunt in Delhi. Her son was going to school. He should send them something. The next week is Roop Chand's daughter's wedding. Shouldn't he give some gift? The old man is too hard up . . . He smiled automatically, thinking about all that. He felt a sense of great contentment. What a paltry sum he spends on himself! All the rest somehow erodes this way and that . . .

He called out good-naturedly to the old cabwallah who took the wrong side, as he passed the military camp, 'Mind your precious life, Uncle.'

Stopping the bus near the rest house, Makhan Singh went to the restaurant where he usually ate. He had forgotten the mother and daughter by then. When he returned, the passengers were discussing them. He heard a young man say, 'They were in our compartment till Pathankot.'

There was still time for the bus to start.

Someone asked, 'Are they going to Srinagar?'

'That's what they said.'

'Looks like they are in dire straits.'

'Aren't they refugees?'

'Why are they going there then?'

'Her son in the army is sick.'

'He must be dead by now.'

'Don't say that, brother.'

'Oh.'

'Isn't she his mother?'

'The other must be his wife.'

'God help them.'

Makhan Singh was hurt. They were not to be found anywhere, even if he wished to do them a good turn.

He said to no one in particular, 'It seems they are gone.'

'Where can they go?'

'They are gone for sure.'

'What, walk up two hundred miles?'

'They might.'

'They'd have to have at least two new pairs of footwear to do that.'

'What about clothes?'

'Still, they left.'

'No wonder.'

'They were weeping.'

'They will freeze to death tonight. That's what.'

'Or . . .'

'The young one is pretty. If someone takes a fancy to her . . .'

'Things are like that in Calcutta and Delhi.'

As he was heading for Banihal, what they said resounded in his ears. The form of his aunt swam into his mind.

His aunt in Delhi.

The refugee women of Delhi . . . The thought was revolting.

He was leaving behind the crowded, colourful streets of Jammu. The bus is merely crawling, he felt. When he rounded the bend in front of the 'Palace', he stopped the bus suddenly.

The woman and daughter were walking along the road, which seemed created only for them.

They halted in confusion.

He didn't look at their faces. But asked, 'Coming along?'

The daughter looked away.

The mother's eyes filled with tears. 'We do not have money, son!'

Makhan Singh recalled his dead mother. Only she had called him 'son' with such feeling and love.

He said, 'You come along.'

They still hesitated.

'Get in.'

Ramlal opened the rear door.

'God will reward you.'

The old woman's voice faltered. The bus moved. Makhan Singh thought in wonder about them. He was melancholy too. He sighed. Alas! Punjab's offspring are orphaned thus.

Families are broken, relationships wrecked.

But here, a mother has set off, without a second thought, to meet her sick son hundreds of miles away.

She has only love in her heart.

That young woman must be craving to meet her husband. He also must be longing to see her. When their eyes meet . . .

That relationship will never be severed.

Like the mother and wife of that sick young man in Srinagar, had his father and wife survived . . .

He was sad and angry at the same time.

He loved to see life putting forth fresh buds in that fertile soil. The beauty and freshness of those hillsides sporting lofty pines and the hillocks dotted by fruit-bearing pomegranates had never been lost on him. He used to glance around occasionally as he passed them. But not that day.

The storm of memories created a lump in his heart.

He had met refugees from Punjab on earlier occasions too. But he had never felt anything like this before. What is past is past. One can never return to old times. So, survive somehow in the new circumstances . . . this was what he felt on those occasions. He had decided not to ulcerate his mind thinking about the past. But now, witnessing such love and self-sacrifice, he was led back to the past of his own relationships. He knew very well that he couldn't do so, but still he yearned: if only he could return to the past!

Familiar faces paraded before the windscreen.

He heard voices of old time through the wind.

His father is calling him. He braked suddenly. It was heading for a chasm! The bus shook violently.

Makhan Singh perspired. How many lives were in his hands!

He remembered his old resolution. He wouldn't think about anything.

Meeting that mother and daughter did it. He shouldn't have seen them.

The bus was moving very slowly.

They failed to reach Banihal before nightfall . . .

Makhan Singh rose as the first rays of dawn fell on the hills.

People were preparing to leave.

Panditji was making tea.

Makhan Singh said, 'Panditji, I am in trouble.'

Putting down the teapot, Panditji looked at the face of the tall Punjabi driver. He had never heard him say anything in that tone.

What had happened? Is it the beginning of some illness? Then he should not stay in the restaurant.

'Panditji, I need some money. As soon as I get my wages, I shall pay it back.'

He was asking for a loan for the first time in his life.

Opening his empty palms, Panditji said, 'Money, Sardarji? I don't have any! And look at the time you thought fit to ask for money. Hardly dawn yet.'

Makhan Singh's face fell. He thought, I shouldn't have asked. Humiliation for nothing. He stood in front of the restaurant, immersed in thought.

After the lethargy of the night, the noisy life of Banihal was pulsating once again. Shops opened. The shepherds with reddened faces were coming out of liquor shops, although it was early morning. The shepherds, their flock, their dogs, their women and children. What a commotion!

The trucks began to leave one by one.

The racket of the porter-urchins. People went down to the stream with neem twigs in their mouths, and sleepy eyes.

Gurgling springs.

Makhan Singh was in low spirits. It was time to start.

With a heavy heart, he got into his seat and started the engine. Heaving and swaying, the bus somehow reached the road. As he proceeded a few yards beyond the toll gate, his legs suddenly seemed paralysed!

The inspector!

Makhan Singh began to sweat.

He did not have a blot on his career, as yet.

But now . . .

What accursed moment let this devil in!

Was he lying in wait?

Damn him!

The inspector took the register from Ramlal's hands and counted the passengers.

'There are two persons in excess.'

Ramlal looked in the direction of Makhan Singh. And Makhan Singh studied the inspector's face.

'Who are they?'

The mother and daughter were in the back seat. The eyes of the passengers turned towards them. They hung their heads.

The inspector asked, 'Where are your tickets?'

There were no tickets.

'Get down.'

The inspector noted down the driver's number.

Makhan Singh thought, I will lose my job.

What if . . .

Let it go!

He remembered that young man in a sickbed in Srinagar. He must be waiting expectantly for them.

The bus is to reach there by midday.

But that Panditji . . . Makhan Singh was enraged. Now there is this inspector halting them!

None of these people can understand human misery.

He went near the inspector and said, 'They have to reach Srinagar by noon today. That old woman's son is ill.'

The inspector said contemptuously, 'So what?'

Sparks flew from Makhan Singh's eyes. 'So what? So, you should permit them to travel in this bus. They are poor. Let alone how they became poor! If I had some money, I would have helped them. But I don't.'

Makhan Singh stopped. The passengers were taken aback. His voice was still booming . . .

Again he said, 'I shall cut the tickets right in front of you. I will arrange for the money when we reach Srinagar.'

The inspector turned round and walked off without a word.

He then said to a policeman who arrived from the toll gate hearing the commotion, 'These Punjabis can't be trusted.'

The blood boiled in Makhan Singh's veins.

'Can't be trusted, eh? I will show you.' His pent-up emotions broke loose like the deluge in a dam-burst. Pain, sorrow, anger and hatred blinded him.

Makhan Singh lunged forward with raised fists.

The inspector side-stepped. Some people stopped Makhan Singh. Ramlal caught him round his waist and begged, 'Sardarji, Sardarji . . .' Ramlal was seeing that good man in such a condition for the first time.

Makhan Singh blurted out as if in delirium, 'Leave me! Let me slash open his entrails! I will die after that.'

The policeman intervened, 'Let it be, Sardarji. What he said is absolute rot. I apologize on his behalf. Enough . . .'

Makhan Singh did not hear him. He said, 'I don't want this job. Let another person take the bus away.'

'Sardarji, don't say so. You . . .'

Makhan Singh didn't let him complete his sentence. Raising his palms, he asked him, 'Do you see these calluses? It is not by hitting people that I got them. Not by holding the steering wheel either. It's by tilling the soil that I got them. My father and grandfather were farmers. We have not cheated anyone. Now this fellow says we Punjabis can't be trusted.'

He was terribly angry. The policeman appealed, 'Let it be, Sardarji. It is all over; forget it . . .'

'Forget?'

He thought for a moment. 'I used to forget. But now? No!'

The policeman was worried.

'How many persons must be waiting for these people? Just imagine.'

How many? There is a sick young man. But he will not be able to meet his mother and wife. Why should I then . . .

Perhaps there might be other similar cases . . .

Many such persons would be waiting for their loved ones.

'Go, Sardarji.'

Makhan Singh thought it over for a moment. Then he started the bus without uttering a word. With a drone, the new bus started to climb the pass. Its wail, as it climbed along the belly of the mountains where the mellow morning sun played hide-and-seek, was painful. Hills towered, one behind the other. No end to them.

The wind whistled and howled.

Hot springs of memories boiled over in Makhan Singh's heart.

A small hill was darkened with a shadow. Another hill in the distance seemed to move in the sun.

Are the hills alive?

Do the hills die?

People were killed in Punjab. Bachan Singh said they had hacked Father into slices. Shall I too kill everyone in this bus? Oh, my chest pains. I feel suffocated. Is the bus going to overturn?

If it overturns . . . jackals will carry off everyone at night . . . from Madhopur. The bus won't fall off. It will hang suspended in the sky. I will then ask, aren't the Punjabis trustworthy?

Oh, such pain. I think I will die . . .

I will go to Lahore. I had gone to Lahore taking Preetham along. But . . .

Oh, what pain . . .

The bus is due to arrive at noon. But I won't arrive. I won't find any of those early migrants in Delhi. If I die declaring I have calluses on my palms, wheat would be ripening in Lahore. If anyone in childhood . . . for me . . .

I feel cold, terribly cold. This corduroy from Lahore . . .

The bus was approaching the tunnel . . .

Makhan Singh's memories stopped. He felt a great fatigue. He was being carried off in a current. The bus passed into the tunnel without waiting for the sentry's signal.

Makhan Singh was choking. The dim lights in the tunnel were like the stars of some other world.

As soon as the bus passed through the tunnel and reached the other end, it slowly came to a halt. Opening its door, Makhan Singh fell out.

In the beautiful Kashmir Valley, waves of sunlight were spreading.

When Ramlal and the sentries came running, he was lying on the raw earth. Tears rolled down and soaked the cloth that held his beard tight.

Someone among the passengers said, 'God saved us. Otherwise, we would now be there, fifteen thousand feet below!'

Ramlal went on crying, like a child, 'Sardarji, Sardarji . . .'

Ramlal's Sardarji did not hear that call. He was dreaming of the ripe wheat fields of Punjab.

[*Translated by A.J. Thomas*]

The Razor's Edge

Kshuraasyadhaara

C.V. Sreeraman

He listened to everything. His eyelids, which always remained half-closed in ceaseless meditation, lifted. Waves coursed through the sockets of his eyes. Straightening the angavastram that lay loosely over a body that had the reddish hue of a jnaval fruit, the brahmachari said, 'I have sympathy for you. But what is this I hear? In bed with more than one woman at the same time . . . blinded by the intoxication of more than one kind of liquor at the same time as well . . . Liquor as fluid, as smoke, as a tablet. Maybe you can get away by calling it perversion in English. But to me, this is my religion. The furies are in possession of your tastes. Violent furies . . .'

The brahmachari grew thoughtful, then said, 'Those who feel lust have neither fear nor shame.'

'Tell me, brahmachari, will I never be free of this?'

'Do you desire salvation?'

'I think it will be impossible.'

'It's not that—do you desire it? Answer that.'

'I do. I desire it very much indeed . . .'

'Then that means you have arrived on the road to salvation. No matter how far away it may be. Have you read the Gita?'

'No.'

'Read it at least as a researcher. Do you know who wrote the preface to the first English translation of the Gita? You will be astonished to know. Warren Hastings. You will be even more astonished when you read what he wrote: "The writers of the Indian philosophies will survive when the British domination in India shall long have ceased to exist and when the sources which it yielded of wealth and power are lost to remembrance . . .'"

He had been sitting for hours, numbed by the brahmachari's torrent of words. This was what had persuaded him to visit this ashram. He nourished no vain hope that his life could be uprooted and replanted on the right path in a minute. But if he could have the occasion to talk to a highly intelligent man for a few hours, it would be an achievement in itself . . .

The brahmachari was gazing out, lost in thought again. Trees with dense foliage as far as the eye could see. The cows of the ashram grazed freely everywhere. A cow rubbed its back against a tree and flowers rained down, scattering white blossoms on its neck and face.

The brahmachari said, 'I was searching for those lines in my mind. The Gita says, *yatatohyapi kaunteya / purushasya vipishchita / indriyani pramathini / haranthi prasabham mana*—O son of Kunti, the senses with their capricious nature destroy even the mind of a hardworking and intelligent man.'

'You must advise me, brahmachari. On how to retrieve at least once the mind I have destroyed . . .'

'You can do it. Have you heard the story of the sage of Vilvamangalam?'

'Forgive me. My knowledge of such matters is very poor.'

'Listen, then . . . Vilvamangalam, a Brahmin, lost his head over the prostitute Chintamani, who was a dancer. Not even bothering to perform his father's funeral rites, he swam across the river with a log as support in order to get to her. What he had imagined was a log was really a corpse, his own wife's. And what he had thought was a rope was a serpent. Chintamani did not like what he did and she counselled him . . .'

As he listened to the story, the beautiful face of a woman in the nether world rose before him. She spoke sweet words in a rough voice.

'Yes, I'm sitting here to sell my body. But it's so late, why don't you go home now?'

'Is it then that Vilvamangalam had a change of mind?' he asked impatiently.

'Just for a short time. Desire woke in him again, for a woman with a husband and a family. He grieved over her. He accepted blindness, wandered endlessly before he attained salvation. This is the story of everyone who goes astray. But one can hope for release, if one makes an effort. In what way? If one tries ceaselessly . . .' The brahmachari was lost in thought again.

Then he said, 'Do you know what the way to salvation is like? The *Kathopanishad* says, *kshurasya dhara nishata duratya / durgam patha tat kavayo vadanthi*—sharp as the edge of a razor, hard to cross, difficult to tread is that path, so sages declare. Somerset Maugham uses these lines in his novel *The Razor's Edge*.'

Suddenly, the brahmachari smiled. A very winning smile. He said, still smiling, 'You must be wondering whether I know literature. There was a time when I used to read three to four hundred pages of fiction a day. I took my first MA in English literature and MAs in Sanskrit and Malayalam later.'

He looked at the time. The brahmachari said, 'Stay here tonight. You can go tomorrow.'

He felt really happy. To spend a night in this ashram, this sacred spot that was so calm and beautiful, immersed in the peace of the brahmachari's words, forgetting everything . . .

'So, as I said, the way of salvation is not very easy. Still . . .'

The next question the brahmachari shot at him was very sudden, 'What reduces you to greater slavery? Intoxication or . . .'

'Brahmachari, all I know is that both, at the same level . . .'

'Intoxication is not new to the puranas. Balabhadra's white radiance used to run away and hide fearing intoxication.'

Someone called out from outside the window, 'Shall I ask for water to be heated for the brahmachari?'

'No, I haven't had fever the last four days, after all. I'll have a bath today in the tank.'

The brahmachari said, as she was about to leave, 'Wait,

Amma.' He looked at his visitor and went on, 'This woman is the reflection of sorrow. She fell in love with a man from another religion while she was still pursuing her studies in college. She ran away with him. He cheated her and, in the end, she came here. See then, how strange the starting points are of the way of action.'

The brahmachari paused for a while and then went on again at greater speed, 'Look at the many flowers in this ashram. Then look at Amma with the same eyes. You will see her only as a flower. Remember the old poem *kusume kusumolpathi shrooyathe na cha drishyate* . . . One flower cannot give birth to another. I have neither seen or heard of such a thing happening. But a woman's face proves that it does happen. For the face can be a lotus, and in this lotus-face there can be two eyes that are karimkoovala flowers!'

He stared at the woman. She had beauty, and even more nobility than beauty. She seemed like a heap of jasmine flowers to him as she stood there in her pristine white clothes. He gazed steadily at the detachment on her face.

It was the brahmachari's voice that woke him up.

'By the way, let me ask you a legal doubt. I studied law, but then thought it was not necessary, so I did not take the exam. Isn't there legal provision to insist on a wife staying with her husband? Something that starts with the word "restitution"?'

He completed it, 'Restitution of conjugal rights.'

'Will a man who goes through a registered wedding have this right? Isn't a registered wedding only a contract?'

'I don't think he will have that right. Since it is a contract, I think all the man is entitled to if she will not stay with him is compensation.'

The brahmachari looked out and said sadly, 'Forgive me! Were you standing there all this while, Amma? Please go now.'

She walked away beyond the thick bushes, her expression still detached.

The brahmachari got up, had a bath, changed his clothes and sat down again cross-legged, immersed in prayer and meditation.

What a fine body he had . . . one shaped by yoga. When he saw how still he looked, he thought, God! If I could sit like this for just a minute! In total concentration. Holding my mind in the palm of my hand . . .

The brahmachari got up after many hours and said, as if only a few minutes had gone by, 'All the avatars took form according to the need for them, the whole as well as the partial ones. But it is this that I worship the most.'

He did not follow what the brahmachari said. Understanding this, the brahmachari pointed to the idol near him. 'Do you know who this is? The form of the great Varaha. The aim of this avatar was not to protect the animate and inanimate things in the universe. It was to take back Mother Earth herself, reclaim her from the asura Hiranyakshan, who had snatched her away . . .'

One of the ashram dwellers came in and said, 'Brahmachari, they request you to go to the hermitage.' The brahmachari continued, paying no attention to him, 'I made this idol with my own hands. With clay . . .'

How marvellously skilful his hands were! When he learnt that the brahmachari was a sculptor as well, he was filled with infinite respect for him.

'Come, swamiji is calling me. Come with me; let us offer him greetings.'

They walked over the green carpet of karuka grass, under the shade of the tamala trees.

'We call the place where the swamiji lives the hermitage.'

He felt the place was truly a hermitage.

Swamiji was seated on the cot. His fair skin gleamed. Although he did not look like a foreigner, he could be mistaken for a North Indian. He wore a woolen cap and a pullover under his ochre shawl.

The brahmachari introduced him. He made an obeisance to the swamiji, who said to the brahmachari, 'I cannot go for the Gita class in the Gnanodayam hall today. I have had an asthma attack. You must go, brahmachari. There will be seventeen foreigners participating. So you must make your speech in English.'

He would have actually liked to go with the brahmachari and listen to his Gita class in English. When he started to go out of the room, the swamiji said, 'Sit down. There is something I want to tell you.'

He saw an old, heavy wooden chair in the room and sat on it. Swamiji asked him to draw up the chair closer and he obeyed.

'Did you go round the ashram? I would have liked to show you round, describe everything to you. But I can't go out at all. I've had asthma for a long time. Do you know of any medicine for asthma?'

He admitted his helplessness.

'There isn't any medicine.' Swamiji's voice was very weak.

Bells rang somewhere outside and there was the sound of collective chanting. Maybe there was a hostel nearby. Evening prayers chanted in many voices lent a new quality to the calm of the place.

'I have seen a thousand and ten full moons now,' said the swamiji, controlling his asthma. 'But I still feel afraid. Not to die. God himself has given us a reason for death, after all. *Jathasya hi dhruvo mrityu / dhruvam janma mritasya cha . . .*'

Swamiji stopped with the first half of the verse and scrutinized his face. Then he said, 'Everything that is born dies. It is also certain that all that dies will be born again. Why should he who knows this grieve? That is the truth. But it is I who established this ashram. At the time when I arrived, there was not even shade for a crow here. I cleared the whole place, planted all that you see. I supervised every stone and tile that was laid. I created the ashram. But let me tell you the truth: I am anxious—what will happen to this after I die? Who will care for it?'

He could not speak for quite some time, either because his throat was blocked or because of an asthmatic spasm.

'I passed my FA in 1916 and took up a government job. I was not content with it. While going to enroll for my BA, I met a holy man in the train, one of the greatest of this era. It was with his blessing that I established this ashram. I have always had only one prayer—the boon Prahlada asked of God: let not desires take shape in my heart.'

He interrupted, 'Swamiji, my mind always slips out of my control. What shall I do about it? I came to find out . . .'

'Give you a way out of that in just one word! First of all, you must learn this: those who have true knowledge see the body as two. The body which is apparent and the body after it has overcome the senses. The second stage is called atmasamyamanam. It can be attained only through ceaseless effort. And to achieve it, you must first destroy the senses . . .' Swamiji had an attack of asthma.

One of the ashram servants brought upma and jeera coffee and placed it before him. Swamiji wound a muffler round his neck and pulled down the sleeves of his pullover.

'When I have an asthmatic attack, I can't eat anything. Actually, I get very hungry and long to eat until I'm full. What can I do . . .'

He gazed at the swamiji. He looked so pathetic.

The swamiji loosened his muffler and said, 'The Upanishads tell us, *vayuranilamamrithamathedam / bhasmantham shariram* . . . The life-breath of he who is dying merges with the breath of the universe, which never dies. The body ends as dust. This is the story of him who dies. So what should he who lives do for he who is dying?'

Suddenly, the swamiji said with great contempt, 'Will there be anyone to remember me when I die? Do you know the situation here? I asked them to give my name to a building constructed here last year. No one liked the idea. In the end they decided that the ashram would give the land for the building as its contribution. The building itself would be put up at my expense. The area has been marked out.'

The swamiji paused.

'I asked you to sit down here to ask you about a legal problem. Can I evict a tenant on my property?'

'Yes, if you want to build a house there for your own use.'

'I inherited a piece of family property as my share when the land was divided. There is a tenant staying on that land. Someone has offered to buy the land at a very good price to put up a cinema theatre, but I will have to first have the tenant evicted. I have made over the land to someone I know well with a deed of gift. He will argue the case saying that he wants the land in order to build a house for himself.'

The swamiji got up with great difficulty, went to the cupboard and brought the file containing the documents. He glanced over the papers quickly.

'Swamiji, all you need to do in these cases is furnish full proof that you need to build your house on that land. Then you can certainly evict the tenant.'

'So I can evict him . . .' The swamiji smiled, a smile that challenged his asthma.

'Once he's evicted, I can sell that land and have a prayer hall built here in my name . . .'

The swamiji looked out of the window. He saw a prayer hall coming up somewhere outside with satisfied eyes.

While consecrating the greater part of his life to uprooting his desires and casting them away, the man had been nursing these insubstantial fancies in secret . . .

'Go and lie down,' said the swamiji, opening the cupboard and taking out a sheet and a mat for him.

'Go and lie down in the brahmachari's room. I never sleep: I spend the time coughing and wheezing. If you stay here, you won't be able to sleep either.'

He went to the brahmachari's room, unrolled the mat, which smelled of camphor, and lay down.

The surroundings were very peaceful. The mingled fragrances of many flowers wafted on the faint breeze. Not even the sound of a night bird disturbed the silence.

He did not think about the prostitutes waiting in the streets. The faces of those he had betrayed did not appear to frighten him. The faces of those who had betrayed him did not lurk anywhere in his mind, laughing wildly.

God!

Why had he not wanted to come here earlier? It was not sleep that came to him but a kind of indolence, in which he slumbered lightly. In a little while, he felt pleasantly cool. He covered his head completely with the sheet. Suddenly, he felt something press against his body, and the warmth of softly spoken words.

'Why did you describe my face and eyes to that man who came today? Aren't you ashamed to say such things? Get up, come on . . .'

She shook him awake.

'No, no, not that. Why did you ask that man who came today about the law? Are you afraid someone will come here and take me away? Imagine me going . . . Haven't you understood me, after all this time?' When her taut breasts pressed against the sheet, he felt disgusted. Her long fingers reached into the sheet, played over his cheeks and crept up to his hair. They froze there for a minute. Then she sprang up as if she had been stung by a snake and fled. There was the sound of her hitting against the table. Something fell from the swaying table and broke into pieces. Maybe the great Varaha's image . . . He lay flat as if he was dead. When he thought of the helplessness of the creature called a human being that made such heroic efforts to uproot desire, he burst into violent weeping.

[*Translated by Gita Krishnankutty*]

After the Hanging

Kadalthiirathu

O.V. Vijayan

As Vellayi-appan set out on his journey the sound of ritual mourning rose from his hut, and from Ammini's hut, and beyond those huts, the village listened in grief. Vellayi-appan was going to Kannur. Had they the money, each one of them would have accompanied him on the journey; it was as though he was journeying for the village. Vellayi-appan now passed the last of the huts and took the long ridge across the paddies. The crying receded behind him. From the ridge he stepped on pasture land across which the footpath meandered.

Gods, my lords, Vellayi-appan cried within himself.

The black palms rose on either side and the wind clattered in their fronds. The wind, ever so familiar, was strange this day—the gods of his clan and departed elders were talking to him through the wind-blown fronds. Slung over his shoulder was a bundle of cooked rice, and its dampness seeped through the threadbare cloth on to his arm. His wife had bent long over the rice, kneading it for the journey and, as she had cried the while, her tears must have soaked into sour curd. Vellayi-appan walked on. The railway station was four miles away. Farther down the path he saw Kuttihassan walking towards him. Kuttihassan stepped aside from the path, in tender reverence.

'Vellayi,' said Kuttihassan.

'Kuttihassan,' replied Vellayi-appan.

That was all, just two words, two names, yet it was like a long colloquy, in which there was lament and consolation.

O Kuttihassan, said the unspoken words, *I have a debt to pay you, fifteen silvers.*

Let that not burden you, O Vellayi, on this journey.

Kuttihassan, I may never be able to pay you, never after this.

We consign our unredeemed debts to God's keeping. Let His will be done.

I burn within myself; my life is being prised away.

May the Prophet guard you on this journey, may the gods bless you, your gods and mine.

The dithyramb of the gods was now a torrent in the palms. Vellayi-appan passed Kuttihassan and walked on. Four miles to go to the train station. Again, an encounter on the way. Neeli, the laundress, with her bundles of washing. She too stepped aside reverentially.

'Vellayi-appan,' she said.

'Neeli,' said Vellayi-appan.

Just these two words, and yet between them the abundant colloquy. Vellayi-appan walked on.

The footpath joined the mud road, and Vellayi-appan looked for the milestone and continued on his way. Presently he came to where the rough-hewn track descended into the river. Across the river, beyond a rise and a stretch of sere grass, was the railway. Vellayi-appan stepped on to the sands, then into the knee-deep water. Schools of little fish, gleaming silver, rubbed against his calves and swam on. As he reached the middle of the river, Vellayi-appan was overwhelmed by the expanse of water. It reminded him of sad and loving rituals, of the bathing of his father's dead body and how he taught his son to swim in the river; all this he remembered and, pausing on the river bank, wept in memory.

He reached the railway station and made his way to the ticket counter and with great care undid the knot in the corner of his unsewn cloth to take out the money for the fare.

'Kannur,' Vellayi-appan said. The clerk behind the counter pulled out a ticket, franked it and tossed it towards him. *One stage in my journey is over*, thought Vellayi-appan. He secured the ticket in the corner of his unsewn cloth and, crossing over to the platform, sat on a bench, waiting patiently for his train. He watched the sun sink and the palms darken far away, and the birds flit homewards. Vellayi-appan remembered walking with his son to the fields at sundown; he remembered how his son had looked up at the birds in wonder. Then he remembered himself as a child, holding on to his father's little finger and walking down the same fields. Two images, but between them as between two reticent words, an abundance of many things. Soon another aged traveller came over and sat beside him on the bench.

'Going to Coimbatore, are you?' the stranger asked.

'Kannur,' Vellayi-appan said.

'Is that so?'

'The Kannur train will be at ten in the night.'

'Is that so?'

'What work do you do in Kannur?'

'Nothing much.'

'Just travelling, are you?'

The stranger's converse, inane and rasping, tensed round Vellayi-appan like a hangman's noose. Once you left the village and walked over the long ridge, it was a world full of strangers, and their disinterested words were like a multitude of nooses. The train to Coimbatore came, and the old stranger rose and left. Vellayi-appan was again alone on the bench. He had no desire to untie the bundle of rice. Instead he kept a hand on the threadbare wrap; he felt its moisture. He sat thus and slept. And dreamt. In his dream he called out, 'Kandunni, my son!'

Vellayi-appan was woken up from his sleep by the din and clatter of the train to Kannur. He felt for the ticket tied in the corner of his cloth and was reassured. He looked for an open door; he tried to board the compartment nearest to him.

'This is first class, O elder.'

'Is that so?'

He peered into the next compartment.

'This is reserved.'

'Is that so?'

'Try farther down, O elder.'

The voice of strangers.

Vellayi-appan got into a compartment where there was no sitting space left. He could barely stand. *I shall stand; I don't need to sleep; this night my son sits awake.* The rhythm of the train changed with the changing layers of the earth, the fleeting trackside lamps, sand banks, trees. Long ago he had travelled in a train, but that was in the daytime. This was a night train. It sped through the tunnel of darkness, whose arching walls were painted with dim murals.

The day had not broken when he reached Kannur. The bundle of kneaded rice still hung from his shoulder, oozing its dampness. He passed through the gate into the station yard, the dark now livened by the first touch of dawn. The horse-cart men clumsily parked together did not accost him.

Vellayi-appan asked them, 'Which is the way to the jail?'

Someone laughed. *Here is an old man asking the way to the jail at daybreak.* Someone laughed again, *O elder, all you have to do is steal; they will take you there.* The converse of strangers tightened round his neck. Vellayi-appan suffocated.

Then someone told him the way and Velayi-appan began to walk. The sky lightened to the orchestration of crows cawing.

At the gate of the jail a guard stopped him, 'What brings you here this early?'

Vellayi-appan shrank back like a child, nervous. Then slowly he undid the corner of his cloth and took out a crumpled and yellowing piece of paper.

'What is that?' the guard enquired.

Vellayi-appan handed him the paper; the guard glanced through it without reading.

Vellayi-appan said, 'My child is here.'

'Who told you to come so early?' the guard asked, his voice irritable and harsh. 'Wait till the office is open.'

Then his eyes fell on the paper again, and became riveted to its contents. His face softened in sudden compassion.

'Tomorrow, is it?' the guard asked, almost consoling.

'I don't know. It is all written down there.'

The guard read and reread the order. 'Yes,' he said, 'it's tomorrow morning at five.'

Vellayi-appan nodded in acknowledgement, and slumped on a bench at the entrance of the jail. There he waited for the dark sanctum to open.

'O elder, may I offer you a cup of tea?' the guard asked solicitously.

'No.'

My son has not slept this night and, not having slept, would not have woken. Neither asleep nor awake, how can he break his fast this morning? Vellayi-appan's hand rested on the bundle of rice. *My son, this rice was kneaded by your mother for me. I saved it during all the hours of my journey and brought it here. Now this is all I have to bequeath to you.* The rice inside the threadbare wrap, food of the traveller, turned stale. Outside, the day brightened. The day grew hot.

The offices opened, and staid men took their places behind the tables. In the prison yard there was the grind of a parade. The prison came alive. The officers got to work, bending over yellowing papers in tedious scrutiny. From behind the tables, and where the column of the guards waited in formation, came rasping orders, words of command. Nooses without contempt or vengeance, gently strangulating the traveller. The day grew hotter.

Someone told him, *sit down and wait.* Vellayi-appan sat down; he waited. After a wait, the length of which he could not reckon, a guard led him into the corridors of the prison. The corridors were cool with the damp of the prison. *We're here, O elder.*

Behind the bars of a locked cell stood Kandunni. He looked at his father like a stranger, through the awesome filter of a mind that could no longer receive nor give consolation. The guard opened the door and let Vellayi-appan into the cell. Father and son stood facing each other, petrified. Then Vellayi-appan leaned forward to take his son in an embrace. From Kandunni came a cry that pierced beyond hearing and when it died down, Vellayi-appan said, 'My son!'

'Father!' said Kandunni.

Just these words, but in them father and son communed in the fullness of sorrow.

Son, what did you do?

I have no memory, father.

Son, did you kill?

I have no memory.

It does not matter, my son; there is nothing to remember any more.

Will the guards remember?

No, my son.

Father, will you remember my pain?

Then again the cry that pierced beyond hearing issued from Kandunni, *Father, don't let them hang me!*

'Come out, O elder,' the guard said. 'The time is over.'

Vellayi-appan came away and the door clanged shut.

One last look back, and Vellayi-appan saw his son like a stranger met during a journey. Kandunni was peering through the bars as a traveller might through the window of a hurtling train.

Vellayi-appan wandered idly round the jail. The sun rose to its zenith, then began the climb down. *Will my son sleep this night?* The night came, and moved to dawn again. Within the walls Kandunni still lived.

Vellayi-appan heard the sound of bugles at dawn, little knowing that this was death's ceremonial. But the guard had told him that it was at five in the morning and though he wore no watch, Vellayi-appan knew the time with the peasant's unerring instinct.

∗

Vellayi-appan received the body of his son from the guards like a midwife a baby.

O elder, what plans do you have for the funeral?

I have no plans.
Don't you want the body?
Masters, I have no money.

Vellayi-appan walked along with the scavengers who pushed the trolley carrying the body. Outside the town, over the deserted marshes, the vultures wheeled patiently. Before the scavengers filled the pit Vellayi-appan saw his son's face just once more. He pressed his palm on the cold forehead in blessing.

After the last shovelful of earth had levelled the pit, Vellayi-appan wandered in the gathering heat and eventually came to the seashore. He had never seen the ocean before. Then he became aware of something cold and wet in his hands, the rice his wife had kneaded for his journey. Vellayi-appan undid the bundle. He scattered the rice on the sand, in sacrifice and requiescat. From the crystal reaches of the sunlight, crows descended on the rice, like incarnate souls of the dead come to receive the offering.

[*Translated by the author*]

Wind Flowers

Preema katha

O.V. Vijayan

When Chandran had packed and was ready to leave, Beeran, the caretaker of the travellers' bungalow, lost all interest in him, the only visitor who had not given him an opportunity to be a good host. After the military had wound up the hilltop camp, the travellers' bungalow which adjoined it had lost the purpose for which it had been built, and attracted only occasional guests who sought pleasure in the privacy of the mountain country. The previous night Beeran had held forth on Visalakshi, describing her excellence, going over her every limb in the style of classical erotic poetry. Mistaking Chandran's silence for interest, he had waxed eloquent. But now this good-for-nothing visitor was getting ready to leave, and Beeran realized his poetry had been wasted.

Chandran rose and went to the balustrade. The dawn lit the valley below. It was just as he had seen it in his childhood, the trees blue-green in the mist and the river showing through the areca palms.

It was to this river that you took me, Visalakshi, to show me the blood of the Namboodiri slaughtered by the Muslim rebels, blood which, the legend said, still eddied in the water. I shall presently drive back over this gravel road, the road we walked as eight-year-olds. We had walked hand in hand, and were grateful for that touch. I go without seeing you, without bidding you farewell; the ingratitude of my departure oppresses me. But perhaps it is just as well, because if we met today we might not recognize each other, and were we to look beneath the changed contours of our faces for the lost innocence of our childhood, it might cause us inconsolable sorrow. I ask myself, why then did I come here? Perhaps, it is because we revisit our innocence like a criminal visits the scene of his crime. Forgive me the hubris of this journey.

Chandran walked back into the room, and Beeran followed, to be of help if it was needed.

'There is nothing more to pack, Beeran,' Chandran said. 'I shall be obliged if there is some coffee.'

'By eight, shall we say?'

'Yes, thank you.'

Beeran went out of the bungalow and disappeared into the annexe that housed the pantry and the kitchen.

Permit me to remember. Memory shall be our colloquy.

*

It was Chandran's first week in the Muslim school. During lunch break Visalakshi said to him, 'Do you want to come out with me?'

'Where to?' Chandran asked . . .

'To the areca plantation. I shall show you bunches of areca nuts.'

Chandran agreed to go with her. It was the first time he had gone anywhere but home from school. As they entered the plantation they encountered an elderly Muslim in a red mundu.

'Who is that, Visalakshi?'

'It is Mohiddeen-kaka.'

Chandran was nervous. Stories of Muslim rebels clad in red mundus came to his mind. Mohiddeen-kaka greeted them, 'What brings you here, children?'

Chandran became even more nervous.

'This is the saheb's child,' Visalakshi said. 'He wants to see the areca bunches.'

Mohiddeen-kaka laughed. 'To see the areca bunches? By all means!'

Chandran's fear of the red mundu passed. 'Child of the major saheb, aren't you?' Mohiddeen-kaka asked.

'Yes, he is,' Visalakshi said.

'And you, aren't you old Raman Nair's daughter?'

'Yes.'

Mohiddeen-kaka led them to the areca palms.

'There!' Mohiddeen-kaka pointed to the top of a palm. 'A ripe, red bunch. Shall I get it plucked for you?'

'No, thanks,' Chandran said. 'I just wanted to see it.'

It was then that they saw the big spider. It had fastened its web between two palm trees.

'Look at that, Chandran!' Visalakshi cried.

Chandran had never seen a spider so big. Mohiddeen-kaka flung a twig at it and brought it down.

'This is a bird-eater,' Visalakshi said. Chandran flinched from the spider.

It was time to be back at school.

'Let's go,' he said.

'Yes, let's.'

Visalakshi walked a few paces, and turned back. 'Look at its tail, Chandran!'

The spider was crawling away, trailing a length of tough and opaque web.

'It is not the tail,' Mohiddeen-kaka said. 'It is the web of the evil one.'

Visalakshi picked up the web and the spider dangled helplessly at the other end. 'Chandran, are you scared?'

'Leave him,' Mohiddeen-kaka said. 'He's poisonous.'

Mohiddeen-kaka accompanied them up to the stile in the boundary fence. 'Give my salaams to the major saheb.'

'I shall,' Chandran said.

But Chandran could not convey that message to his father without letting out the secret that he had wandered out of the school compound, in sly disobedience of his father's injunction. The camp on the hilltop was the authority of Occupation, and his father had forbidden him to fraternize with the children of the village. Even the teachers treated Chandran with deference: he was the child of the major who commanded the camp.

Chandran was sent to the school of the Muslims because that was the only school around, and his father wanted Chandran to get used to children his own age. It was a school of the poor, and its teachers themselves did not have much education. To offset this Chandran had a tutor who lived with the family and taught him Browning and Coleridge.

The teachers often visited the camp to pay their respects to the commandant. So broken was the spirit of the Muslims after their crushed rebellion, and so awesome the power of the military, that the teachers would hesitate to sit before his father. But Chandran's grandmother treated them to lavish teas, and invoked their blessings for her grandchild. Her favourite was Mohammed Haji, Chandran's class teacher.

'He is a pious one,' she would say.

Mohammed Haji was a placid being with a round face and a corpulent body. Those were times when one could study up to the fifth standard and on the strength of that scrappy literacy train oneself to be a teacher. Mohammed Haji was one such. But this did not bother Chandran's grandmother.

'He is your teacher, your preceptor,' she would tell Chandran. 'Listen to his words of wisdom.'

The words of wisdom came in abundance. The first period at school, since it was a school for Muslims, was the teaching of the Koran. Mohammed Haji was theologian, historian and scientist rolled into one. Every day after the scripture lessons, he wrote out a few problems in arithmetic on the blackboard, and then moved on to history. History was a matter of conjecture, and science daring discovery. Teaching science one day, Mohammed Haji asked, 'What is this thing that we call air? You answer, Usman!'

'Wind,' Usman said.

'Can you see the wind?'

'You cannot.'

'Then listen to me, O child of the devil! You can see the wind. Go to the riverside at noon and slant your head and watch; you can see the wind rise up like flowers.'

After this lesson, when the class broke for lunch, the children trooped to the riverside. They cocked their heads to one side, as the teacher had instructed them to, and looked over the beds of sand. And sure enough, they saw the wind flowers rise layer upon layer!

Chandran stayed behind. So did Visalakshi, working out a sum. She looked up from her book and asked him, 'Aren't you going, Chandran?'

'No.'

'Don't want to see the wind flowers?'

Chandran contemplated saying no. But he said, 'Let us see them.'

'Then come with me.'

'But mother has told me not to go to the riverside.'

Visalakshi laughed. 'Ayyee! What is there to be scared of? Am I not with you?'

She closed her book and came over and took his hand. 'Come, Chandran.'

When they reached the riverside, the rest of the children had left. The sands were deserted.

'Look!' Visalakshi said.

Chandran cocked his head and looked over the hot sands.

'Chandran, do you see the flowers?'

'I see them.'

Every day during lunch break, after the other children had returned, Visalakshi took Chandran out to see the wind flowers. Chandran liked to be alone with her in the spaces of the river, to breathe her fragrance in the river breezes. But the wind flowers disturbed him. He had read that air was invisible. At last he asked his tutor. The tutor explained to him how heat created the mirage, and recited Sanskrit poetry which described the mirage as the pond of the deluded wild deer.

Chandran did not say anything of this in class: he was reluctant to contradict Mohammed Haji. But he let Visalakshi into the secret.

'But don't tell anyone,' Chandran said.

'Why not?'

'I don't know myself. But my grandmother said something about the preceptor's blessings.'

She did not understand it either, but both realized that it would hurt their teacher if they told the others; so they decided to keep the mirage to themselves, a secret kept in tenderness and trust.

*

After these twenty years Chandran experienced the benediction of that trust, the grace of his grandmother and of his unlettered teacher. His grandmother slept at the foot of the hill, the banyan they planted over her must have grown into a big tree. Mohammed Haji too was gone.

'It is all over with the village,' Beeran said as he came to remove the coffee cup. 'The village died with the camp, and the school too was closed down. The tigers returned to our mountains, and the big spiders to the hilltop.'

Beeran withdrew with the tray, leaving Chandran alone. Chandran sat on in the veranda, and the sun climbed towards its zenith.

*

A few days after the incident of the wind flowers, Chandran composed a poem in English on butterflies. He had taken the first couplet from a book of nursery rhymes, but wrote out the rest himself. He showed it to his tutor.

'The first two lines are not mine,' Chandran confessed.

The tutor smiled, 'It does not matter.' He read through the poem and said, 'It is well done.'

Chandran took the poem to school and showed it to the headmaster. The headmaster read it out to the children of the eighth standard, the highest class in the school. When the poem was written out in the school's manuscript magazine, there were sceptical whispers. How could a boy of the fifth standard know so much English? Even Mohammed Haji could not have written that poem. Raghavan, the overgrown back-bencher, swore that Chandran's grandfather had written the poem.

It was then that another incident brought the children's resentment out into the open. Mohammed Haji was spelling out the word 'depot', and wondered aloud whether the final 't' was sounded or not. He came up to Chandran and said, 'You read.'

Chandran read the word out, with the 't' silent. A murmur went through the class, and Khadija, the Muslim landlord's daughter, said, 'Why do you ask him?'

Mohammed Haji caressed Chandran's shoulders, and told Khadija, 'O child of the devil, isn't he the one who is learning English at home?'

The English lesson ended and Mohammed Haji, tapping the table with his cane for silence, announced the next lesson, 'Now, all of you go down into the lane and chase butterflies. It is nature study till lunch break.'

With shouts of joy the children tumbled out of the classroom.

'Anyone to the riverside?' Khadija called out. Hymavathi, Amina and Aisu joined her.

'Shall we go too?' Visalakshi asked Chandran.

'Yes.'

When they got to the river Khadija said to no one in particular, 'It is depot! The "t" is not silent. My brother told me.'

'What about the teacher then?' Hymavathi asked.

'All that is like the poem,' Khadija said.

Amina asked Chandran, 'Did you write it yourself?'

Chandran flushed. He said, 'Yes, I did.'

Amina feigned surprise, 'Ya Rahman!'

Khadija, who was listening, said, 'A lie!'

Visalakshi lashed out, 'Didn't the headmaster read it out? Are you calling the headmaster a liar?'

That silenced Khadija.

'Chandran, let us go,' Visalakshi said. She led him back to

school, and the other children who remained behind on the river bank dared not snigger. Walking up the lane between embankments of fern, Visalakshi paused. 'Chandran,' she said, 'don't be sad.'

At this, Chandran's tears came rolling down.

'Ayyee!' she said. 'Why do you cry? I shall take you to the orchard and pluck you the ambazha fruit.'

'No.'

'Come along,' she said, grasping him by the shoulder. 'Don't you want to see the orchard?'

A narrow lane led to the orchard, and one had to cross a steep stile to get among the trees.

'Are you scared, Chandran?' Visalakshi asked, as she helped Chandran over the stile.

'No, Visalakshi. But aren't we getting late for class?'

'Don't worry.'

Chandran entered the enchanted grove; he had never been inside an orchard before. He looked up at the branches arched beneath the sky and listened to the tumult of the cicadas as they jingled their mysterious hoards of silver.

Visalakshi was familiar with the secrets of the orchard. 'Karinagattan lives here.'

'Who is that?'

'He is a god. The snake-god.'

'Will he bite?'

'I don't know. Perhaps, if we step on him. Are you scared?'

'No.' But Chandran was afraid not so much of snakebite as of his father coming to know of this expedition. He was the commandant's son, and it was not proper for him to have gone into the orchard foraging for the wild ambazha fruit. If the snake-god bit him all his secrets would be out, the forays into the areca plantation, the journeys to the riverside. O serpent-god, he prayed, help me keep my secrets.

Visalakshi plucked the ambazhas and gave them to him. Chandran bit into them. Some were sour, yet others bitter.

'Aren't they tasty?' Visalakshi asked.

'Yes.'

They were busy plucking fruit when the bell rang for reassembly.

'Chandran!'

'Shall we run?'

'It is the geography teacher's class. He will cane us.'

They left the orchard and broke into a run. In the embarrassment of truancy they hesitated at the entrance to the classroom. The geography teacher turned from his map and asked them, 'Where have you been?'

Neither Visalakshi nor Chandran replied. But from the back bench an informer piped up, 'They were in the orchard, Sir.'

Chandran was terrified, for the orchard was forbidden territory. The cane lay on the table. The geography teacher regarded the delinquents in indecision for a while and then said, 'Get inside.'

That evening the car did not arrive to take Chandran home. Instead, an orderly waited with biscuits and a flask of milk. After he had eaten, Chandran set out. He found Visalakshi waiting at the gate.

'Where is your car, Chandran?'

'My father has taken it. He's on tour.'

Chandran and Visalakshi walked behind the orderly.

She said to him softly, 'We escaped a caning because of you.'

The road to the camp climbed steeply. Midway was Visalakshi's house. This was where old Raman Nair ran his village hotel and place of entertainment. It had an austere look compared to other tea shops. There was no glass front, no funnelled gramophone. Still, soldiers frequented the place, and so did landlords from the deep countryside.

As they reached her house, Visalakshi said shyly, 'Will you come in, Chandran?'

He had dreamt of going into that charmed house every time he drove past it. He would see Raman Nair seated in the veranda, or at times catch a glimpse of Visalakshi's mother, her face fair and bright. Today he was at its very threshold. The temptation was irresistible. He would be late getting home but could pacify his mother with some alibi. But there was the orderly—he would never consent to the visit. Taking a desperate chance, Chandran asked the orderly, 'Nambiar, can I go with her?'

Nambiar consented with unexpected readiness. In exuberant joy, Visalakshi bolted in, crying, 'Mother! Look who has come!' Visalakshi's mother emerged from the kitchen through a smoky corridor. Her face was flushed with the fires of the hearth, and reddened a little more as she blew her nose. Chandran saw the drops of sweat under her lips, the patch of soot on her dimple and sensed her fragrance like Visalakshi's in the river breeze. Flashing a seductive smile at Nambiar, Janakiamma turned to Chandran tenderly, 'We are honoured!'

Visalakshi insisted that he have coffee. Chandran's confusion increased. This visit was in defiance of his parents' ban on fraternizing. He wondered if the orderly would turn informer. Visalakshi returned with a tray of biscuits and coffee and said, 'Let us go to my room.' She led the way into a little room in the corner of which were stacked her worldly possessions: a seashell, a bronze Krishna, a few marbles, a collection of copper and silver coins. Above this treasure hung a garlanded photograph.

'Whose picture is that?' Chandran asked.

'It's my father's.'

The reply struck Chandran as odd. 'Then,' he asked hesitantly, 'who is Raman Nair?'

'Aw,' she said, 'he keeps my mother.'

Her reply baffled him. He asked, 'Doesn't your father stay here?'

'He stays far away, in Manjeri.'

Janakiamma came in and stroked Chandran's cheeks. 'Have some biscuits, child. It is poor fare.'

'Oh, no,' Chandran said, and hastened to eat the biscuits, which were stale and damp. Janakiamma smiled as she watched him and the dimples deepened on her cheeks. As she smoothed back her curls her face was like Visalakshi's, and so were her large, black eyes, her delicate feet and the soft touch of her hands.

Janakiamma left the children and went away to entertain the orderly.

'Don't you like my mother?' Visalakshi asked.

'Yes.'

'Isn't she pretty?'

'She is.'

'Her thighs are very fair.'

'You have seen them, have you, Visalakshi?'

'Yes,' she said. 'Mother is very young, and Raman Nair is old. Mother says he is ninety.'

'And how old is your mother?'

'She is sixteen.'

'Is that true?'

'It is. All her visitors say so.'

Chandran ate the rest of the stale biscuits and hard bananas with relish.

'Why doesn't your father stay here?'

Visalakshi did not reply. Chandran asked again, 'Doesn't your father visit you, Visalakshi?'

A sadness misted her face, a sadness beyond Chandran's understanding.

Visalakshi said, 'He did come some time ago, when Raman Nair was away. It was sad seeing my father—he was so poor and worn. He works in a plantation in Manjeri, and they pay him scanty wages. Mother sat with him in her room, and they talked till evening, when he wanted to go away by the last bus. *Oh, no, don't,* mother said, *you don't love me!* She kept taunting him, and father agreed to stay the night. When mother went for her evening bath, father put me on his lap and told me, *You must study well, my child, and become a teacher in the big school at Manjeri.* He said he was saving from his wages so that I could go on with my schooling. He misses supper to save this money for me, and that has given him an ulcer. He said he will move on to larger estates in the mountains where they pay better wages. He is doing it all for me. That evening he wept over me, and said again, *You should become a teacher, my child. You should not become like your mother.* What did he mean, Chandran?'

'I don't know, Visalakshi.'

Visalakshi went on, 'That night I couldn't sleep. In my mother's room I could hear them whispering. And father repeating her name, sobbing, *Janu, Janu!* I pressed my face into the pillow and cried myself to sleep. When I woke up, father was gone.'

When the story ended, Visalakshi was greatly depressed. She asked, 'Does your mother have another man, someone who keeps her?'

'No.'

Visalakshi fell silent for a while, then went over to her treasure trove. 'Chandran . . .'

'Yes?'

'Take a gift, Chandran. Anything you like.'

'Oh, no!'

'Aren't we friends?'

'Of course, we are.'

'Then choose your gift.'

She placed the bronze Krishna before him. It was her father's gift and she polished it every day with sour tamarind.

'Not that, Visalakshi,' Chandran said. 'That is too precious.'

Reluctantly she put the Krishna back. 'Then at least this seashell,' she said.

'If you insist.'

Chandran put the shell into his satchel. It was getting late. 'Visalakshi, I must go.'

It was the orderly that Chandran was anxious about, but Nambiar showed no sign of impatience. He sat in Janakiamma's room, chatting with her and bursting into peals of laughter. That reassured Chandran. Surely if the orderly was so friendly with Visalakshi's mother, he would not turn informer.

'What do they call you at home, Chandran?' Visalakshi asked.

'They call me Kunchu.'

'And me they call Chinnu.'

The visit ended. That night Chandran tossed sleepless in bed for a long while. And when he slept, strange dreams came to him. He dreamt that he was Janakiamma's child, a nurseling. Janakiamma was only as big as Visalakshi, and had the same riverside fragrance. Yet she had big pale breasts with which she suckled him. He slept clutching those breasts with an infant's hands.

*

Beeran waited in ill-tempered patience: Chandran had said he would be leaving after breakfast, yet he sat on. *Forgive me, Beeran. This is a wait I cannot help, a wait for noontide, for the river sands to become hot.*

*

The visit to Visalakshi's house could not be kept a secret for long. The orderly was severely reprimanded and Chandran received another sermon on dignity: he was the commandant's son and ought to keep his distance from the village children. But, once in school, this oppressive dignity gave way to freedom.

'Kunchu, let's go!' Visalakshi would call at lunch break.

'Let's,' he would say. They wandered in the neighbourhood during lunch break, taking in the magical sights of the village. They watched old Muslims sit stooped, hollow goats' horns stuck on their shaven heads to let barber-surgeons draw out impure blood. Visalakshi taught Chandran to climb over the stile, and they foraged in the orchards. They hunted among ferns for cocoons, watched giant dragonflies plummet into the river and rise, and schools of tiny silvery fish churn in the deep eddies. Chandran often slipped on the riverside rocks of quartz with their cover of velvet moss. But Visalakshi, sure-footed, always held him. It was while watching the eddies once that Visalakshi narrated the story of how the Muslim rebels murdered the Namboodiri landlord and flung his body into the river.

'It was my father who shot the rebels,' Chandran said. He

had seen his father wear a silver medal with King George's head embossed on it. His father had been decorated for suppressing the rebellion. Visalakshi's eyes widened in wonder. 'Is that so, Kunchu?'

'He shot them with a big gun. Have you seen a big gun, Chinnu?'

'How could I?'

'Ayyee! You haven't seen a Lewis gun? It has a magazine of forty-seven rounds and can kill two thousand people. It was with the same gun that the leader of the rebellion was shot too. My father shot him.'

'Kunchu, will you take me to see this gun some day?'

'Of course.'

It was in the days after the promise that Chandran was terrified by what he had let himself in for. How could he invite Janakiamma's daughter home—what would he tell his father? It was then that an opportunity presented itself. The commandant left on a tour of inspection and was expected to be away for a week. Chandran trailed his mother round the house, his heart beating fast.

'What is it, Kunchu?'

'Mother, this classmate of mine . . .'

'What about your classmate?'

'She wants to see the camp.'

'Why do you have to ask me?'

'She wants to see the Lewis gun.'

'Who is she?'

'Chinnu,' the word slipped out of his mouth.

'Chinnu who?'

Chandran's face reddened in confusion.

'Visalakshi, Raman Nair's daughter.'

Chandran's mother laughed. 'Why don't you wait till your father returns?'

That would ruin everything; Chandran was on the verge of tears. Unexpectedly his mother said, 'Call her if you want to.'

The next evening Visalakshi came home with Chandran.

Chandran's mother received her with effusive courtesy, but Chandran himself shied away.

'You ought to be chaperoning her, Kunchu,' grandmother chided him. 'Isn't she your friend?'

Mother was amused. 'Come, Kunchu, pass her the cake.'

After tea his mother called the orderly and said, 'Nambiar, could you take the children to see the guns?'

The gun-room was a narrow corridor dimly lit by high ventilators, its still air heavy with the smell of grease and oil. It held row upon row of rifles along with stacks of magazines and grenades and, laid out on cement racks, the heavy Lewis guns, sombre like the trunks of elephants.

'Ayyo!' said Visalakshi, holding her breath. Chandran felt a great tide of love rise within him and sweep over her.

'Are you scared, Chinnu?'

'Ayyo!'

She stood awhile in silence and asked him, 'Is that the big gun your father used?'

'Yes,' Chandran answered hastily. He was not sure, and did not want to risk talking about it in the presence of the gun-keeper.

'Ayyo!' Visalakshi repeated.

*

There were a number of factions in the class, led by Abu, by Salim, by the muezzin's daughter Mariam and so on. Each of these factions had tried to claim Chandran, but he had rebuffed them all and, consequently, all of them turned against him. It did not matter; he would not condescend to belong to any faction. He was the commandant's son after all. Despite the reclusive, superior air he adopted, Khadija ventured to call him a liar a second time. Her uncle, who traded in Malaya, had brought home a silver inkpot. She brought it to the class and proclaimed, 'There is no inkpot like this anywhere in the world.'

Chandran laughed. On his father's table was an identical piece.

'We have one at home,' he said.

'Oh, ho! Here is the one who has everything!'

'I shall bring it to school tomorrow.'

'Let us see you bring it!'

Chandran realized the predicament he was in. He dared not displace anything on the commandant's table. When he came without the inkpot to school the next day, Khadija shouted, 'Liar!'

Chandran turned pale. If he wanted he could complain to the headmaster, but he reasoned himself out of such a course. More than the humiliation, it was isolation that Chandran found hard to bear. No faction came to his rescue. In despair he glanced towards Chinnu. 'What is it all about, Khadija?' Visalakshi asked, pretending not to know. There was a titter in the class. Visalakshi said, 'Chandran didn't lie. I have seen the inkpot myself.'

God, she hadn't.

'How did you see it?' Khadija asked, the sparring now heady. 'Have you gone to his house?'

Embarrassed, Visalakshi admitted, 'Yes.'

'Ho, ho,' Khadija and her friends set up a chorus, 'ha, ha!'

Chandran and Visalakshi had kept the story of her visit a precious secret. It was now revealed before a leering, hostile class. An insensate courage seized Chandran. He would bring the inkpot, come what may. Let his father shoot him down with the Lewis gun, like he had shot the Muslim insurgents!

Chandran came to the class the next day with the inkpot. Visalakshi did not bother to show her triumph. Khadija was silent. Hymavathi, Amina and Aisu turned away from the glittering object.

Then events took a disastrous turn. The inkpot slipped from his hand and fell, and its engraved latch came off. Chandran despaired. Now his father would discover his transgression!

'We shall set it right, Kunchu,' Visalakshi said with confidence.

'How?'

'Just you wait.'

When the bell rang for lunch break, Visalakshi led Chandran into the orchard. There was a tree in the orchard whose bark oozed an adhesive resin. It was called the tholi gum, and could fix practically anything. Visalakshi scraped off chunks of the resin and smeared it on the metal.

'Will it stick?'

'Of course.'

The gum made a mess on her palms, elbows and arms.

'Chinnu . . .'

'Yes?'

'The gum is all over you.'

'Where?'

'Here.'

'Where?'

Chandran wiped it away from her palms and from her elbows and arms. Traces of the resin lingered on her cheek. Tenderly, he began wiping it away.

'Is it going, Kunchu?'

*

God, if only it had ended there, this ballad of my love, with the ministering palm on the fair cheek! But it was destined for a grosser completion, by an intruding pimp.

*

'All that is left of this village,' Beeran said, 'is Raman Nair's hotel. The old man died, and after him his woman, getting rid of an inconvenient pregnancy.' Here Beeran paused and laughed, a pimp's idea of comic relief. 'Now the daughter reigns, and if she goes away that will be the end of this travellers' bungalow. She is worth her weight in gold.'

Chandran smiled in forgiveness, and rose. It was noon.

'Thank you, Beeran. I must go now.'

Dispirited, Beeran helped with the boxes and stood by.

'Salaam,' he said.

'Salaam.'

The car sped down the hill and climbed up another. On either side of the road were mud walls with their veneer of moss and their mouldering smell. At the top of the hill, Chandran stopped his vehicle. This would be a brief tryst with the noontide. Were he to linger on he would disturb the slumbers of many. Of his grandmother, who had invoked for him the benediction of an unlettered teacher; of the beautiful girl who had filled the river breeze with fragrance; of himself, the child suckled by the pale breasts of innocence. *Let me leave all this undisturbed; let me resume my disconsolate journey.*

Far away, in the depths of another river, schools of fish churned with the eddies. Far away, on strange sands, in the heat of the noontide, in the grace of the preceptor, rose the splendorous wind flowers.

[*Translated by the author*]

A Colony of Hermaphrodites

Napumsakangal

Kamala Das

There is in Bombay in the slums of Koliwada in Sion a colony inhabited solely by hermaphrodites. A village that overflows with huts made of zinc sheets, rope cots, rotting vegetables piled in stinking heaps and human beings who are forced to shave their faces even though they wear women's clothes. Brandishing their drums and anklets, these hijras rush to any house where a baby boy has been born and perform a dance so that health and long life may be granted to the child. As compensation, the lady of the house usually gives them the wheat, jaggery and coconut to which they are entitled. If these gifts are not given them in plenty, they retaliate by shouting obscenities. And if they are provoked to fury, the hijras lift their skirts and expose the curse they normally keep concealed. Most people consider that sight a terrible punishment.

The hijras come into the city every Friday with dotted skirts or sarees draped round them and terrified women hurriedly throw them coins. The hijras laugh delightedly at the fear they inspire and describe the beauty of these respectable women's organs using the most obscene words . . .

The people of Bombay believe that hermaphrodites steal infants and transform them by cutting up their private parts with knives. But there are no witnesses to this. Or if there are, they do not have the guts to speak about the matter. The hermaphrodites most certainly steal babies, for how else would new faces continually appear in their ill-reputed colony? Innumerable hijras live there, tapping idly on their drums, jingling their anklets and singing in rough voices. All day, they wander around. Like everyone else, they too have a machinery of government and a chief who runs it. A hijra named Ram Kinkari. A black creature they call Ram Bhavu.

Six feet in height, Ram Bhavu always wore white sarees. His flat teeth showing like gravestones between lips reddened with betel juice, Ram Bhavu was a pandit of obscene language.

Ram Kinkari usually had an oil bath at dusk. He needed four ounces of brahmi oil and his dear friend Shakku Bhai to assist him at this ritual. Lying flat on his rope cot, he would give himself up to the caresses of Shakku Bhai's gentle hands. Once the oil had been rubbed into his body, the hijra leader would get up and walk to and fro in the moonlight, and while he walked, he would find out everything that concerned the welfare of the folk who lived there.

It was one evening, at dusk, when he was lying on his cot like this that the old woman arrived there. A Sethani woman wearing her saree the Gujarati way. There were no jewels on her neck or ears. Her eyes had a strange glitter and Ram Kinkari knew at once that she was mad.

'There's an old woman here,' said Shakku Bhai, 'a Gujarati woman, a Sethani.'

Making no effort to get up from where he lay, Ram Kinkari asked in a rough voice, 'What do you want, old woman? Don't you know this is a colony that belongs to us hijras? You have no right to be here.'

The old woman sat down on the ground and stretched out her legs. 'I've been walking since noon,' she said. 'I've taken a vow that I won't go back home until I find my pretty little child.'

'Your pretty little child?' asked Ram Kinkari. 'What is the point of looking for her here? Only hermaphrodites live here.'

'She was born one,' said the old woman. 'I waited seventeen years after I was married for her to be born and made innumerable offerings to temple after temple. Her face was as bright as the rising moon and she had a tender birthmark on her lips. It must have been your people who stole her from her cradle and took her away. I will not go back until I find her . . .'

'We don't steal children, old woman,' said Ram Kinkari. 'Families often sell their children to us. We may pay large sums for them but we are not in the habit of stealing them. Hijras are more honest and straightforward than you people. We are the children of Bhumi Devi, the goddess of the earth.'

'When did you lose your child?' asked Shakku Bhai.

'It will be nineteen years next Deepavali. It was on a Deepavali day that she was found missing. A thief came and took her away when I went out early morning to have a bath. I was sleeping in the servant woman's room. My husband and his mother had not been happy at all that I had given birth to a hermaphrodite. They were ready to wring the child's neck and kill it. It was because I wept and wailed that they let the child live. But they told me that I had to bring the child up secretly in the servants' room. They told our friends and relatives that the baby had died. And as for the mother, Anasuya, they said she had gone to her doctor brother's house for treatment.' Ram Kinkari sat up. The old woman's eyes kept searching even in the dark.

'Then your child must be eighteen years old now,' said Ram Kinkari. 'A beautiful girl with a face as bright as a full moon. There's no one like that among us.'

'I'm not going home without my child,' said the old woman.

'You're not allowed to enter this colony—it belongs to us,' said Shakku.

A group of hijra queens arrived at that moment, brandishing their drums. Some of them stared at the old woman. They were all different from one another. Some had male faces with stubble on the chin; some had beautiful bodies that moved with feminine grace. Some wore sarees, others skirts with red dots; some had tattooed foreheads and arms; some were deformed . . .

'Who is she?' one of them asked. Ram Kinkari smiled. 'The old woman says her pretty child is here, the child she lost nineteen years ago. A child that had a face as bright as the moon and a birthmark on her lip.'

'Could it be our Rugma?' asked one of them. 'She is a beauty. And she has a birthmark on her lip.'

'Don't say foolish things,' said Ramu. 'There's no one like that here. And Rugma doesn't have a birthmark.'

The hijras muttered to one another, sounding displeased.

'How much did you make today on the dancing in Dadar? Didn't the child's mother give you jaggery and wheat?'

Ram Kinkari untied their bundles and examined them. 'A boy was born on Sunday in Gadkopar,' said one of them. 'We'll go and dance there next Monday. They're rich people—they're in business.'

'Get up, old woman, and go back home quickly,' urged Shakku Bhai. 'Don't you see how dark it is? We don't like the idea of your folks coming in search of you, or the police. This colony belongs solely to us.'

'I won't go back home without my daughter,' said the old woman. She lay down on her side on the ground and closed her eyes.

'Are you going to sleep?' asked Ramu. 'We'll lift you up and take you to the station. You're not permitted to stay here.'

'If my daughter can live here, so can I,' said the old woman. 'I'll cook for you. I'll make you tasty dhoklas and khandvi. Don't send me away from here.'

'You're a Sethani from a rich house,' said Shakku. 'And we are simple folk. If your people know you're working as a cook for us, they'll be angry.'

'None of them need me,' said the old woman. 'All of them call me a madwoman. And a creature of ill omen. If my mother-in-law catches sight of me first thing in the morning, she goes into the bathroom to have a purificatory bath, even if she's already had one.'

'Who is this, Ramu Bhavu?' asked a beautiful girl in a red skirt, pointing to the old woman. 'I just heard Sulu say there was a Gujarati woman here.'

'Go in, Rugma,' shouted Ramu. 'Go in this minute!'

Rugma's nose-ring glittered in the moonlight. Everyone

could see a birthmark on her upper lip. The old woman stared at her.

'Let me relax here in the moonlight for five minutes,' said Rugma. 'My feet are hurting. How many hours I danced on the hot concrete floor! If I continue to dance like this without any rest, I will be dead before next Deepavali.'

'Do not speak inauspicious words, my child,' said Ramu. 'How can I live if you die? Aren't you my little green parrot?'

The old woman got up and stood by the rope cot. Staring at Rugma's face, she asked, 'How old are you, child?'

'She is twenty-four,' said Shakku. 'She's from Mysore. It's only four years since she came here. She's not your pretty daughter.'

'That birthmark . . .' murmured the old woman.

'That's not a birthmark. It's the chandu that dripped down when she was placing a pottu on her forehead with it,' said Ramu. 'Rugma has no birthmarks.'

'I have a birthmark in a place no one can see!' said Rugma, laughing. 'Isn't that so, Ramu Bhavu?'

'That's true.' Ramu laughed, holding his stomach tightly. 'Ha, ha! That's not a birthmark she can show you, old woman!'

The old woman asked, holding Rugma's face in both her hands as she sat on the edge of the cot swinging her left foot and displaying the elegance of her ankle, 'Tell me, daughter, aren't you my pretty child? Weren't you the baby that lay sleeping close to me, suckling my breasts? Am I not the mother that bore you?'

'No,' said Rugma crossly, gathering up her hair into a knot. 'No, my mother is Bhumi Devi, Mother Earth.'

She scrambled up hurriedly and began to dance, her red skirt swirling. It seemed to the old woman that in the moonlight the silver zari on the border rose and fell like the waves of the sea. The girl kept smiling as if recalling some delightful secret. Her hands were transformed into white doves beating their wings. Her anklets tinkled.

Ramu Bhavu picked up his drum and put it on his lap. Its beats began to induce a faint headache in the old woman. The moonlight grew steadily brighter and hung like emeralds on the golden branches.

'O Bhagavathi, Yellamma, protect me,' sang Rugma. 'My body burns and blazes. Who has placed two stones under my feet and lighted a fire there? Who has built dams in the rivers of my blood? O Devi, Yellamma, protect me . . .'

Innumerable hermaphrodites streamed out like shadows from the huts made of zinc sheets. Within them was a dryness that looked out at the world from eyes blackened with kajal. The earth flew up in red specks beneath their dancing feet. Suddenly, it rained. A light shower that lasted a minute or two. The old woman thought the rain had the odour of rats' urine. She shook her head.

'It's true, you're not my child. My child was fair-skinned,' she said. 'Your skin is the colour of the earth. You must certainly be the daughter of the earth.'

As the sound of the drums grew louder, the old woman left the colony and began to walk towards the railway station. Even in the dark, she could see its red lights clearly. The drumbeats of the hijras followed her.

[*Translated by Gita Krishnankutty*]

Elder Sister

Oppol

M.T. Vasudevan Nair

Oppol was crying.

Appu did not like to see Oppol cry. She was crying with her head pressed against the window sill, in the northern room. She cried and cried, all the time! Perhaps Valiamma, his grandmother, had scolded her. Valiamma used to scold Appu as well. But he never cried—he would just feel angry. If he were as big as Oppol, he would have shown Valiamma! Grown-up as she was, Oppol listened silently when she was scolded. Her face would darken with sorrow. Her eyes would fill with tears. When he saw this happen, Appu would usually leave the place quietly.

Appu could not bear to be near Oppol when she cried. She would hug him while she wept. He loved it when she put her arms round him and hugged him close. But while she murmured 'little one' and rained kisses on his head and forehead, hot tears would drip on Appu's body. Then he would feel like crying too.

He never paid much attention when Valiamma scolded him. She scolded him a great deal. Right from the morning, she would start, 'The fellow gets up only at noon. Do you know, boy, no sooner was your head glimpsed outside your mother's womb than the foundation of the house crumbled!'

If a little water spilt on the ground while he sat near the grinding stone on the veranda cleaning his teeth, Valiamma would begin, 'Good-for-nothing fellow! I break my bones, sweeping and mopping the floor.'

If there was even a speck of dirt in the courtyard, if he flung a stone into the well or drummed a bit on the copper water pot, Valiamma would scold him unceasingly. Now that he had started going to school he had a little respite. At least she couldn't abuse him in the daytime.

Why couldn't Oppol give Valiamma a couple of blows? But Oppol was even more frightened of Valiamma than Appu was.

When she heard Valiamma scold him, Oppol would sometimes say, 'You'll kill him with your cursing!'

'Phoo!' Valiamma would retort. And she would not stop with that. 'Swallow him up then, if he's so sweet.'

'When it's your own . . .' If Oppol went towards the child, Valiamma would come charging angrily at her like Karambi, the cow, tossing her horns.

'Listen, girl, if some stranger . . . Don't make me say things now.'

At this point, Appu would always go quietly down into the courtyard. He would wander around the compound with Chakkan. Sometimes he would try to catch the red-tailed dragonfly that hid between the ash gourd creepers. He had never been able to lay his hands on it. What a sly little fellow he was, that dragonfly, fluttering around, and his tail flashing red. Appu would not go back into the house for a long time. He would think from time to time about Oppol, who must be sobbing wildly, her face pressed against the window sill in the northern room.

Chanting prayers at dusk was a difficult task. Appu usually sat in the corridor to chant them. He had to repeat '*Namah Shivaaya*' innumerable times. Then the birth stars in Malayalam, 'Ashwathi, Bharani' and so on. He never made a mistake with them. After the twelve months in Malayalam, he needed Oppol's help. She had to recite the names of the months in English and the numbers, one, two, three, to him.

Oppol knew English. She could read everything printed in English on the calendar with the picture of the infant god Unni Krishnan that hung on the front veranda. Oppol had studied up to the eighth standard.

After he had recited everything, he would go and sit near Oppol, silently. Oppol's fingers would wander through his hair. It was around that time that they would hear music from their neighbour's house. The house next door was very big. Appu had not been there. He had only seen it from his side of the fence. There were a number of people there.

It was only recently that they had begun to hear music from there. They had bought a box that sang songs and talked. How could a box sing and speak? Chakkan said someone must have crept inside it. Chakkan didn't know a thing! He didn't go to school after all. But he was the only one Karambi, the cow, never tried to butt. Not because he was special in any way, but because of the stick he carried to chase the cattle.

They said the songs were all from films. Appu had never seen a film. Yashoda and Mani, who were in his class, had seen some. He had seen a bag with pictures from the films on it.

When she heard the songs, madness would possess Oppol. She would no longer answer any questions. Why did she suddenly turn so sulky? Sometimes Oppol would remain absolutely silent and not say a word. She was terrible, Oppol!

Still, he loved Oppol. It was she who gave him a bath before he went to school in the morning. He didn't like his body being scrubbed with the rough surface of a dried ridge gourd. It tickled him when the finely twisted edge of a towel was inserted in his ears. It was Oppol who always served him kanji, rice gruel. When he had eaten his kanji and washed his hands, she would wipe the water off his chest with a wet towel and help him put on the shirt and the shorts with the suspenders that she had washed and folded the previous day. Once she had combed his hair and wiped the oil stains off his face for the last time, he could set off for school.

Oppol would sit with him when he had dinner at night. He liked it best when she fed him. But she would not feed him if Valiamma was around. Because Valiamma had said once, 'Imagine, putting the food into his mouth! As if he's a baby!'

Oppol seldom answered back. If ever she did, Valiamma

would grow more furious. Then there would be a quarrel. After they'd said many things to each other, Oppol would cry. Sometimes Valiamma would cry too.

He didn't care if Valiamma cried. He had felt sorry for her when she cried only once. She hadn't quarrelled with Oppol that time.

He had never forgotten the event or the man who had made Valiamma cry.

Appu was playing in the courtyard with a ball that Chakkan had made him out of palm leaves. Someone called out at the gate, 'Amma!'

He saw a man standing there, his hand on the fence. He wore a long-sleeved shirt and had a bag tucked under his arm. Valiamma came down to the courtyard and walked up to the fence. She spoke to him. 'It's your mother, after all, who says it: Can't you come in, Kumara, having come this far?'

Appu thought Valiamma was right to say this. Who was this arrogant fellow? Did he have to call Valiamma to the fence to talk to her? Couldn't he have come into the house?

He said, 'It's almost six years now since I went away saying I'd never set foot here again, remember? It's not going to happen, Amma.'

Why didn't Valiamma scold him, shout at him?

But Valiamma, who usually sprang angrily on everyone, was pleading again with that arrogant fellow, 'She came out of my belly, didn't she? How can I kill her?' Appu did not follow what he said in reply.

'At least until I die and am cremated in the southern field . . .' she said.

'After that there won't be even this.'

Valiamma lowered her voice and said something more. He was shouting again, 'You should have preached this philosophy to your daughter earlier.'

In the midst of all this, the man looked at Appu. It wasn't a pleasant look at all. Appu had not felt so frightened even when the gosayi, the wandering beggar who wrung the necks of little children and stuffed them in his bundle, had stared at him. Was this man going to wring his neck?

He went up slowly to the front veranda. Oppol had gone in. She was standing at the kitchen door, gazing into the banana grove. Appu clung to the end of her mundu and asked, 'Who's that at the gate, Oppol?'

Oppol didn't seem to have heard. 'Oppol, who's at the gate?' Oppol began to say something, and then stopped. 'Who is it, Oppol?'

'That is . . .'

'Will he wring my neck?'

'Who?'

'He—doesn't he wring children's necks?'

He thought Oppol was finding it hard to breathe. 'That is . . . your Ammaman, your uncle.'

This was something new! If the man was his uncle, was this the way to behave? Imagine standing at the gate and calling out to Valiamma! And then staring at Appu as if to frighten him . . . 'What a terrible Ammaman!'

Was Oppol joking?

'Really, Oppol?'

'Yes.'

'Why doesn't Ammaman come in?' Oppol didn't answer. He was about to ask again, 'Why doesn't he come in?', when he saw Oppol dab at her eyes. She was mad, this Oppol . . .

Valiamma came in just then. Appu was aghast to see her. Valiamma was sobbing. In between her sobs, she kept mumbling something. Appu felt very sad. However much she scolded him, she was his Valiamma after all, wasn't she?

He came out quite confidently and glanced at the gate. Ammaman had gone.

It was good to have an uncle. But no uncle had the right to frighten him like this. Or stand at the gate, call out to Valiamma and say all sorts of things to make her cry.

Janu, who lived in the house on the western side, had an uncle. He was somewhere far away. You had to cross the seven seas to get to his place. There were lots of silk dresses there and fancy umbrellas. He had brought Janu both these when he came. The umbrella was very pretty. It was not heavy at all. She used it only when she went to the temple with her mother. She had put the dress away in her box because it did not fit her.

She had an uncle at home but he had never given her anything. She liked the uncle who had crossed the seven seas much more. She said he would come the following year too.

Appu felt sad that his own uncle was such a troublesome fellow. Oppol said he would never come home. Were fancy umbrellas available in the place where he lived? Even if they were, he wouldn't bring one. The look he had given Appu! He had even made Valiamma cry. Maybe he hadn't come into the house because he was angry. With whom was he angry?

Appu decided to ask him when he came next. But he did not come.

Where was Ammaman? Oppol would not say. Janu did not know of such a person. She found it difficult even to believe that Appu had an uncle. Chakkan knew vaguely of him. 'He has a house and land near the river.'

Chakkan said he had seen him. Ammaman had been laying tiles on the roof of his new house when Chakkan went that way.

'Why doesn't Ammaman come here?'

'He quarrelled and went away, didn't he?'

Chakkan didn't know why there had been a quarrel. Appu could not make out what it was all about. He had so many doubts to clear. But whom could he ask?

It was Oppol who usually cleared his doubts, when they went to bed at night. By the time he had dinner, she would have spread his mattress in the northern room. She used to spread a red saree patterned with big white flowers on the mattress. That's why he liked to lie down on it, because it was Oppol's saree.

Oppol had another saree too, folded and put away in her box. He had never seen her wear it. When the box was opened, there was a wonderful smell. The fragrance of screwpine flowers.

How good it would be if Oppol walked around wearing the saree that spread the fragrance of screwpine.

Although Appu always lay down as soon as he finished his dinner, he never went to sleep until Oppol came. Oppol would join him only after she had swept the kitchen and washed up. He would lie down with his arms around Oppol and ask her to clear his doubts, one by one. Most of the time what he wanted to know was whether what Janu had told him that day was a lie.

What lies she sometimes told! She said there was a snake that had eaten nine children in the serpent shrine south of her house. Wasn't that a shameless lie? Not even seven children would fit into a snake's stomach.

Once Janu said she had seen God. Appu did not believe her. Appu had not seen Him. Nor had Chakkan. Not even Oppol had seen God. Janu had seen Him at night. God had a thicker moustache and beard than the priest who came to do the puja for Lord Subramanya. To find out if she was telling a lie, Appu asked, 'And what did he have on his head?'

'What head?'

'On God's head!'

Janu thought hard then said, 'Hair.'

'Phoo!' shouted Appu. 'It's a crown that God has on His head.' Janu hadn't seen it. She was ashamed.

Although she told lies, Appu liked her. He had had someone to play with when she was around. Now she had gone too. Janu's father had taken her away. They had gone to a place full of forests and mountains. But if you crossed the seven seas, it was the place her uncle lived in that you would reach. When her father took her, they went by train. It was said that the train bored a hole in the mountain's stomach and rushed through it.

Janu came to Appu's house the day before she left. Her mother came with her. When she said, 'We're going to get into the train tomorrow and go away,' he felt quite jealous. How many things she would see! There might be fine rubber balls and bicycles in the place where she was going.

Appu would have liked to go somewhere. But how could he do so unless someone came to take him?

At the Thalappoli festival, the girls walked in procession carrying platters that held lighted wicks and auspicious objects, and these platters were emptied under a pala tree on a hill nearby. Appu had never gone beyond this hill. The lands beyond the seven seas . . . The train that bored a hole in the big mountain's stomach . . . What fun it must be for children who lived in places filled with fancy umbrellas and silk dresses!

Janu's mother said goodbye to Oppol. They had gone to school together. Janu's mother had a lot of sarees. She had gone to many places with Janu's father. Do you want to hear something funny? Janu's mother spoke of her husband as 'Ammu's father'.

Oppol's eyes filled with tears when Janu's mother left. Maybe Oppol too wanted to travel by the train that rushed through the mountain, boring a hole in it.

Oppol never went anywhere. Not even to the temple tank to bathe. She had a bath by the well in the house. When there was a festival in the Bhagavathi temple, and all the girls walked in a procession holding platters with lighted wicks in them, Valiamma went to see it. Appu went as well. But Oppol didn't go.

'Won't Oppol come, Valiamma?' Valiamma pounced on him. 'Shut up, you rascal!'

He had started going to school last Edavam. In two months he would have examinations. If he passed he would go to the second standard.

Janu said she would go to school when she arrived in her father's place. Maybe there were schools there. Appu wondered, would there be a Kelu Master there? May there not be. Then she wouldn't be beaten.

He had a friend who was in his class. Kuttisankaran. His house was on the other side of the fields. They went to school and came back together. Kelu Master sometimes called Kuttisankaran

'Kuttichathan', little demon. Appu liked to hear Master say that. But the blows Kelu Master gave were unbearable.

Kuttisankaran once gave Appu a lime as a gift. He had brought it from his house. He said there had been a lot of limes in his house the day before. The younger of his elder sisters had got married.

'Why limes for a wedding?'

'Stupid, don't you know?' asked Kuttisankaran with an air of having witnessed many weddings. Kuttisankaran described a wedding. A lot of people would come to the house. Rose water would be sprinkled from a bottle on all those who were seated in the pandal. Rose water smelt very good. Later, sandalwood paste and limes were given to everyone.

Appu did not believe any of this. But if he said openly that they were lies, Kuttisankaran would ask, 'Have you seen a wedding?' He would have to admit that he hadn't. Appu said to comfort Kuttisankaran, 'When there's a wedding in my house for my Oppol, I too will give you a lime.'

But Kuttisankaran said, 'And do you have an oppol, an elder sister?'

It made Appu furious to hear that. He wanted to call him 'Kuttichathan' four times in succession and give him a whack on his cheek. But Kuttisankaran was bigger than he was, so he didn't.

'Then whose elder sister is my Oppol?'

'You fool, your Oppol is your mother. Didn't you know?'

He laughed, thinking how foolish Kuttisankaran was. No wonder Kelu Master said he had no brains.

'Go on, you don't know a thing,' said Appu.

'And what do you know? My mother told me.'

'And what does your mother know?'

It ended in a quarrel. Kuttisankaran asked him to give back the lime. Appu threw the lime at him and made a face.

He thought about it while coming back from school. How could Oppol be his mother? He didn't have a mother or a father. He had only Oppol and Valiamma. And Valiamma didn't count.

Boy, don't do that; boy, don't do this . . . from the moment your head was glimpsed . . .

Oppol was all he wanted. What should he do with that Kuttichathan, that little demon, who said his good Oppol was his mother?

He didn't want a mother. He knew how unpleasant it was to have a mother. Valiamma was Oppol's mother, wasn't she? And did she give Oppol any peace?

The last few days, Oppol had been crying day and night. Valiamma had not been scolding her, but she kept crying all the time. She was mad, this Oppol!

Oppol was not angry with Appu. She told him many things when they lay down at night, hugging each other. Not stories. It was stories that Appu liked to listen to. Oppol knew a lot of stories. The story of the prince who had found a ruby. It was after he had heard this story that Appu learnt the secret of how to hide a ruby if he found one. It had to be wrapped in cow dung. Then its radiance wouldn't be visible. Then there was the story of the princess who was turned to stone. When he heard of how a child was cut up and its blood poured over the stone to make it come alive, he felt like crying.

Nowadays, Oppol did not tell him stories. She would lie quiet. After a while, she would ask, 'Are you asleep, little one?'

'No.'

'You must study well, little one.'

'Umm . . .'

'And be a good boy.'

'Umm . . .'

'When you grow up, won't you take good care of Oppol?'

What a meaningless question! But he grunted all the same, to say yes.

'Oppol has no one but you, little one.'

Oppol had been ill the last two or three days. She would not speak to him at all while she gave him a bath or mixed his rice and vegetables together or combed his hair. She would keep looking at his face. And then sit down as if she was dazed.

She was mad, this Oppol . . .

One day, when Oppol and Valiamma were lying down on the floor in the middle room, he heard Valiamma say, 'Don't worry so much about him.' Oppol didn't say anything.

'What happened, happened. If you think of all that now, you'll lose your mind. If this goes through, we'll be fine.' Oppol said nothing to that either.

'Sankaran Nair will manage it. He's very reliable.'

'What do you mean, Amma?'

'You know,' Valiamma's tone changed a little. 'Don't plan too much. If something goes wrong now, you'll have to spend your whole life like this.'

'Isn't this treachery?' said Oppol.

'What?'

'This thing that you're doing.'

'You don't have to worry about that.'

'But I'll have to pay for it.'

'Sankaran Nair knows all that. A fellow who lives in Wyanaad won't have any idea that . . .'

'Amme, Appu's . . .'

'Appu-kuppu indeed! Malu, it's I who am telling you. When I think we can put an end to this troublesome situation . . .'

Oppol had stopped speaking. He could hear only her sobs. Valiamma repeated, 'Sankaran Nair said he'd take care of everything.'

Who was this Sankaran Nair? If he was such a great fellow, Appu wanted to see him. And then one day he heard Sankaran Nair was coming.

Sankaran Nair seemed a nice person. While he sat on the platform in front, talking to Valiamma, Appu admired the elegance of the circle of grey hair that stood round as a pappadam round his head. He had so many things to tell Valiamma.

Appu didn't want to hear. A wedding was going to be conducted in Wyanaad. So what, let him conduct it, thought Appu. You must take care, said Sankaran Nair, that he doesn't get to hear about the boy. So what, let them take care. All Appu wanted was to gaze at that hair, standing up in a circle as round as a pappadam. He thought it would look real good if he could place four long strands of hair in the centre of it. It would look as pretty then as the horsetail plant that stood in a pot in the middle of the garden at school. He put his head out and took a good look again.

Sankaran Nair lowered his voice. Valiamma turned round and saw Appu. 'Appu, go and play in the yard.'

He went into the house. They and their gossip! What did he have to do with a wedding in Wyanaad? He wouldn't even get a lime. Let whoever wanted conduct the wedding. What did Appu care?

He opened the wooden box in the inner room in which rice was kept, and then closed it. A cockroach that had not yet grown its wings glared up at him from inside it. He climbed on to the window sill and peered inside the basket hanging from a nail on the wall—there was mustard in it.

He heard the sound of a bell-metal glass falling in the kitchen. Oppol was in there. Valiamma called, 'Malu!'

Was it to scold her because the glass had fallen down?

'Malu, girl!'

Oppol went to the outer door. Appu strained his ears, wondering what he was going to hear.

'Didn't you tell her everything, Amma?' That was Sankaran Nair. 'Don't worry at all. I'll take care of everything. He's a good fellow. And he's all by himself; he doesn't have relatives. He's never going to know.'

Oppol was not saying a word.

'We'll conduct the thing there. We must invite a few people.'

'Won't he say that's unusual?'

'You're my relatives. You don't have people of your own. And I've been living there nearly twenty years. You understand, Devaki Amma?'

'What, Sankaran Nair?'

'Ha, ha . . . that's what I said to him. What's wrong if I conduct the wedding modestly at my place?'

'That's all right. Sankaran Nair, you're the only help I have.'

'Isn't that why I took so much trouble to arrange this? He said he wants to see the girl. What about that?' Valiamma mumbled something. 'I'll see he doesn't get to hear of all that.'

'If everything goes well, I've vowed I'll make an offering of payasam at the temple in Tazhathekkavu.'

'Everything will go well, I tell you. Your daughter won't have anything to worry about. He's got four acres of land from the government. If he works hard, they can live comfortably . . .'

Appu suddenly caught sight of a little horned fellow hiding inside the empty tray below the outlet in the makeshift bathroom. It was not a cockroach. It was some new species of warrior. He couldn't let him go like that. He could never lay hands on a broom when he wanted one. He needed a thick broomstick.

They were still talking, Sankaran Nair and Valiamma. About something secret—that's why they were talking so softly.

Let them talk! Where was the broom? He must give the horned one lurking there a blow.

He went to the kitchen, looking for the broom, and found Oppol there. Hadn't she gone to listen to Sankaran Nair's gossip just a little while ago? When he asked her where the broom was, she gathered him up in her arms. And kissed his forehead and his head over and over again. Her tears dripped all over his head and his face.

He hadn't heard Sankaran Nair scold her. Valiamma had not lost her temper with her. Then why was she crying? She was mad, this Oppol . . .

At night, Oppol asked him, 'Will you sleep with Valiamma if Oppol isn't here?'

'I'm your child, Oppol.'

'And if Oppol goes away?'

'Where are you going, Oppol?' Oppol didn't say where. He asked her over and over again and she answered, 'Nowhere. Oppol was joking . . .'

Ah . . . Appu was relieved.

One evening when he came back from school, there were sweet ottadas to eat. That was unusual. Appu always made sure that whenever there was something special like that to eat, he ate it in front of Chakkan. He liked to watch Chakkan's greedy expression. Chakkan was terribly greedy. Oppol had told Appu never to eat while Chakkan looked on. Still . . . Chakkan knew how to make a mudingol-stick to chase cattle and he was the only one Karambi cow never butted. He could even put his arms round Karambi's neck and hug her if he wanted.

He hid the ada in his hands and stepped into the courtyard stealthily. Chakkan was pulling out straw from the haystack. He didn't plead as usual: 'A tiny bit for me, little master.'

'The mistress gave me some,' he said.

'Lies!'

'It was me who went to buy the tea and sugar when he came.'

'When who came?'

'A visitor. Look, little master . . .'

Chakkan showed him what he had tucked into his waist: three beedi stubs!

'The thampuran who came smoked them.'

He must be a respectable man if he smoked beedis. Even though Sankaran Nair had a circle of hair as round as a pappadam, he didn't smoke beedis. When he came last week, he had just chewed betel, like Valiamma, and spat it out. Shameful!

Where was the visitor? He ran into the house to ask Oppol. Oppol was outside, in the yard. Valiamma was peeling vegetables.

'Where's the visitor, Valiamma?'

'Which visitor? Who comes here visiting, boy? Kaalan?'

Chakkan hadn't told Appu his name. Kaalan, then, if that was the name. Where was he? That was what he wanted to know.

'Look here, you rascal, I'll beat you to death if you come here saying impudent things.'

He didn't want to hear. How could he have known Kaalan was the name of the God of Death? How arrogant Valiamma was being, just because there had been a visitor! Appu didn't ask about him again.

When he woke up suddenly at night, Oppol was not on the mattress, next to him. A lamp was burning in the room. Oppol had opened her box and was arranging something in it. There was the fragrance of screwpine in the room. Oppol had been lying next to him when he fell asleep. Why had she got up? Why was she sitting there with a lighted lamp near her, stuffing mundus and blouses into her box? He wanted to get up quietly, creep up softly to Oppol, grasp her neck and frighten her. But he could not get up. His eyes kept closing. He thought of the forest where the prince had found the ruby. The faint scent of screwpine . . . he closed his eyes again.

Appu didn't wake up on his own in the morning; Oppol had to wake him. When he had had a bath by the well and had his kanji, Oppol put on his clothes for him. While she combed his hair, she said, 'Be careful when you go to school. There are cattle; they'll come at you . . .'

She used to say that often, so he said yes.

'Don't quarrel with other children.'

'Uh-umm . . .'

'Valiamma will take great care of you, little one.'

'Umm.'

'You must do as Valiamma says and not be naughty.'

'Valiamma's bad; I want only you, Oppol . . .'

'My little one . . .'

Gasping for breath, holding him close to her, Oppol called to him feebly, 'My little one . . .'

Appu was afraid Oppol would cry. But no, she didn't cry this time. So he was not upset.

Suddenly he wanted to tell her something. 'Look, Oppol . . .'

'Call me Amma, little one, just once.'

He didn't like that. 'Why, Oppol?'

'Just like that.'

'Where's my mother, that you ask me to call her, Oppol?'

Oppol didn't reply to that. Her hands slackened slowly. She turned her head away and stood there silently. After a long while, she took his bag off the nail, gave it to him and said, 'Go now, little one . . .'

Appu laid his palm leaf umbrella across his shoulder, hung his bag on its painted handle and went down to the courtyard. As he was going out, he slipped and nearly fell. He turned to find out if anyone had seen him. Oppol was standing with her hand on the front door, staring at him. Why did Oppol have the same look as the gosayi, the wandering beggar? Oppol caught sight of him and suddenly withdrew her head like a tortoise.

She was mad, this Oppol . . .

When he got to the other side of the field, Kuttisankaran was waiting for him, blowing up the leaves of the castor plant. He had two gooseberries in his bag. He gave Appu the smaller one. Even though it was small, it was very sweet. They had to cross a dry canal, a lane and a small hillock before they got to school.

He was afraid to go over the hillock. There were so many buffaloes and cows there. That was not so bad. There was a rumour that the big bull from Manamakkavu was sometimes seen there. Appu had never seen him. He hoped he never would.

In the afternoon, Narayanan's pencil fell down from Appu's hand and broke. Narayanan cried and was about to tell Master when Kuttisankaran made a pact with him. If the matter went to Kelu Master, Appu would have a bad time. If he wanted to avoid trouble, all Appu had to do was give Narayanan a quarter-anna coin the next day. Appu was relieved.

He would certainly get a quarter-anna if he asked Oppol for it.

When he got home in the evening, he threw his bag on the platform and called out to Oppol.

'Is it Appu?' It wasn't Oppol who answered; it was Valiamma. Valiamma came out from the kitchen and asked, 'You're back early today?'

Appu was tempted to ask her, 'Why are you being so pleasant today?', but he didn't. What if she hit him?

'Where's Oppol?'

'I've served your kanji. Take off your shirt and come on.'

It wasn't kanji he wanted, it was Oppol. If he didn't get a

quarter-anna by tomorrow, he would lose his standing at school.

'Where's Oppol?'

He went into the northern room. Oppol was not there. A faint scent of screwpine clung to the room.

'Where's Oppol, Valiamma?'

'Oppol . . . isn't here.'

'Where's she?'

'She's gone to a place . . .'

'Where?'

'Oppol . . . will be back. She'll bring you a ball when she comes.'

She could bring him a ball if she wanted. But why had she gone away without taking him along, without telling him? He was furious. What a terrible Oppol! Why had she done this? Appu would never talk to her again . . . What was he going to do with her?

There might be a quarter-anna coin in Oppol's box. He would take not one but two coins. He'd show her, if she came to scold him for doing that. But where was the box?

He wanted to cry. Valiamma called him again. Appu didn't want any kanji.

He went down into the courtyard, took out a stone that was loose from the platform round the kuvalam tree and threw it at the front steps. Then he walked to the western side of the house.

'Appu, little one, Valiamma will give you your kanji . . .'

He didn't want Valiamma to be nice to him. Let Oppol come. If she gave him a rubber ball, he would fling it away, that's what he would do.

Valiamma called him again . . . Appu didn't want anything. All he wanted was to cry. Cry loudly, to show how angry he was with Oppol.

And what if it was a ball with a cover round it, and sweets, that Oppol was going to bring him? What would he do then?

Still, hadn't Oppol gone away without telling him?

She was a terrible Oppol. She was mad, this Oppol . . .

[*Translated by Gita Krishnankutty*]

Sherlock

Sharlok

M.T. Vasudevan Nair

Chechi had said that he could get up late.

Chechi usually got up at five-thirty and was ready by seven. It took her an hour and fifteen minutes to drive to work.

The door had not been locked. Balu woke up when someone pushed it open. It was the cat. And it was seven o'clock.

When he came downstairs, Chechi was just leaving.

'You're up? I've left a note for you on the fridge.' Chechi had forgotten to tell him two things last night. One, that the front door key was under the statue of Nataraja. The door locked by itself and he must remember to take the key when he went out.

'I'm not going out.'

'Good. Read something. There are lots of programmes on TV. You can use the set in my room.'

The second thing he had to take note of was to always leave the door of the downstairs bathroom open because the cat's feeding tray and toilet box were there.

Chechi went out and closed the door, saying she would be back at four-thirty. Vaulting on to the window sill which held potted plants, the cat gazed out. When Chechi had driven out of the parking lot, the cat jumped down and looked at Balu.

Its look seemed to say, 'It is I who will reign here now.'

Chechi had arranged Balu's ticket in such a way that he had landed in Philadelphia on a Friday evening. He could therefore familiarize himself with the house and the machines in it through Saturday and Sunday, while Chechi was at home. And that had been enough for his Indian body to adapt to the

American clock. By now he knew exactly where all the food was kept and what vitamin pills were available. He had learnt how to operate the buttons on the microwave. Chechi had been meticulous by nature even as a child.

Chechi said to him, 'You must rest a lot. And read.'

She had decided to re-activate his mind and body in a space of two months.

'You can write if you want. Your impressions of America. How do you think you can earn a living if you write ten lines of poetry every six months?'

Balu did not answer.

'A master's in English literature. A diploma in journalism. Highly qualified. There is so much you can do.'

Chechi sighed with an air of disappointment. Balu was not prepared to argue, having just arrived. He said to himself, something went wrong somewhere in the dealings between God and me.

Chechi was trying to arrange a scholarship for him. Jayant would tell him where to send the applications.

'In America, you can't get anywhere unless you work really hard. And the peak of success is higher than the sky.'

After that, Chechi spoke in Malayalam to comfort him.

'Never mind. Something will turn up. We'll manage it.'

Maybe miracles would happen in this his twenty-seventh year. Chechi still had faith in her younger brother.

He had learnt eventually that Chechi had telephoned many times when he lay in the hospital, vomiting blood. Valia Chechi, his eldest sister, had often reminded him of how he had circumvented death only because of the many prayers that had been offered for him.

As soon as the cat disappeared into the bathroom, Balu went to the kitchen to make tea. He lit the remains of a broken cigarette. When he stubbed it out against a potted plant that was kept on the kitchen table, along with the music system and cookery books, he heard a growl of protest. The cat. Evidently, no one smoked here.

The day he arrived, Chechi had talked most of the time about this cat. She had asked after Valia Chechi and the children. She had also mentioned the hundred dollars she had sent for Kutti Ammama's daughter's wedding. After that she had chronicled the virtues of the cat, which had been seated on her lap. It was a comfort to have a living creature around the house when she was alone. Jayant was sometimes away for months together.

'He says months, but who knows?' Chechi's voice was full of resentment.

While coming from the airport she had extolled the marvels of being able to buy a house and a car by paying ten- or fifteen-month instalments. When houses sprang up in this elegant area, she had bought one, although it had been difficult for her. There were huge spaces around it and a golf course beyond. There was no crime in this suburb. It was strenuous driving for an hour and fifteen minutes to work, especially in winter when it was still dark even at seven. But Chechi's friends had all told her that she had been lucky to acquire this house.

Until Jayant left for San José on the West Coast, they had had no problems. Even after all their expenses, they had been able to save a little money. But now they had to maintain two establishments.

Chechi said, 'I've started to talk to Sherlock when I am alone. I need to hear my own voice sometimes.'

He felt distressed.

Sherlock was a strange colour. Light blue. No. You could describe it as a light blue tinged with ash. He asked, to change the subject, 'So what does the Siamese say?'

'He's not Siamese. He's some other breed. The veterinary doctor had told Jayant. I don't remember.'

Last winter, she had seen it lurking outside the parking lot but had taken no notice of it. One night, it had come and scratched at her door. When she opened the door, it had come in, delighted to have escaped the cold, and curled up on her sofa. She had given it some milk.

It was probably somebody's pet cat. It had certainly been

house-trained. She had put up a notice on the board next to the mailbox outside the colony to say that she had found a cat. No one had come to claim it.

It was Jayant who had named it Sherlock.

'Sherlock?'

'Jayant used to read a lot of detective novels as a child. Its full name is actually Sherlock Holmes. Sherlock Holmes Shinde in the veterinary doctor's register!'

Chechi laughed. It occurred to Balu suddenly that it was years since he had heard Chechi's loud laugh.

In America, even pet cats were astonishing creatures. Even if you left food containers open, they would take no notice. They ate only the cat food bought in packets from the store. The only country where cats did not steal!

Balu examined the arrangements made for the cat in the bathroom. Food in one dish, water in another. It climbed into the big basket every time it wanted to defecate. Pet cats never soiled the house.

'Remember Nandini? Dr G.K. Nair's daughter, Nandini?'

Balu remembered her. One of her younger sisters had been in his MA class.

Nandini was in New Jersey. She had two cats in her house. Neither of them ever ate the cat food bought at the supermarket sales. They recognized it as old stock by the smell. Chechi laughed again.

'We'll call Nandini and visit her over a weekend. After Jayant is back.'

The cat walked up slowly to Balu and put a paw in his lap. Chechi said, 'Don't worry. He doesn't have claws.'

The cat's claws had made marks on the furniture when he jumped over it. So Jayant had taken him to the hospital and had an operation done to remove the claws. Balu looked at the cat with a twinge of sympathy.

'It's cruel. But the furniture is costly. The operation did not hurt at all. And his claws will never grow again. Nandini had the same thing done. Everyone does it here.'

At night, Sherlock slept on Chechi's bed. He had a habit of tapping and pushing her to wake her up even before her alarm rang.

When Chechi went to San José for a week's holiday, she had left the key next door so that the neighbours could change Sherlock's water and feed him regularly.

Balu observed that the intelligent Sherlock constantly followed him. Indeed, the cat had been assessing the visitor ever since he arrived.

Balu had a bath and ate some cereal with cold milk. Then he went to Chechi's room. Most of the space in it was taken up by Jayant's computer books. There were a few novels in a small cupboard. John Le Carré, Robert Ludlum, Martin Cruz Smith and some other novelists whose names were not known in India. All were stories of daring espionage. In the old days, Chechi used to track down the finest books to read.

Princess Diana's biography lay on the bed. Chechi must have been reading it. On the wall was a photograph of Jayant and Chechi with bouquets in their hands. It must have been taken on their wedding day.

Jayant had looked much younger than this in the photograph that she had sent Valia Chechi. At thirty-six, Chechi still looked like a little child.

As he looked at the pictures in Diana's biography, the cat came to the door. He turned on the television. A case was being tried in a family court. An old Wild West movie was showing on another channel. He turned it off. Sherlock stood at the door, growling.

Did cats lose their voices along with their claws? He had never heard Sherlock mew in cat language. Yet another marvel!

Balu took a book and went out. He lay down in the little bedroom that had been set apart for him. Sherlock lay outside the door for some time with his legs in the air, battling with an invisible adversary, and then went to sleep.

Chechi had described the deck at the door. The washing machine and Jayant's exercise tools and bicycle were kept there.

There was a heap of bottles on the carpet in the centre, all wine bottles. There must have been about sixty of them. Every label was marked and signed JS. Jayant Shinde.

Most of the labels bore the name of Californian wine companies. As he picked up a bottle with a French label, he felt someone standing behind him.

Ah, Sherlock had got up from his sleep and come looking for him. He scrutinized Balu through half-closed eyes, yawning. Balu tried to threaten him with a look.

'Get out! Out!'

Sherlock stretched out beside the bottles and drew pictures in the air with his tail.

Get out!

If it was Jayant who had trained him, the cat must understand a little Hindi. So he said, '*Baahar jaa!*'

Balu wondered whether the cat was going to stay here until Chechi came back in the evening, in order to bear witness to his having opened the basement and explored it. He went upstairs, consoling himself with the thought that the cat was sure to come out when he was hungry.

He saw little golf carts make their way towards the course. He could not see them play through the window.

The cat came up from the basement as he was heating lunch. He hurried downstairs and locked the basement door.

Chechi came back at the time she had said she would.

'What did you do all day?'

'I just sat around.'

'You must rest a great deal. Your health will improve by itself. That is why I insisted on your coming here.'

Chechi had a wash, changed her clothes and came into the bedroom with two cups of coffee.

'Jayant has a collection of wine bottles in the basement. It's his hobby. He keeps a register.'

Why was Chechi talking about the wine bottles? Maybe she had guessed that he would open the basement and find them.

'We buy liquor only when we have visitors. Sometimes, Jayant has a glass of wine. I deliberately did not keep any up here so that it would not be a temptation for you.'

'I've stopped. Didn't I write to you, Chechi?'

'Mm . . . People who stop can always start again. Valia Chechi wrote and told me why they did not confirm your post in the newspaper office. Who would appoint senseless employees?'

Balu did not say anything.

'You'll have to work hard here. No matter what field you are in, you can't survive unless you work really hard. America is no heaven.'

Balu said, 'I know.'

'I had said I would arrange for a green card for your Kumarettan. You know that.'

'Mm . . . I heard.' Why did Chechi want to recall a separation that had taken place eight years ago?

'He said that the month he spent here was like being in prison. The very day he arrived, he complained that there were no human beings on the road, only vehicles.'

Balu made an effort to smile.

'Listen to a bigger joke. Valia Chechi and Mala Chechi seem to think I did something terribly wrong. But the ultimatum he gave me was that if he could not live in a place without learning to drive, he would never stay there.'

Balu did not say anything. Kumarettan had been promoted and had become a professor. He had built a house near the college. He had two children now. Chechi must have heard. Chechi had acquired engineer Shinde. No one had any reason to complain.

At night, Chechi took him to the Chinese restaurant next to the supermarket. After dinner, fortune cookies containing predictions for the future were served.

Great things happening . . .

Chechi looked at the curl of paper, crumpled it and put it in the ashtray. He was sure she would ask him what his said. He told her that he had been told that great things would happen.

'It's good fun for the children, this . . .'

At night, he put the prediction away in a previous year's empty diary, which he had kept in his handbag in case he wanted to jot down something.

Maybe wonderful things would happen. A fellowship in mass communication, perhaps. After all, China had a tradition of wise men which could not be underestimated. Was not the arrival of Ariyambadath Balakrishnan in America a great event in itself?

Achan had been sure that the son who came after three daughters had been born at a moment blessed by the navagrahams, the nine planets. As a child, when he went out with his mother or his elder sister, he used to find all kinds of things by the roadside. Coins buried in the sand, the broken bits of an anklet, the stem of a gold nose ring. 'Balu will come upon a treasure one of these days,' Amma's jesting tone had concealed a profound hope.

She had been certain that good fortune would always come in search of her son.

That night, Balu wrote in the old diary:

'14-7-92. I had a dream on Saturday night. I woke up with a start in Heathrow airport. The signboard said that passengers had begun to board the flight for Philadelphia. Where was Gate 27? I ran down an interminable passage and came to Gate 26, only to find that there were no more gates. I turned and ran desperately to the opposite side. The gates there started with 28. Where was 27? I kept running. Where was Gate 27, my way out? Twenty-seven is my age as well.'

The fact that the number of the gate and his age were the same was not part of the dream. He reread it and scored it out. Then he tore out the page and threw it in the waste-paper basket. A travelogue always had to start with a beautiful hostess.

He heard Chechi talk for a long time on the telephone in the next room. He could not make out what she was saying. She might have been speaking to Jayant. That night there was sudden lightning and thunder and a light shower. The cat came to the door and peered in. Balu closed the door, bolted it and lay down.

When Chechi left next morning, he was lying awake. He came down only after she had left.

He decided to write to Valia Chechi after he'd had coffee. He had promised to write to Bhaskaran Master as well. 'I am trying to come to terms with America.' That was how he would start.

He found Chechi's letter pad, sat down at the high stool in the kitchen and began to write at the semicircular counter. The cat jumped up and settled down next to him. It stared at the paper, anxious to know what Balu was writing.

Balu got down from the stool and sat down on a corner of the sofa. No sooner had he started to write, balancing the pad on the coffee table, than the cat arrived and continued to stare at the paper.

Balu was irritated. Filthy creature! What did it expect to see?

The cat gave him a mocking look and growled softly.

He took a decision and walked to the dining room. He opened the front door. If the cat wanted to leave in the same manner that it had come, this was the way out. The front yard was right here. Then the car park. Beyond that was the golf course and then other houses. Freedom! You can go.

'Sherlock! You can go!'

The cat stood at the door for a few minutes, looking out, then came back, lay on the carpet and rolled over and over playfully. After a while it opened half an eye and looked at him mockingly.

Balu bathed and changed, dusted his shoes and put them on. He looked back as he took the front door key and went out. The cat lay as if it was half-asleep.

He turned left at the golf course and walked up to the market. Then he turned back. The sun was very hot.

When he entered the house, the cat was still asleep in the same spot.

That evening, Chechi was in the process of making a chicken curry for the night. He helped her chop the onions.

'Where did you go?'

'Just a little way down the road.'

He shuddered as it struck him. Sherlock. He was no ordinary cat. He was a spy. Jayant must have trained him to spy on Chechi when she was by herself. And now Sherlock considered it his responsibility to act as a spy for Chechi. How else could Chechi have known that he had gone out?

He glared vengefully at the cat, making sure Chechi did not see him. The cat turned its head away indifferently as if it had not noticed.

The cat's eyes followed him all the time. Even if he locked his door, the cat stayed on the other side. Balu had discovered this when he woke up suddenly once and opened the door to go to the bathroom.

Chechi said that Jayant would be back on Friday night. She came back early from work that evening.

'Come, let's buy some fish. Jayant likes our Malabar-style fish curry. And you can see the supermarket. Indians always marvel at the supermarkets here. They are really worth seeing.'

First, he witnessed the marvel of driving up to the bank and putting in a card to take out money. Then came the supermarket. When they had bought vegetables, Sherlock's food packets and fish, Chechi said, 'We'll buy a bottle of wine. For Jayant's homecoming.'

Jayant's flight was at nine o'clock. The telephone rang at seven-thirty, as Chechi was hurriedly trying to finish the cooking.

'Hullo.' After that he did not hear Chechi say a word. All she did was grunt. As Balu entered the kitchen, Chechi put the telephone down and walked slowly to the back door. Then she came back, sat down on the sofa and said, 'Jayant is not coming.'

She opened the wine and poured out a glass. 'He is busy.'

She served Balu his dinner. 'I'll eat later. I have a bad headache. I'm not giving you any wine since you've stopped drinking.'

Chechi finished almost half the wine and went up, taking the bottle with her. Sherlock did not follow her. Instead, he lay down at the kitchen door. He too seemed uneasy.

Chechi spent most of Saturday and Sunday in her bedroom.

When Balu went to bed on Sunday, he decided to tell her that he was going back. The marvel of the fellowship was unlikely to happen soon. It was Jayant who had said he would try to arrange it. This brother-in-law whom he had never met was far away in San José. Balu did not know how many days he would have to spend here with Sherlock. It was not for nothing that Kumarettan had called this a prison. Sherlock, after all, was no company.

Sherlock seemed to know that Balu was thinking about him. Balu pushed the cat out and shut the door.

Chechi said to him before she left in the morning, 'It will be all right. Be patient. I've contacted a lot of people on my own as well.'

This Sherlock Holmes could read even his thoughts, and convey them to Chechi. Balu was not quite sure how.

I have very, very little left over after the instalments for the house and the car and the household expenses.

I sent the PTA for your ticket because I wanted to rescue you. Two thousand dollars is not a small sum.

Balu said nothing.

'Do you want some dollars?'

'For what?'

'Well, if you want to go out . . .'

'No.'

'Once summer is over, the cherry trees will begin to blossom. The whole place will look beautiful. This region is called the Pearl Buck country. We'll visit Pearl Buck's place one day. After Jayant comes.'

Chechi had made innumerable plans and was waiting for Jayant to get back. Weekend trips, places Balu should see. Chechi described all of them to him.

It was not the boredom of loneliness that troubled Balu. He was afraid of the cat: its eyes followed him everywhere. But he said nothing.

He decided to ignore that cat. When he had read the whole of Princess Diana's scandalous story, he started Greta Garbo's biography. Then he went on to one of Jayant's spy stories.

The cat continued to watch him from a distance. He now had the air of contempt with which one looks at a reptile that has crawled into its hole, admitting defeat.

As the days went by, he felt that Chechi no longer had anything much to say to him in the evenings. She had no new questions. She said once that her work in the office was growing more burdensome. She rarely fondled Sherlock now. She scolded him if he tried to snuggle against her. 'Out, Sherlock, out!'

Balu kept strict count of the weeks. Chechi stayed at home all Saturday and Sunday. She spent the whole of Saturday vacuuming, washing clothes, cleaning the carpet. He lost count of the dates, however, and had to calculate them.

Another Friday was drawing near. Balu asked, 'Did he call?'

'Who?'

'From San José. Jayant.'

How was he to address Jayant Shinde? Jayant Ettan, Jayant Dada. The North Indian term for brother-in-law was jeejaji or something like that. The Marathis probably used another word.

'No. He said he would call if he was coming.'

Then she muttered, 'He had work to finish.'

Balu discovered that time passed quickly if he slept during the daytime as well.

He had a shave that morning after a gap of four days. Chechi had brushed the jeans and jacket he had worn when he arrived and hung them up. They could be used once more. He had twenty dollars left in his purse after what he had spent on breakfast at Heathrow.

He went out. Kumarettan's conclusion was correct: there were no human beings to be seen, only vehicles rushing along the road. He passed a group of red-coated workmen repairing the road and came to the shopping centre. He stood near the car park, reading the nameboards on the stores. There were seven restaurants in the area. The most widely advertised products on every television channel were food articles. He decided to note down in his diary that America was one enormous stomach.

He bought a packet of cigarettes. The next store was a wine shop. A half bottle of vodka cost nine dollars twenty-five cents. No. He had an idea. If he spent ten dollars more, he would have nothing left. And no more room for temptation. He would be completely free. Eternally free. Was it to be Popova or Smirnoff? Popova won. *Mir druzhba*!

When he got back, Sherlock growled at him angrily. He placed the vodka in front of the cat. He poured one-third of it into a glass, added orange juice and cold water. He might as well put in ice cubes. Do it in style. Sherlock seemed baffled. Balu drank a mouthful. He added a little more water. Popova was full of music and dance.

'Sherlock, do you want a drop?'

But Sherlock only bent his head. It was not yet time to heat the food. Balu took out two cans from the cupboard above the sink. One of peanuts, the other of almonds. Sherlock did not want either. He sniffed, then rejected them. He was a law-abiding cat.

'Do you want a drop?'

He poured a few drops from his glass into a saucer. Sherlock sniffed it cautiously, then gave it a lick. Then he smiled gratefully and licked up the rest. Balu laughed triumphantly. 'See now, you've broken the law as well. So how will you be able to tell your owner this secret in the evening?'

Balu drank the second glass by himself. Sherlock growled impatiently when he finished it.

'All right. I'll give you one more drop. Don't ask for more.' A hot wave of pleasure coursed through him and he started to speak.

'Eda Sherlock, you must learn Malayalam. Ma-la-ya-lam. What do you know about this youngest sister of mine? This Kochechi, who speaks English through her nose, brought me up. Do you understand? You, who can read even thoughts, must understand.

'In the old days, when I was a child, we did not have a latrine in the house. So I had to stand guard over this Kochechi when she went to relieve herself on the hillside, behind the snake shrine.

'The Bombaywala who taught you espionage, Jayant Shinde, Shin-de. Tell him that at Kochechi's wedding, when the bridegroom came with his retinue, wearing a full-sleeved shirt and a kasavu mundu, with a sandal paste mark on his forehead, it was I who washed Kumarettan's feet. I!

'Of course you can understand my language. You're just pretending you can't. Tell me, is Jayant a finer fellow than our Kumarettan?'

Balu showed Sherlock the bottle of vodka and asked, 'Where shall we hide this, Mr Sherlock Holmes?'

All he had to do was get it into the dustbin outside the colony by four-thirty in the evening.

Balu took the rice out of the fridge, sprinkled water over it and put it in the microwave with a dish of chicken curry that had been made a few days earlier.

He poured a little more vodka into the saucer and sipped what was left in his glass slowly, savouring it. He did not quite finish it.

He transferred the heated rice and curry to his plate. And said, 'We'll have lunch together today, Sherlock. We'll settle all accounts today.'

He put some rice on a plate, placed it before Sherlock and said, 'Try some. There are a whole lot of countries outside America—India, China, Japan, Thailand, Burma—where people eat this. And cats too. Therefore, cats raised by Indians can eat it as well. Rice . . . It is for rice that the Indian prays to God. Did you know that?'

Sherlock's eyes were on the glass.

Balu laughed. 'We'll go halves on the last few drops. In our arrack shops we call them the lucky drops. I'll give you these on condition you eat some rice, Sherlock!'

A miracle happened in America at that moment. Sherlock began to eat the rice with a sly smile. And with great relish too.

Balu washed the dishes and lit a cigarette. He thought he had given Sherlock too large a share of the vodka. The American half-bottle seemed to contain less than the Indian one. It had been finished so quickly!

Suddenly, he was angry with Sherlock for having curried favour with him just to share the Popova.

'Come here. Go and look at the outside world.' Balu opened the front door and called out. But Sherlock did not come. Balu feigned affection and stroked him. When he lifted him up to take him to the door, Sherlock jerked out of his grasp. Furious, the cat stood in front of him with a muffled growl in his throat.

'Sherlock, it's me, little one.' Balu went closer to him. The cat raised its paws and hissed, ready to do battle. That was when Balu saw with a start of fear the long, pointed claws on Sherlock's paws.

Shocked, Balu collapsed. Sherlock gave him a look of contempt, drew back his claws and walked upstairs slowly.

Balu went and lay down in his own room. The cat came in and smiled at him as if they had reached a mutual understanding.

Sherlock climbed on the bed and lay down near him. Balu smiled and stroked his feet with their hidden claws. Then his neck. A laugh echoed through the room.

Who laughed, Sherlock, you or I?

Balu tried to get up. The cat put a leg over him to prevent his getting up, pushed him back on the mattress and murmured, 'Sleep. Sleep soundly.'

Sherlock stroked his chest to comfort him. He murmured softly in Balu's ear, as if it was a great secret, 'I'm here. Sleep without fear.'

Balu wanted to weep aloud. When he found that he could not, he sobbed quietly and closed his eyes.

[*Translated by Gita Krishnankutty*]

The Sixth Finger

Aaraamathe viral

Anand

When he learnt his brother was sparing his life, Kamran ceased offering resistance. He asked for a pillow and, when it was brought, he slid it under his head.

The gatekeepers showed in the five soldiers who were commissioned to do the job. It was a large room. Besides the gatekeepers, there were only the five soldiers in the room, a priest who stood huddled in a corner and Kamran himself. No one uttered a word.

Two of the soldiers pinned Kamran's hands to the floor. One tied his legs together and sat on them. The fourth one twisted a piece of cloth into a ball and gagged his mouth with it. The fifth soldier was Ali Dost, who had six fingers on both his hands. He came in only after the others had taken their positions. Ali Dost folded his legs, sat down at Kamran's head and took out a lancet from a bag he was carrying with him. He held back Kamran's eyelids with one hand and applied the lancet fifty times to each of his eyes. He then took out a lemon from his bag and squeezed its juice into the eye-sockets from where blood was gushing out. At that moment Kamran left out a muffled cry, as much as his gagged mouth would allow—according to historian Gulbadan, who also happened to be both Humayun's and Kamran's sister.

His work done, Ali Dost got up and came out of the room. The four soldiers were still holding tight Kamran's hands, legs and head. The priest continued to stand motionless in the corner. Kamran was groaning. And Humayun was pacing up and down in his chamber, restless and anxious to know whether the task had been completed.

It was an exceptionally warm day in the Hindukush Valley. The year, 1553. Month, August. It was the seventh day of Ramzan (Kamran, it is said, regretted he could not carry on with the rest of his fast).

In the outskirts of Kabul, the battle had raged for days. When Humayun sent his emissaries of peace, Kamran arrested them. Some of them were beheaded, while others were hung down the ramparts of the fort in order to stop the fusillades of Humayun's artillery. It was also during this war that Hindal, who was brother to both Humayun and Kamran, was cut into pieces by Kamran's men. Humayun's mind at last hardened like a stone against his brother. Kamran began losing the battle and had to flee. One by one all his friends left him. No one offered him refuge. The sultan of Gakkar caught him and handed him over to Humayun.

With the war over, Humayun wanted to embark on a campaign to retrieve Hindustan. Before that, he camped at Pirhala in the Hindukush Valley to celebrate his victory. Discussions on the fate of Mirza went on for days. Amirs, muftis, imams and qazis were all of one view: Kamran did not deserve any mercy and should be put to death. Humayun's mind wavered. Rejecting everyone's advice, he finally decided it would be sufficient to effectively incapacitate him. Thus, this hot August, on the seventh day of Ramzan, a day before the emperor's campaign to retake Hindustan, Kamran was blinded by Ali Dost, who had six fingers on both hands.

Coming out of the cell, Ali Dost paused for a moment to look at himself, his hands and clothes soaked in blood. He had carried out a variety of punishments in his career but this was the first time he had blinded somebody. The blood that had gushed out had fallen on his face and almost blinded him. Wiping his eyes, he had continued his work. When he looked at Kamran's face after completing the job, it dawned on him that his victim would no longer be able to see him. He did not know why, but he was not relieved by that knowledge. When the slaves poured water on his hands, he washed away the blood mechanically. Then he wiped his hands with the towel they held out.

After such deeds people like Ali Dost are entitled to a treat in the drinking place. Ali Dost did not go there. He walked towards the barracks. But he didn't go in. Instead he untethered his horse, walked with it for a while, and mounted it.

The horse galloped through new pastures, new lands and the darkness of the woods. At sunset he reached a village on the edge of vast fields. Ali Dost was exhausted. Dismounting from the horse, he sat on the ground against a hayrick. The hay and the earth were comfortably cool, probably from the previous day's rain. Suddenly Ali Dost had a bout of nausea. He retched violently. A great relief swept over him when everything inside was thrown out. He took deep breaths to tide over the exertion.

The commotion brought an old woman out of her hut. When she found it was a soldier, her curiosity changed to anger. Flailing her hands, she yelled, 'After plundering the poor of their little paise and getting drunk, you fellows get only this place to come and empty out your bile?'

'No, mother, I am not drunk,' Ali Dost muttered, still gasping for breath. 'Someone else is. I am vomiting for him.'

This was the first time he had opened his mouth after carrying out the deed. But he didn't know what he meant by those words. Like the bile he was spewing, a few words too spilled out of him. That was all.

What might have been on Kamran's mind when he said he had to abandon his Ramzan fast? Couldn't he have continued it even after he was blinded? Or, was it because he did not want someone else's help to know the rising and setting of the sun? Kamran lay prostrate before his tormentors for his eyes to be plucked out. That, however, did not mean he repented his deeds and was accepting the punishment gracefully. In fact, Kamran was never one to willingly lose anything. It's just that in the circumstances, he chose his life rather than his sight. That was all.

The victor in a battle kills the vanquished. Kamran too had done this. It is done to prevent the enemy from gathering strength and rising once again. For the same reason it is necessary for the vanquished to save his life so he can take another chance. Babar built an empire just with his strength and skill. Sher Shah Suri took it away from his son. If fortune had favoured him, Kamran too could have achieved what Sher Shah did. He had staked his claim to the empire not as Babar's son, but as a strong soldier. He could not therefore understand the 'crime' people said he had committed. If an ordinary Afghan—not a Turk or a Mongol or any relation of Babar—could defeat Humayun and occupy the throne, then why not he? If captured, Humayun would have been beheaded by Sher Shah or Sher Shah by Humayun and no one would have seen the necessity of any trial for that. Why, then, had all these amirs and muftis and imams and qazis arrayed against him with all their books and laws?

Kamran sent a message through Munim Beg to Humayun that he wanted to meet him. Humayun agreed on the condition that Kamran would not betray the least emotion. When he heard this, though his head was splitting with pain, Kamran laughed loudly.

As expected, it was Humayun who burst into tears when he saw the bandaged face of Kamran. 'Oh, the vanities of this perishable world! I stained my hands with my brother's blood. I did not listen to the dying words of my revered father,' he cried.

'If this is how you feel, why did you do the deed?' Kamran asked dryly.

'It was not my decision, Kamran. It was the verdict of law. I am an emperor too, the same way I am a brother. I too have to obey the law.'

'How beautiful!' Kamran exclaimed. 'Protecting the position of the emperor is the necessity of the emperor and not of the law, Humayun. Law serves the one who sits on the throne. It does not ask how he reached there. But it comes down heavily on those who claim it. I too have beheaded people and burnt them at the stakes. I did not quote books for doing that, Humayun. I have not come to you with this splitting headache of mine to hear your philosophy.'

'What have you come for?' Humayun asked submissively.

'I have come to congratulate you. To celebrate the death of brotherhood. I spat on its face long ago. Even if the reasons are different, you too have done just that today.'

'Don't say such things, Kamran. Your greed for power made you forget you are a brother. Yet, I saved your life, on that count.'

'You will not understand, Humayun,' Kamran waved his hands to show it was useless to talk to him. 'You have always been polluting politics with your foolish sentiments. You spoiled its purity by inducting fathers and sons and brothers into it . . . At least today, I thought, you had finally liberated yourself from it. No brother will any longer be a threat to your throne.'

Speech had exerted pressure on the muscles of Kamran's face. He pressed his hands against his head and groaned.

Humayun could not stand the sight. Nor could he understand his brother's arguments. He called the guards and asked them to take him away from there. When they had left, Humayun fell into a deep reverie. In one way, he felt it would have been better to have killed his brother. A dead Kamran might still haunt his thoughts. But where is the time for an emperor for such musings? And if they persisted, there were always the opium pills for him.

Humayun called his chief and announced the ceremonial opening of the campaign to take Hindustan.

Hindal is dead. Askari defeated and imprisoned. Kamran blind. Riding on his favourite horse, in the midst of the army moving towards Hindustan, Humayun was suddenly engulfed by solitude. The Mughal army was a moving city which includes not only soldiers and officers and ministers but also the wives, servants and cooks of the king, traders, courtesans, dancing girls and even moneylenders who followed the soldiers. A confusing mass which raised a deafening noise and clouds of dust.

Humayun has led this army a number of times—sometimes as a victor and sometimes as a fugitive. These three brothers of his were never with him then. Perhaps the brothers were his worst enemies, not the sultan of Gujarat or the Rajputs or the Afghans. Separately and jointly, they kept attacking him even when he was wandering in the deserts of Thar and Sindh alone, after being driven out of the country by his enemies. And yet, it was not during those days of running from pillar to post but now, when he was confidently on his way to regain all that he had lost, that he yearned for the love of brothers who already were blinded or imprisoned or dead.

Once, as young boys on a ride, Humayun and Kamran saw a dog lifting its leg against a tombstone. Kamran observed, 'The man who lies buried here must be a heretic.' 'Yes,' was Humayun's reply, 'and the dog's soul that of an orthodox brute.'

There were many complexities and contradictions in the character of Humayun. He was not orthodox, nor was he a heretic. He could melt sometimes with benign brotherly love and, at other times, could commit the most cruel deeds. Again and again he forgave his brothers who had raised their swords against him. When a battle was won or a city captured, clad in red garments, he would sit on his throne. Till his anger subsided and he put on his green garments—and that would often be days after his soldiers had been out in the city plundering, killing, raping and doing whatever they liked with the population. Humayun was a very good soldier but a highly incapable ruler. He always delayed his decisions. Opium had blunted his brain. Mughals who claimed descent from both Timur and Genghis Khan had shown interest in collecting works of art along with their professional skill in cutting heads. Humayun too was interested in arts and pleasure. But he rarely got any time to remain in one place and lead a peaceful life. Whenever he found time he was absorbed in astronomy and literature. He wrote poems.

Even with his willingness to accommodate other points of view, there was one area in which he had no confusion—that empires should be ruled by dynasties and that the right to the throne belonged to the eldest son of the deceased emperor. He would not compromise on this.

After fourteen long years, today Humayun was going to re-establish the correctness of that doctrine. Shaking off the loneliness that had overcome him for a moment, Humayun marched ahead. It was a cloudy day. It would be raining all over Hindustan, he thought. Rivers would be overflowing. Towns and villages would be engulfed by waters. Till the rains subsided, winter began and the festivals of the Hindus concluded, he should spend his time on the banks of the Indus, organizing his army, training his soldiers and planning the operation. Humayun tried to compose a poem in his mind.

Way back in Pirhala, guarded by soldiers and attended on by physicians, in his world of darkness and pain, Kamran too was trying to compose a poem. (Kamran was better than Humayun in poetics, says Gulbadan.) These two brothers simply did not understand each other. One believed that the right to rule a people belonged to a dynastic hierarchy. The other believed it went by right to the strongest person. They were blind men who opened their eyes only before mirrors.

There was yet another blind man whose eyes failed him even before a mirror—Ali Dost. He could see everything else, but not himself. Standing behind the cluster of huts, he watched Humayun's army marching in the distance. Villagers shuddered at the thunder and the clouds of dust which enveloped men, horses, elephants, everything. It was like a moving thundercloud. When convinced that the army was moving away from the village, the villagers sighed in relief and returned to their huts. Ali Dost alone stood and stared.

It was the first time he was dropping out when an army moved. He had no explanation for it. The onward march had been announced days in advance, yet here he was this night, beside the haystacks in the village, eating the bread offered by the villagers and staring at the endless play of clouds in the sky.

No battle was alien to him. He had never looked upon any

king with feelings other than of docile submission. There was a category of people those days who had no attachments to family or country and no roots or relations to claim obligations, and whose only consistent activity was to follow this direction or that, with this king or that. Ali Dost was one of them.

He had reached Hindustan as a little boy, in circumstances he himself could not recollect. He grew up serving Turks, Afghans and Mughals. It was the sultan of Gujarat, Bahadur Shah, who had first exploited the induration process in this soldier. Every soldier kills in the battlefield but that is to save his own life. To kill or maim a man who has done nothing to you, or who cannot do anything to you since he is in chains, is something that not everyone can do. So kings always retained such people as their palace guards without wasting them in the battlefield. Their duty started after the battle was over. Ali Dost, from his tender years, specialized in jobs such as cutting prisoners' limbs, castrating them with boulders and impaling culprits on stakes.

When the artillery commanded by the Ottoman Turks and Portuguese soldiers smashed the fort of Chittor, Bahadur Shah's victory was assured. Ali Dost and his friends stood by waiting for the sultan's orders on things to be done after the battle was called off. Rani Karnavati and other women remaining in the fort jumped into flames. The males, to the last one, rushed out of the gates to end their lives by the swords of their enemies. Left behind were the children. When the soldiers cleared the wells after the battle, Ali Dost stood by and counted their bodies. When the number exceeded three thousand they stopped counting. The Rajputs did not leave much for Ali Dost to do.

When Humayun's forces captured Champanir from Bahadur Shah, Ali Dost and friends were inherited by the Mughal emperor as part of his 'war loot'. Led by Alam Khan, one of the principal officers of Bahadur Shah, they were brought to Humayun's camp for a banquet. Softened with food and drink, Alam Khan revealed the treasures hidden in the fort. So immense were the treasures that the emperor almost danced. The whole camp burst into celebration. In the disorder, a clique of palace underlings did something indiscreet. Extremely incensed with what had happened and intoxicated with drugs, the emperor, clad in blood red, sat on his throne. He ordered a variety of savage mutilations to be inflicted upon the revolting soldiers. Ali Dost and friends dutifully complied. With the deafening shrieks of soldiers roasting in the flames and the wail rising from the town, the emperor's mood was ecstatic.

It all quietened by evening and an eerie silence fell over the palace. Sitting in a corner of the durbar room which had been cleaned after the day's macabre doings, in the sullen light of a candle, the imam on duty foolishly read that chapter of the Koran which speaks of the ruin that befell the masters of the elephant from their attempt to destroy the sacred building at Mecca. Humayun, who took this as a reflection upon himself, ordered that the imam be trod to death by an elephant. The interceding of the moulanas was in vain. The strong hands of Ali Dost twisted the imam into a ball and carried him to the elephant. Since he stood at a distance, Ali Dost's body was not soiled. The mahout was dirtied all over with splattered pieces of brain and intestine.

This was how Ali Dost had grown up.

In the battle for Bengal, Ali Dost came over to Sher Shah, but then, in the battle of Chausa, he found himself among Humayun's men.

From then on it was flight, for five long years. Along with a routed and demoralized army, looking for refuge, they moved across plains, mountains and deserts. Till, at last, on the other side of Hindukush, Humayun bowed his head before the Shah of Iran.

That night at Chausa, had he cared, Ali Dost could have managed to stay behind in Sher Shah's army. He would then have been around to rout the army of Maldeo of Jodhpur and to kill Puran Mal of Malwa by deception. Who can say, Ali Dost might have been assigned the task of capturing the surviving daughter and sons of Puran Mal. He might even have been the man selected by Sher Shah to violate the girl and to sell her to the *bazigaran* and to castrate the boys. But people like Ali Dost never speculate in this manner. They are not particularly concerned about whom they serve.

As the emperor's convoy moved on, the dust gradually settled. The rows of trees on the other side of the maidan again became visible. But Ali Dost did not see anything. His eyes, perhaps, were still clouded with dust.

The old woman came out and took his hand in hers. She said, 'What is it that is troubling you? You never told me. If it is the thought of sin, my dear boy, you must understand why no retribution can ever fall on you with so many sultans, rajas and subedars to bear that burden on their heads.'

'It is not sin, no; it is something else,' he said.

'I can give an anwer only if you tell me, is it not?'

'It is not the answer that is eluding me, mother; it is the question itself. I cannot see anything, mother. I have gone blind!'

'Do one thing, son,' she placed her hand on his shoulder. 'Get your horse. Go to the next town. There will be drinking establishments there. And also dancing girls. Cool your head for some time. You will be all right.'

He looked at her through his vacant eyes.

Delhi and Agra fell into the hands of Humayun. Thus he proved again that the right to the throne belonged to the Mughal dynasty and, within the dynasty, to the dead ruler's eldest son.

Victorious and satisfied, he withdrew to a quiet and happy life in the palace in Delhi built by Sher Shah. Though he was barely fifty, he had grown old and exhausted. He might have started seeing his end nearing. The sight of the old graves and sepulchres of Delhi often brought to his mind the thought of the Great Beyond and he felt an inclination to depart from this world. He made all arrangements, through Bairam Khan, to install Akbar, who was only thirteen years old at that time, as the emperor after him. He spent most of his time in prayer and reading. He reduced his dose of opium to four pills a day and planned to further reduce it to two. After drinking a portion of his dose for the day mixed in rose water, while coming down the stairs of Sher Mandal, the octagonal red sandstone and granite palace built by Sher Shah which Humayun had converted into a library, on that fateful Friday evening of the first winter after his settling in Delhi, Humayun stumbled and missed his footing and fell down and died.

Kamran lived for another year. Discoursing with the ambient darkness, he gradually came to terms with the fact that he had lost the game. He decided, finally, to journey to Mecca along with his faithful and devoted wife Chuchak Begum. The costs were met by the emperor. En route, pirates looted the party. Again the emperor helped him. Favoured thus by the emperor, the blind man performed three pilgrimages to the holy city. The third time he did not return. He died at Mecca.

The dispute between these two men came to pass in this way. But don't believe even for a moment that the notion of the eldest son's right to the throne has triumphed over that of the right of the strongest contestant. Who can say, the story might have swung completely the other way round. Irrespective of the conclusions, at least some of you might argue that the discussion is totally irrelevant to us today as we firmly believe the rightful ruler is someone elected by the country's citizens through a free franchise.

What is left to be told is the story of Ali Dost. What happened to this man jaunting from villages to towns to inns to liquor shops to dancing girls? Could he locate the question which was evading him? Or did he sink from darkness to even deeper darkness? We do not know. Jauhar, Gulbadan, Bayazid and Abul Fazl do not say anything about it. In fact we hardly know anything about the man. Also, historians abandon this wretched man at the point where they say he applied the lancet fifty times to each of Kamran's eyes. Whatever was said of him thereafter is our creation. But there is one thing all of them wrote in their histories—that Ali Dost had six fingers on each of his hands. We do not know the significance of this small detail nor what they wanted to convey by it. Yet, taking a cue from this tiny unconformity, we went ahead to create this little story. Since we have now reached a stage from where it is impossible to proceed further, we too will have to drop the story here, as the renowned historians before us had done at, perhaps, a more appropriate stage. Who can say, Ali Dost might actually have gone along his usual path, the narrow, lonely and probably sad path his type of people are condemned to follow.

Coming out of his cell, he might have entered the drinking place to celebrate the treat that was due him. He might have been enriched by the customary gifts he received from the emperor. Raising dust and clamour, he too might have moved with the troops of the emperor to Hindustan. He might have taken a valiant part in the battle of Sirhind. He might have toiled hard in the gigantic test of sawing off the heads of man after man to build the acclaimed *sir-i-manzil*. People with freakish physiques need not necessarily veer off the beaten track to become men of moments. Nor is it mandatory for supermen to emerge to alter the form and pattern of practices which are common to specified periods in history.

[*Translated by the author*]

The Bathroom

Kulimuri

M. Mukundan

Purushottaman has a wish.

> O Bhagavati of Korom, please make Purushottaman's wish come true—
>
> Guruvayurappa, please fulfil Purushottaman's wish—
>
> Lord Ayyappa, please bring Purushottaman's wish to fruition—

He never wishes for anything. The poor fool. Even as a child, he never wished for anything. Merchants from distant places used to sell whistles, balloons, balls and such at the Thira festival in Korom.

Purushottaman never demanded anything.

'Mummy, get me a balloon. A red balloon.'

He never demanded.

'Daddy, get me a ball.'

Never.

'Mummy, get me a whistle.'

Even when he grew up, Purushottaman never had a desire.

He didn't want a terrycloth shirt.

He didn't want a watch.

He didn't want money for a movie.

Purushottaman is a man who has never desired anything. Well, now this same Purushottaman has a desire—he wants to be a housefly.

> O Bhagavati of Korom, please make Purushottaman a fly—
>
> Guruvayurappa, please make him a fly—
>
> Lord Ayyappa, please make Purushottaman a fly—

Most High and Benevolent God. If you could please fulfil
Purushottaman's humble desire—

Purushottaman wants to be a fly.

Everyone has a wish. One person wants to win the lottery.
Another wants a beautiful wife. Others want children. Some
people long to find a job.

And the just Lord grants their various wishes. If he didn't,
how, in his whole life, could Madhavan the horse-cart driver
hope to have such great luck?

Madhavan bought the one-rupee lottery ticket from
Abubakkar's luggage shop. He tucked it in his waist. As he
walked to his shack, he prayed, 'God, let me win the lottery this
time!'

Would the Most High and Benevolent God refuse to make
Madhavan's wish come true? Or allow only Madhavan's wish
come true? Buck-toothed Bhaskaran had also made a wish, 'I
wish I had a beautiful wife.'

By the time Bhaskaran's desire reached his mind, God had
already sent a beautiful wife his way. A beauty with lots of hair
and pearls for teeth.

Gopalan Master wished, 'If only I had a son . . .'

When Gopalan Master's wife delivered, it was a baby boy.
Would the God who so graciously blessed Madhavan, Bhaskaran
and Gopalan Master fail to bless Purushottaman?

Purushottaman has a wish.

Purushottaman wants to be a fly.

The desire to be a fly crept into Purushottaman's mind
yesterday. Just yesterday. Nevertheless, he suffers as if it's been
a thousand years. The fire of his desire crackles hot and bright.

'Is Vasanta here?'

Lifting his head from the newspaper, Gopalan Master looked
through his glasses, 'Purushottaman? What's the matter, son?
Sunrise is pretty early for a visit?'

Gopalan Master was stretched out in his chair.

'Sit down. Lakshmi, my dear! Look who's come for a visit!'
There was no answer from inside.

'She's probably at the well.'

Master again populated his chair. Purushottaman stood up and walked inside. He didn't see anyone there. He pulled up his lungi and tied it. Then, with a little whistle he proceeded towards the well.

Lakshmiamma was standing next to the well, brushing her teeth.

'What's the matter, my dear?' she said politely.

'Is Vasanta here?'

'She's taking a bath.'

Purushottaman noticed only then that the bathroom was closed shut. He could hear the splash and plunge of water being drawn and poured, drawn and poured.

Vasanta was taking a bath.

Purushottaman felt ill for some reason. The smile on his face, that permanent smile, instantly vanished.

Lakshmiamma was talking and brushing her teeth at the same time.

Purushottaman did not understand what she was saying. Nor did he hear her laugh.

He just stood there staring at the closed door. The only thing his ears heard was the sound of water being drawn and poured, drawn and poured.

The sound of the water stopped. The door opened.

Untied hair. Wet, red glass bangles on her wrists. White drops on her neck and cheeks.

A smile blooming in the wetness!

'Ettan?—'

'He's been waiting for you,' Lakshmiamma reported.

'I'll be right back, okay?'

Vasanta went back inside with her wet towel and soap dish.

That was when he saw it: in the bathroom filled with the aroma of soap and oil, a fly was flying around in circles.

The fly who can see everything.

Purushottaman anguished, envious of the fly.

His heart beat like a big drum. His feet quivered. His face

went pale like paper.

That lucky fly! That very lucky fly!

Why was Purushottaman born a man? Forget being born a king—forget being born an emperor—Purushottaman yearned to be born a fly.

In the bathroom permeated with the scents of medicated oil and soap, lurking along the wall, watching Vasanta . . .

O God, make me a fly.

Bhagavati, Ayyappa, Guruvayurappa, Mathappumuttappa, hear my prayer. Make me a fly. I want nothing else in this life. I will never ask for anything else.

Please make me a fly.

Please make me a fly.

Can God refuse?

The Most High and Benevolent God created gods specifically for the purpose of fulfilling human desires. A god was born specifically to make Madhavan the horse-cart driver win the lottery. To give buck-toothed Bhaskaran his beautiful wife. A god was born specifically to give Gopalan Master a boy.

And God had to create a god specifically to fulfil Purushottaman's desire. If that god could not fulfil it, God would again create himself. He would recreate himself into another god capable of fulfilling Purushottaman's desire. Another god more powerful than the first.

Purushottaman prayed. He prayed night and day. Please make me a fly. Please make me a fly.

He begged the trees and the seedlings, 'Dear trees and seedlings, please make me a fly.'

He begged the crakes, 'Dear crakes, please make me a fly.'

He begged the animals of the earth, the birds and the snakes, 'Please make me a fly.'

The trees and seedlings called out, 'O Lord, make Purushottaman a fly.'

The crakes flew up to the sky with prayers in their beaks, 'Most High and Benevolent God, fulfil Purushottaman's wish.'

'Make Purushottaman a fly,' the animals howled to God.

'Make Purushottaman a fly,' the birds sang to God.

'Make Purushottaman a fly,' the snakes hissed to God.

'Make Purushottaman a fly,' the insects buzzed.

God opened his eyes and smiled.

Thin, fibrous legs attached to his belly—on tiny little wings—Purushottaman flew toward Vasanta's house.

As usual, Gopalan Master was sitting in his easy chair reading his paper. Master didn't see Purushottaman fly by with a whistle.

Purushottaman exited the house through the back door and flew towards the bathroom.

Inside the bathroom, he stuck himself against the wall. From here, he could see everything. Everything.

With a palpitating heart, eyes wide open, he awaited Vasanta's arrival. Seconds, seconds which lasted aeons. Or aeons like seconds that splintered and tumbled down in the bathroom.

Someone's footsteps. Are they Vasanta's? O Lord, let it be Vasanta. I can't bear to wait any longer . . . I simply can't . . .

I'll die if I don't . . .

Vasanta entered, soap dish and towel in hand. The glass bangles on her wrists chimed as she unbraided her hair.

She fastened the lock on the door.

She poured the medicated oil in her hands and rubbed it into her hair. Thick hair, black like eyeliner, rolling down to her waist.

Accompanied by the music of the bangles, she undid the buttons on her blouse . . .

Purushottaman saw nothing. Heard nothing. He had gone mad.

Purushottaman did not see the lizard prowling, creeping quietly towards him from the other corner of the wall.

And he did not know it was the lizard who devoured him.

[*Translated by Donald R. Davis, Jr*]

Bhaskara Pattelar and My Life

Bhaaskara Pattelaarum ente jiivithavum

Paul Zacharia

I saw Bhaskara Pattelar for the first time one evening in Udina Bazaar. Squatting on the edge of a shop veranda, I was thinking about my sorrows. The sound my frayed mundu made as it gave way little by little at the back kept pace with my thoughts. Suddenly I heard someone call from the other side of the road.

'Hey!'

I looked up to see who it was.

The man who called me was seated on a chair in the veranda opposite. He must have been about thirty-five years old. He was as tall as he was large. He wore a silk jubba and was fair-skinned. His eyes and hair had a coppery tint. He had a big moustache which curved downwards and his lips were stained red with betel juice. His big body barely fitted into the chair. Half a dozen people stood around him respectfully.

'Come here, you whore's son!' Pattelar called out in Kannada. I sprang up with joined palms. Who could this be? What did such a great man want of me?

As I jumped down from the veranda, my mundu tore along its entire length. I held the torn ends together behind me with one hand, covered my mouth respectfully with the other and crossed the road.

The giant got up from the chair and came to the edge of the veranda.

'What is that in your hand, rascal?'

'Nothing, master,' I said.

'Why then, dog, are you holding one hand behind you? Do you want to shit? Don't you know how to show respect to those who deserve respect? Come closer, you rascal.'

I quickly took away the hand that held the mundu together, joined my palms and bowed deeply, and moved closer. My torn mundu fell apart like the halves of a stage curtain. With a loud laugh, Pattelar gave me a kick that took in my folded hands, face and all. I fell backwards, naked and staring skyward. Pattelar spat betel juice in a wide arc, spraying it all over me. 'Thoo!'

I rolled on to my stomach, pressed my face into the sand, joined my palms and begged, 'Show me mercy, yejamanare!'

It was then that I saw the gun leaning against Pattelar's chair. It was as large and terrifying as Pattelar himself. The people around him said something in Malayalam and laughed. What! They were Malayalees!

'Get up, dog,' said Pattelar.

I got up and tied one of the pieces of the mundu around my waist.

'Where are you from, rascal?'

'From Kochi, master.'

'Where do you live?' He switched to Malayalam.

'In Ichilampadi, master.'

'How many acres have you encroached on?'

'Only five, master!'

'Are you married?'

'Yes, master.'

'How old is your wife?'

'Twenty-one, master.'

'Good,' said Pattelar. 'Is she pretty?'

I said nothing.

'Speak, son of a dog, is she a beauty?'

'No,' I managed to say.

'Ha, ha, ha,' laughed Pattelar. His men laughed with him. I could hear people in the other shop laugh as well.

'You liar!' Pattelar took his gun and aimed it jestingly at me.

He said, 'I'll have a look and see if she's pretty, and give her a certificate.' The betel-juice-stained teeth smiled through the stubble on his pink face.

'Run!' he said.

I began to run in the direction of Ichilampadi.

'Not that way! This way.' Pattelar pointed with his gun in the opposite direction. I gathered my mundu with one hand and ran along the road he pointed to. The sun was setting. I looked back once.

'Don't look back, rascal!' Behind me, I heard the loud report of the gun. I sobbed aloud and kept running towards a bend in the road some distance away. When I had rounded it, I stopped and leaned against a tree, gasping. Then I clambered down the slope to the river bank and lay on a big, flat rock. I saw a star fall from the sky. When I got my breath back, I rolled down into the water, shivering, and washed away the spittle from my body. I wrung out my torn mundu and wiped myself dry with it. Then I crossed the river and ran to Ichilampadi. Even as I neared my hut, I heard Omana sobbing. On the other side of the hut, torch beams went down to the river and crossed it.

Pattelar sent for me the next day. He bought me a mundu and Omana a sari from the jauli shop. He said to me, 'From today you can work in the toddy shop as server—I've spoken to Varkeychettan. Omana is pretty. You lied to me. Will you tell lies again?'

'No, yejamanare,' I said.

Everyone knew that it was the Malayalee hangers-on who had corrupted Pattelar. He had been just another proud janmi and a man of pleasure. When he sat on the shop veranda, the hangers-on would sometimes point to a woman and say, 'Yejamanare, look at that one, she's so beautiful! Why don't we have a word with her?'

Pattelar would say in Kannada, 'Why bother? It's not worth it.'

They would then say, 'Maja madanna, let's have fun, Pattelare! We are with you!'

'All right.' Pattelar would get up and go after the woman.

If someone walked through the bazaar unmindful of Pattelar and his group, they would whisper, 'Pattelar, look at him, he's behaving as if you're not here. What cheek! Should we give him one?'

Pattelar would gulp his toddy and say, 'No. Let's not have trouble. Galatta beda.'

'We are with you! Give him one, Pattelare. Teach him to show respect.'

'All right.' Pattelar would then get up.

In time, Pattelar came to believe in all this and to go along with it. When I think of it, I feel sad for him. What a pity that such a good man should have come to this! Whose sins was he paying the price for, by sinning over and over again? And what bond from a previous birth was it that brought me to him all the way from the land of my birth?

And so I became Pattelar's servant. As soon as he took his seat on the shop veranda, I would bring him a pot of toddy and then wait down in the yard, bowing respectfully, hands folded across my chest. Whenever he went woman-hunting, he asked me to go with him. In a narrow deserted gully somewhere, he would cover some whimpering Gowda girl's mouth with one hand and grip her hands with the other, before pushing her down on the dry leaves. Once in a while, he would ask me, 'Want her, rascal?'

'No, yejamanare,' I would say.

Without letting go of the girl, Pattelar would aim a friendly kick in my direction.

'Go away, scoundrel; go where I can't see you.'

I would walk some distance and wait for Pattelar, look up at the sky and at the mountains in the distance. If someone came by, I would signal to them, 'Pattelar is here!' At once they would take another path. Indeed, people understood what was afoot as soon as they saw me. Whenever I heard a girl cry out, I would think of Omana, of that first day. Omana had stopped crying as time went by. That was a great relief to me. Omana is such a simple soul. So am I. How good it is not to have to cry.

*

One day, at dusk, Pattelar was seated in his armchair on the shop veranda in Udina Bazaar, drinking the evening-fresh toddy. I stood in the yard and filled his glass from the pot. Every now and then I ran across the street to the tea shop and brought him vadas and bolis. The usual group stood around Pattelar, some on the veranda and some down in the yard. I brought glasses for them too from the toddy shop and poured them drinks.

It was then that the last bus from Dharmasthala to Hassan groaned and slid to a stop in the bazaar. One or two people got off. Spreading a reddish glow behind, the bus disappeared into the darkness to make its way up the Shiradi hills, past Sakaleshpuram, determined to reach Hassan somehow before midnight. One of the passengers who had alighted crossed the road and approached us. I recognized him at once. He was a dhani—a rich merchant from Arshanamukki. He had areca nut groves and, with his younger brother, owned a lorry. How come he had taken a bus today? He looked very worried. I ran up to him, joined my palms respectfully and said, 'Ayyo, dhani! Why have you come by bus today and why are you looking so worried?'

He said, 'My brother went to Yenjira early this morning with the lorry and is not back yet. He should have returned at noon. Have any of you seen him? Did you hear of an accident anywhere?'

Pattelar pointed with his foot at the newcomer from his armchair and asked me, 'Who is this, rascal? Why are you grovelling? Is he your father, dog?'

I stood between them on the roadside, perspiring in the huge shadows cast by the petromax lamp, aware that my joined palms were growing limp with fear and sliding down. I said,

'Yejamanare, this is Yousappicha from Arshanamukki. He's a dhani. His younger brother is missing.'

Pattelar splashed the toddy he had in his hand on Yousappicha's face. He said, 'Do we keep your brother here? Look at the bloody dhani!'

The shops were closing for the day and everyone was going home. Only a few people lingered in the tea shop and the toddy shop. They were listening silently. No one came out.

Pattelar jumped down into the yard, swaying a little. I begged in a trembling voice, 'Please forgive me, yejamanare! Yousappicha is one of our own.'

Pattelar gave me a terrible blow across my right cheek and ear. I slumped to the ground; my ears filled with the noise of a world splitting apart. When I raised my head, Pattelar had Yousappicha on the ground and was kicking him. He kicked him in the head, stomach and spine.

'This dog of a dhani comes to look for his brother here! So late in the evening!' shouted Pattelar. I was too scared to get up from where I cowered. My God, I thought, Pattelar is beating Yousappicha to a pulp. A man he is seeing for the first time! Why hit a man who had come to look for his brother? Yousappicha lay still on the roadside, in the shadows of Udina Bazaar, like a muddy bundle of rags. Not moving and hardly daring to breathe, I stared at the sprawled figure.

Pattelar climbed back on the veranda, sat on his chair and summoned me. My head buzzed violently as I jumped up and rushed to him. In the dark I stumbled over one of Yousappicha's outstretched legs and fell. He knew nothing of all this. I scrambled up again, ran and poured toddy for Pattelar from the pot. Pattelar said, 'A dhani, is he? And he comes at dusk, like a bad omen. You be careful too! Next time you invite people like this, you'll get the same treatment.'

'Ayyo, yejamanare,' I wailed, 'I didn't invite Yousappicha. His younger brother . . .'

'Shut your mouth, dog!' shouted Pattelar.

I shut my mouth.

It was late when Pattelar finally got up to go home. He said to us, 'Put him in the back of the jeep.'

We carried Yousappicha and put him in the jeep. It was I who held his hands. The pulse is beating, I said to myself.

Pattelar's wife, Sarojakka, did not like noisy gatherings in the house at night. So Pattelar usually went to play cards in the watchman's hut in the yard where areca nuts are dried. Tonight, there were six or seven people with him. Yousappicha was dumped in a corner, hands and legs tied up. The blood that oozed from his mouth dribbled in a long thread and vanished into the dusty floor. I sat near him and watched the card game, dozing off occasionally. He knew nothing, not even what had happened to his brother. Now and then, when I woke up and saw the way Yousappicha lay, I felt sorry. Once, I almost whispered, 'Yejamanare, may I give Yousappicha a drop of water?' But my voice stayed trapped in my throat. Sometime near dawn, Yousappicha groaned once. Then I fell asleep. When I woke up, it was daylight and only Yousappicha and I were in the hut. He was cold and dead. 'Ayyo, my Yousappicha, that you had to die this way,' I said sadly, looking at his corpse. Suddenly I thought of Sarojakka. Ayyo, Yousappicha must be moved before she finds out.

Shivering in the morning cold, I ran, slipping and sliding on the areca nuts, to the window of Pattelar's room. I knocked on it softly.

It was Sarojakka who opened the window. 'What is it?' she asked. 'Nothing, nothing, yejamanathi,' I stammered. Then Pattelar got up, came to the window and asked, 'What is it?' I said, 'Nothing, master.' Pattelar looked at my face closely and said, 'I see. Go back now; I'll come.'

I waited near Yousappicha, trembling in the cold. Pattelar came, wearing a shawl, his ears covered with a monkey cap, and said, 'Get two or three people, tie him up in a sack and bury him in the Arabi Majal before Sarojakka comes out to milk the cow. I'll take care of the police.'

I felt very relieved.

*

One day, Pattelar said to me, 'Listen, I'm going to kill Sarojakka. I need you.'

I jumped with fear. Sarojakka was such a good person. She gave me something to eat or drink every day. She knew Pattelar's ways, but always spoke to him with affection. She gave him good advice and never quarrelled with him. I felt very sad. I said, 'Why do you want to do that, yejamanare? She is such a good akka. Please don't . . .'

Pattelar said, 'I want to make it look like an accident. You will be the witness. You will call her out to the veranda. I will sit there pretending to load my gun. It will look as if the gun went off by mistake. She must not know that I shot her. I do not want her to die with that sorrow. There's no need for you to feel sad either. Just think of it as an accident, that's all. You'll have to give proper evidence. Her brothers are nasty fellows.'

I thought sadly, I know why Pattelar wants to kill Sarojakka. To lay his hands on her share of the property.

'Yejamanare,' I said, 'we don't need Sarojakka's share.'

He gave me a long look.

That afternoon, Pattelar sat on a chair in the veranda, put the gun on his lap, opened the bag of gunpowder and pretended to load his gun. I squatted on the edge of the veranda some distance away. The gun turned slowly in my direction. I told myself, Pattelar is just loading his gun, that's all he's doing. There's nothing to worry about. When Pattelar signalled with his eyes, I looked towards the kitchen and called, 'Sarojakka!' She answered. I said, 'Please give me something to drink.'

'Shall I give you some kanji?' she asked.

'All right,' I said. Poor Sarojakka, I thought to myself. She will bring me kanji to satisfy a hunger I do not feel. And she will die.

With sudden fear, I called out again, 'Sarojakka, please don't add salt!' I did not look at Pattelar.

Sarojakka came out. She had the bowl of kanji in one hand and a glass of buttermilk in the other. She gave Pattelar the buttermilk and said, 'Drink this. You did not eat anything this morning.'

Pattelar flinched, but took the glass from her.

Sarojakka walked towards me with the bowl of kanji. My eyes were on Pattelar. He tried hurriedly to put down the glass of buttermilk with one hand. At the same time, he tried to point the gun with the other at Sarojakka. I saw him pull the trigger. The glass fell down and broke. At the same moment, I heard the shot . . . I kept staring at Sarojakka! I looked at her, wanting to cry for her. Suddenly, I felt a searing pain in my stomach, as if someone had stabbed me with a red-hot stick. It felt like a fire blazing inside me. I could not bear the pain and jumped up. Blood spurted from my stomach! Ayyo! Is it I who've been shot! Pattelar sat staring at me with wide eyes. Sarojakka screamed. I wailed, 'Yejamanare, save me. It's I who have been shot!'

'Shut your mouth, scoundrel,' shouted Pattelar, 'or I'll finish you off right now!'

Sarojakka went out into the courtyard and called for help. People came running. I fainted then. When I became conscious again, I was lying on the floor of the grain-shed, with cloth tied around my stomach.

I heard Pattelar say to the others, 'Don't waste time. He's dying. Carry him to the Arabi Majal. I'll bring my gun. We can bury him there.'

I whimpered, 'Yejamanare, Omana will have no one. Don't kill me, please.'

Pattelar looked at me in astonishment. While he watched me uncertainly, Sarojakka suddenly came in and said, 'What are you saying? I'll not allow it. Take him to the hospital!'

I lay unconscious in the hospital for a week. I had many dreams of Sarojakka and Omana. It was while I was dreaming that I lay with my head on Sarojakka's lap that I woke up. My head swam in a wave of happiness. The warmth and softness of Sarojakka's lap clung to me for a long time. I laid my hand on my wounded stomach, feeling very happy that Sarojakka was alive.

A few nights later, I said to Omana, 'Do you know, I had a dream that I lay with my head on Sarojakka's lap?' Omana did not believe me.

*

One night, Pattelar came to my house, woke me up and said, 'Come. We're going to catch the fish in the temple ghat at Arshanamukki.'

'Oh! My yejamanare!' I said, trembling with fear. 'Ayyo, my yejamanare!'

'Why are you scared?' asked Pattelar. 'I am here.' He held up a cloth bag, which contained dynamite sticks, and shook it. 'Just you and I will do it. No one else has the courage. Cowardly dogs!'

I looked out fearfully. A faint moonlight filtered through the Makara mist. This was the time the yakshi of the Arshanamukki temple came out to stroll around. The fish that lived in the ghat belonged to the yakshi. The Udina river flowed wide in front of the temple, looking like a lake. Even in summer, the current was strong enough to make your legs totter. In the rainy season the floodwaters roared and rushed like a stormy sea. But the five thousand fish in the bathing ghat by the temple always lay there undisturbed. They were huge, sleek, gleaming fish, with knowing eyes. They did not fear men, but allowed no one to touch them. They splashed and writhed in the water, clustered together as if they were in a fish basket. If you threw them puffed rice, you could not see the water because of the way they thrashed about. When they jumped and fell back, the sound was like coconuts falling. I have often watched them and felt frightened. What if I were to fall among them? Wouldn't they eat me up in a moment? I would then move two steps back before throwing them more puffed rice. Watching them, sometimes my mouth has watered too. If Omana could get just one of them, it would last her a whole week—to make curry, deep-fry, make roast chutney and also pickle some. Just one fish would be enough. But they belonged to the yakshi. The yakshi caught and ate anyone who caught and ate her fish. She would tear him open, bring her fish back to life from where it lay in his greedy intestines, give it a loving kiss on its pouting lips and, her laughter filling the night like the tinkle of crystal balls, shoot it back into the river like a silver arrow flashing through the darkness. Then, smacking her lips, she would bend down to savour slowly the one who had eaten her fish.

'Ayyo, yejamanare,' I wailed. 'Ayyo! Ayyo!'

Pattelar took the headlamp out of his shoulder bag, put in on his forehead and fastened the belt. He gave me the cloth bag of dynamite sticks and said, 'Carry it carefully.' Then he picked up his gun.

As we went down into the courtyard, Pattelar said, 'Take two or three baskets also.'

All along the way, in the meadows and valleys of moonlight, I thought there was movement and readiness. I heard the tinkling of anklets too. The yakshi was pursuing us to protect her fish. Carefully placing my feet in Pattelar's footprints and trembling with fear, I walked under the moon, to the river by the Arshanamukki temple. Once, I mustered enough courage to say, 'Yejamanare, the yakshi . . .' Pattelar brandished the gun and said, without turning around, 'Fool, the yakshi is afraid of guns. Don't you know a gun is made of iron? She's afraid of you as well. You're from another religion and because of that she doesn't like your blood!' In the darkness, Pattelar shook with laughter.

When we had gone quite a way, I whispered, 'Yejamanare, if anything happens to me . . . Omana . . .'

Pattelar laughed again. 'Don't I look after Omana even when you are there? If you're not there, you don't have to worry at all. Ha, ha, ha!'

We reached the river as I was asking myself whether Omana would grieve if something happened to me. There was only the soft sound of the summer waters. And the moonlight. And the mist drifting over the water. And the stillness of the temple. Shivering with terror, I looked up at the sky, standing on the steps of the bathing ghat. The moon was only a faint glow in the foggy sky. Veils of mist and cloud floated in its shadowy light. In the waters of the river, all was quiet. Where were all the fish, I wondered. Where they asleep? Do fish sleep? Were we going to kill the fish when they were sleeping? Ayyo! That would be so sad. Ayyo, my fish, I said to myself, you doze and dream in still corners under the moving sheet of water. But now you will not be able to complete your dreams. The thunder of these dynamite sticks will, like a hammer, shatter your dreams and your hearts. Then I will jump into the water with my basket. I will stack your gleaming bodies in it till it is full. The moonlight will fill your unclosing eyes. The mist will kiss your gasping mouths. I will weave through the water like an otter, lift up your corpses and stack my basket high, over and over again. The shreds of your broken dreams will cling to me like your white scales. And then, while the yakshi is devouring me, you will fly out of these baskets with throbbing hearts and return to the river through the mist. I will drip from the yakshi's mouth as blood and marrow, dribble down her thighs and become manure for the earth.

I said to Pattelar, 'Yejamanare, I am afraid.'

I looked once towards the temple, took a stick of dynamite and held it out to Pattelar. He said, 'Shitting coward, throw it yourself!' He pressed the switch on the battery-box tied to his waist and bent his head so that his headlamp shone directly into the water. I lit the stick of dynamite and threw it into the centre of the patch of light. It sank and disappeared. Both of us waited for the explosion that would resound from the envelope of water. One! Two! Three! I counted. I counted to fifty and said, 'The stick did not explode, yejamanare!'

'Throw the next one, rascal,' said Pattelar.

I lit the next stick and threw it. When I had counted to fifty, Pattelar said, 'The next one!' I counted to fifty again.

Only the light from the lamp on Pattelar's forehead lay floating on the water.

I took the next stick in my hand and looked at Pattelar. 'Yejamanare,' I stammered, 'you throw this one, yejamanare.'

Pattelar looked at me and muttered something. The beam from his forehead wove its way through the night. I was terrified. Pattelar was growling obscenities. His face was distorted as he hurled dirty words at the yakshi. Then he grabbed the stick of dynamite from me and, spilling light from his headlamp over the steps, he ran up to the temple yard.

'Baddimagale! You whore's daughter!' he screamed, lit the stick of dynamite and threw it with all his might at the closed door of the temple. I covered my ears with both hands and crouched down. Look at yejamanar, he's wrecking the temple. The explosion comes now! I closed my eyes tight, dug my fingers into my ears and sat there, frozen. But there was only silence everywhere. When light filtered through my closed eyes, I opened them and looked up. Pattelar was bending down and peering at me. I thought, Pattelar is mad with rage and is going to kill me. Ayyo! My Omana, I shall not see you again. My God, here I come. Was Pattelar picking up his gun? I sat staring into the blinding light. Suddenly, he switched off the lamp. He stood there without moving for some time. When the ghost-light of the headlamp had faded from my eyes, I stood up. I picked up the cloth bag in which I had brought the dynamite. I put the baskets on my head.

'Shall we go, yejamanare?' I asked.

Pattelar said nothing. He walked up to the temple door and took the unexploded stick of dynamite lying there. Then, with a grunt, he threw it far into the river, as if aiming at the other bank. I heard it fall with a plop somewhere in the middle of the river, beyond where the fish lived. As we were going out through the temple yard, a sound came from the river, 'Bhum!'

The sound of the exploding dynamite pursued us like something awful the river had spoken, making me feel as if a world had ended. 'Bhum!' said the river.

As we walked back under the whirling stars of the midnight sky, I heard footsteps around us and bells tinkling from the shadows, and I shivered in fear. Pattelar moved silently, like a sleepwalker, with the gun on his shoulder. Shadowy forms of bats circled in the sky above us. For a moment I thought they were flying fish.

*

People regularly brought Pattelar gifts so that he would not harass them. They would prod me and say, 'Pattelar might forget who brought this. You must remind him.' I used to put away the balls of jaggery, the dried and salted chunks of deer meat, rough boards of rosewood, ripe jackfruits, fowl and big packets of pickled fish wrapped in spathes of the areca nut palm. In the evening, I usually gave Pattelar the details of who had brought what. Pattelar would clear his throat loudly, spit and say, 'The spineless scoundrels!' I carried all the gifts on my head to Pattelar's house, taking care not to leave anything behind. Sarojakka would say, 'Do people give these things out of love? They give them because they're afraid. I don't like to keep such things at home.' 'Ayyo!' I would exclaim, looking towards the front veranda, where Pattelar was seated. Sarojakka always secretly gave me a portion of all the gifts. And I would take them in a basket to Omana. 'See, Sarojakka gave me these!'

One day, Pattelar said to me, 'You rascal, the fish pickle I ate at your house with the toddy yesterday tasted exactly like the pickle that Kuttapparai brought to my house. How did this happen? Does Kuttapparai also have an account in your house? Tell me the truth!'

I said, 'Ayyo, yejamanare, I don't know.'

Pattelar burst out laughing. 'So you need my help to finish the pickle your Sarojakka gives you with such love, do you?' He shook with laughter.

Early one morning, I was lying with Omana, hugging her close. She was still enveloped in the fragrance of Pattelar's perfume. I breathed in that scent which I loved deep into my nostrils and lay there, pressing Omana to me with great pleasure. I said to myself, although she smells of Pattelar's perfume, she belongs only to me. Some day, I'll buy her this perfume. It was then that I heard a knock. I jumped up, startled, opened the door a little and peered out. There were four or five people standing in front of the house. I made out Kuttapparai, Ahmed— the panchayat president's younger brother—and a couple of Malayalees. I began to tremble uncontrollably. They had come to kill me. Perhaps they had killed Pattelar before they came here. I stood there, unable to move. When Omana peered over my shoulder, her breasts brushed my back. I thought, I will never feel her breasts rub against me again. Kuttapparai said from the courtyard, 'Come out. We have come to ask you something.'

I closed the door without replying, hugged Omana and said, 'If these people kill me, Omana, you must commit suicide. I think Pattelar is already dead.' Then I opened the door and went out.

They caught me by the shoulder, took me under the elanji tree in the compound and said, 'Don't be scared now! Pattelar has to be killed. What is the best way to do it?'

I stared at them. Kill my yejamanar! Ayyo, who would I have then to turn to?

They said, 'Listen, everyone is fed up with Pattelar. You know that no man or woman can walk safely in the village because of him. Pattelar is useful to you, we know. But you're a good fellow, and a harmless one. If you help us, we'll help you. We'll give you a hundred rupees. And the job of a peon in the panchayat office.'

Sunrise had touched the sky. I thought, if Pattelar dies, the village and the villagers will benefit. I'll have a good job as well. But Omana, wouldn't she feel sad? Or would she be happy? I had never asked her this question. Suddenly I was afraid. If Pattelar died, would Omana belong to me? And only to me? I was both thrilled and frightened by this thought.

My mind in a whirl, I asked Ahmed, 'What sort of help do you want, muthalali?' My words tumbled into my ears as if somebody else had spoken them. Ahmed said, 'It's not easy to kill Pattelar, you know. His companions are always with him. All we want you to do is to get Pattelar to sit for a while on your veranda this evening. We will shoot him from a hiding place. It will happen right in front of his men, so no one will suspect you.'

I stared at them, and said, 'Don't let them shoot me or Omana, please.'

They laughed soundlessly. 'We don't shoot as badly as your Pattelar, you fool.'

At noon, scratching my head, I asked Pattelar, 'I wonder if you're going to Ichilampadi this evening, yejamanare?'

Pattelar said, 'What does it matter to you whether I go or not?'

I said, 'Omana is preparing a meal specially for yejamanar. Yejamanar must come.'

'What is she making?'

'Mushrooms fried with coconut, roasted deer meat, fried fish and arrack. She's frying eggs as well, yejamanare.'

'All right,' said Pattelar.

When Pattelar arrived at my house with his men that evening, the lamp had been lit. The men squatted here and there in the courtyard. Pattelar told me, 'I don't feel like drinking arrack. Go and bring me two bottles of fresh toddy.'

I heard suppressed laughter from the courtyard. It doesn't matter, I whispered, you won't laugh after today. Although I'm scared, Omana will soon be mine alone.

I was anxious about the people hiding somewhere outside in the darkness with their guns. What if Pattelar ate and left before I returned with the toddy? Who would get him to sit on the veranda?

I looked helplessly into the darkness around, went down to the road and started running. From the shop I ran back again with a bottle of toddy in each hand. As I set foot in the courtyard, Pattelar opened the door and came out to the veranda. 'Ah, you've come,' he said. 'I've just finished eating.'

His men were dozing in the shadows of the courtyard. I did not have the courage to look farther. What were they going to do now? Would they do something in haste? As I climbed on the veranda, I shrank into myself. Where would they shoot from? My God, don't let them shoot Omana. I kept thinking of a way to make Pattelar sit down. But he stood on the upper veranda, waiting to wash his hands. I knew that the thatch of the hut hung so low that they would not be able to see him from were they hid.

Omana came to the veranda with a lamp in her hand. I put down the toddy and said, 'I'll draw you water to wash your hands, yejamanare.'

The well was next to the lower veranda. It was a deep well which they had had to dig right down to the nether world to find water. Pattelar stepped down to the lower veranda and came to the well. I lowered the bucket into the well, drew water and straightened up. As Pattelar bent and extended his hands to wash them, I heard the shot. I wept silently and looked at Pattelar. Then I looked at Omana. She was running into the house, crying. Pattelar covered his right ear and cheek with one hand, and jumped. The second shot came then, shattering earth and stones from the mud wall of my house. I dropped the bucket and rope. Pattelar had fallen on the well's rim and was slipping off the edge. He was clawing at the earth desperately, trying to get a hold. He was silent. In a moment he would be gone. 'My yejamanare!' I shouted. I leaped forward, caught hold of both his hands, stretched myself out on the ground for support and hoisted him from the mouth of the well. Pattelar lay on the wet earth and breathed through his open mouth like a fish that has been thrown on land. I saw Pattelar's men crashing through the shrubbery, flashing their torches. Shots rang out and there were shouts. I helped Pattelar get up, took him into my hut and sat him on a mat spread on the floor. There was a wound on his ear. His right cheek looked black and blue and he could not open his right eye properly. Omana leaned against the wall, weeping. I poured a glass of toddy from the bottle I had brought from the shop and said, 'Drink this, yejamanare.'

I stood looking at Pattelar and thought, why did I save this man? A small push with these hands of mine would have been enough. I stared at Omana. Was this really my Omana? Who was I? Who was this wounded man, sitting on my torn mat? In the shadows thrown by the wind-shaken flame of the kerosene lamp, it seemed to me that Pattelar and Omana were turning into shapeless, writhing forms. My head reeled. I fell down in a faint.

As I lay in a swoon, I remember seeing, like a picture in a calendar, Sarojakka and Omana flying somewhere through the clouds, looking like white storks.

✳

One rainy evening, at dusk, I was squatting on the veranda of the toddy shop. The shop was closed because the toddy had not yet arrived. Suddenly, Pattelar came in his jeep and asked me to get in. I got into the back and he drove off like a madman. Now and then, the jeep grazed against culverts. At one of the bends, it skidded and nearly overturned. I leaned forward, full of fear, and forcing my face against the screaming wind, I cried, 'Yejamanare, please go slow; otherwise we'll be killed!' Pattelar did not answer. He roared on, soaking the forests on either side of the road in the blaze of the headlights. The jeep rattled over the stones of the rough pathway to his house as he drove in, and stopped. Then he turned to me and said, 'I've killed Saroja. We have to make it look like suicide. You have to help me.'

I stared at Pattelar, unable to take my eyes off his face. 'Ayyo, my yejamanare!' I said. 'My Sarojakka! My Sarojakka!' Crying silently in my heart, I stumbled out of the jeep and started running. Pattelar got into the jeep and tore through the peringalam groves and the thickets of weeds. I heard the jeep roaring behind me, its eyes glittering in the dark. The headlights threw enormous shadows that writhed through the bushes and pursued me. I was sure Pattelar was going to run me over and kill me too. Sarojakka, I cried to myself, here I come. Omana, what will you do? I ran into an embankment, supported myself against it and looked at the shining eyes of the jeep racing towards me. I did not want to die! I screamed, 'My yejamanare, please don't kill me!'

Pattelar stopped the jeep, got down, took me by the hand, pushed me inside and said, 'Don't run away, you wretched rascal. What are you afraid of? I need you. Be a little brave.'

Sarojakka lay on her back on a cot. She had been strangled.

Her tongue was hanging out. Her neck was black and blue. Her face was distorted. I put my trembling hand to my chin and gazed at Sarojakka. Sarojakka, who had fed me sweets and kanji, given me old clothes. Sarojakka, whom I had once betrayed, but whom I loved. Sarojakka, who had refused to let me be killed. She lay dead. At the moment of death, what would she have thought, looking at Pattelar's face? Would she have pleaded for her life? No, she would have looked at Pattelar with eyes full of astonishment and sorrow.

Then Pattelar said, 'She didn't know I killed her. I covered my face with a towel, came in through the window in the darkness and caught hold of her. But she gripped my hands. That's what worries me. Would she have known they were my hands when she touched them?'

I did not say anything.

Pattelar kept quiet for a while and stood looking at Sarojakka. Then he said to me, 'I've run through all my money. So I had to kill her. Don't you know that I have nothing against Sarojakka?'

Pattelar bent down and gazed at Sarojakka's face. He said, 'Saroja, I didn't kill you.'

I drew back, afraid. I thought Sarojakka was going to get up to answer Pattelar with her tongue hanging out.

Then Pattelar turned to me and said, 'Never mind. Come and hold her legs.'

I went up and held her ankles in both my hands. And that is when I first touched Sarojakka. Holding her slim, pale, soft ankles tightly in my hands, I looked at Sarojakka's face. That distorted face was not my Sarojakka's. I looked once at Pattelar, and then I bent down, pressed my face into the soles of her feet and kissed them. Pattelar said softly, 'You liked Sarojakka.'

I climbed on the bed without saying anything, hoisted Sarojakka on to my shoulders, then put my arms around her and lifted her up as one would a child. Pattelar tightened a rope around her neck and pulled her up. I squatted on the bed, pressed my face to her cold feet and sobbed aloud. Pattelar did not scold me. He stood quietly, looking out of the window. I looked back once we went out. My Sarojakka hung from the rafters like a broken branch.

Pattelar said again, 'She wouldn't have known, would she?'

I followed him without replying. All I wanted was to get back to Omana. I wanted to embrace her feet and weep all night, to overcome my sin and sorrow.

As we walked to the jeep, Pattelar said, 'I'm going to the police and to her brothers now to tell them that she killed herself. Remember, you are the witness.'

He stopped near the jeep. I waited in front of him in the dark. Suddenly Pattelar flashed his torch into my face. With dazzled eyes, I searched confusedly for his face behind the torch.

Pattelar shone the light into my blinking eyes and asked in a small voice, 'Tell me, look at my face and tell me. Can one recognize a person by just touching his hands?' I said, 'Who knows, yejamanare?' Pattelar spat out an obscenity and threw the torch on the ground. Its light came rolling towards my feet. I bent, picked it up and switched it off. I heard Pattelar gasp. In the darkness, stretching both his hands towards my blinded eyes, Pattelar said, 'Touch my hands.' My fingers brushed his outstretched hands. 'Is this me?' he whispered. 'Yes, yejamanare,' I said and drew back my hands. Pattelar growled, in a voice that came from deep within him. 'I made a mistake. I should have asked you to kill her.'

*

The next day I heard that Sarojakka's brothers had got some people together and attacked Pattelar's house. I ran there, crept up behind the crowd and peered over their shoulders. The house had been set on fire, but the fire had been put out. Household items lay broken in the courtyard. The jeep looked battered. I did not wait. I ran back like a wounded cat before anyone could recognize me. I reached home, closed the door and said to Omana, 'Omana, it's all over. Pattelar's house has been attacked and burned. I don't know where Pattelar has gone. They are sure to come looking for me now. What will you do?' Omana caught my shoulder and wept.

No one came looking for me. All that day and the next I sat at home not knowing what to do. When I was certain that no one was interested in me, I asked a passer-by, 'Do you have any news of Pattelar?' He looked hard at me, then said, 'Yes. They say he's gone into hiding. It is you who should know, isn't it?' Worried, I sat on the veranda and thought, what should I do now?

At midnight, as soon as I heard a knock on the door, I said to Omana, 'That's Pattelar.' I got up and opened the door. Pattelar stood on the veranda. The rain had drenched him. He did not have a torch. He had his gun and bag of gunpowder. All he wore was a mundu and there were bruises on his body.

'My yejamanare!' I said. I brought him into the hut and shut the door. Pattelar squatted on the ground. I felt very sad, looking at him. I sat near him with folded hands and said, 'My yejamanare, to think that this should have happened to you! Tell me what I must do.'

Omana brought some hot kanji for Pattelar. As I stood by the well in the dark, pouring water for Pattelar to wash his hands and feet, I remembered many things. Pattelar had his kanji, then he asked me, 'Will you go with me?'

'Where will we go, yejamanare?'

Pattelar said, 'We'll go to Kodagu. I can hide in my nephew's house.'

He took some money out of the fold of his mundu, put it on the mat and said, 'This is for your expenses until this fellow comes back.' Then he raised his head and looked at Omana. Her face was in the shadows thrown by the lantern.

Would Omana feel sad, I wondered. It seemed to me that the fragrance of Pattelar's perfume filled the room. Omana came up to me, held my hands and began to cry. She put her face between my palms and sobbed. Pattelar sat staring at the ground. Omana's crying suffocated me. Trying to lift her face, I said, 'Omana, I am there for yejamanar.'

Slinking through the night, we reached the main road, hailed a night lorry passing by and arrived in Madikere.

As soon as we entered the courtyard of Pattelar's nephew's house, he hurried us into the shed used for distilling lemon grass oil, closed the door and said, 'It's dangerous for you here as well. I've just heard that Aunt's brothers are in town with gunmen. You had better go into the forest, Uncle.'

Pattelar's face fell. 'Who told you?'

'People who saw them in town. The story has spread to these parts, Uncle.' His face showed pity and fear.

We stayed in the shed till nightfall. Pattelar spoke to his nephew about the possibility of coming to an understanding with Sarojakka's relatives. He replied, 'What I heard is that they have already taken over Aunt's share. In which case, they'll hardly talk about conciliation now.' Pity touched his face once more. I could not bear it. I squatted in my corner and shut my eyes tight.

At night, we packed up the roast meat, salt, chillies and coconuts that Pattelar's nephew gave us. I put the bundle on my head. Pattelar took the gun, the bag of gunpowder and a torch. We entered the forest.

It was peaceful and quiet. My fears vanished as we moved like two ants beneath the shade of the sky-high trees. Walking briskly and enthusiastically, I said, 'Yejamanare, this is like our old hunting trips.' Pattelar didn't reply. He just turned and looked at me.

That night and the following day we ate our dried meat and coconut chutney, rested now and then and walked. I followed Pattelar, with the load on my head, thinking in wonder of the paths my life had taken.

The hiding place that Pattelar had in mind was on the far side of a river. We heard the murmur of the river from quite a distance. We were then walking under a wild champakam tree full of flowers. With a feeling of uncertainty, I paused beneath the tree. 'Yejamanare,' I called, 'the fragrance of your perfume!' Pattelar turned. He called me by my name, 'Thommi.'

'Yejamanare,' I answered. Pattelar stood on the fallen wild champakam blossoms, gun in hand. The roar of the river filled my ears. Pattelar said, 'You must never again make Omana cry.' 'My yejamanare,' I said, 'Omana is my life. Will I ever make her cry?'

Once again, there was only the sound of the rushing river. Pattelar leaned against the champakam tree. He said softly, not looking at me, 'Saroja would not have known, would she?' For a moment, the sunlight drifting through the leaves cast a net over Pattelar's face. I looked into his eyes, which were caught in the meshes of the net and said, 'No! No! No, yejamanare.' We walked to the river.

*

The river hissed amongst the rocks. From the hills on the other side, a brook sprang down a rocky slope, descending as a waterfall. Pattelar began crossing the river, gun and bag held high over his head. I followed with the bundle on my head, through the chest-deep foaming water. Pattelar was more than halfway across the river when I suddenly saw something strike a protruding rock, making splinters fly. A shot! I had not heard the sound of the shot above the roar of the water. I counted six gunmen running down the hill on the other bank. Pattelar was thrashing through the water towards the same bank. More shots hit the river, flinging up water and bits of rock. 'My God,' I said, 'they are using big rifles!' I turned and waded back like a madman. I stumbled, fell, went under and, flailing about, somehow reached the shore. Crouching behind the thickets at the water's edge, I looked back. Pattelar had climbed to the shore and was running, bent double, under cover of the bushes. Two of the gunmen were just behind him. I saw two others cut across the trees and run to block him in front. Suddenly, Pattelar stopped. He held the gun above his head in both hands and stood still. I cried, 'My yejamanare!' Shots came one by one, then together. I saw blood gush from Pattelar's chest, forehead and stomach. He fell over and lay still. I then proclaimed my great sorrow, my voice carrying across the white expanse of the river, 'My yejamanare! Ayyo! My yejamanare!'

Someone said, 'Don't let him go!' A few gunmen jumped across the rocks, cut through the water and rushed to the bank where I hid. I left the shelter of the thickets and ran for my life. 'Ayyo! I don't want to die! I am afraid of being shot!' Panting like a dog, I raced headlong with the fear of death in me. I heard the gunmen somewhere behind me. Beyond the wild champakam, there was a steep slope. I rolled down the slope into a grove of enormous trees. I clambered up one, clinging to it like a chameleon. The dusk-like darkness beneath the branches wrapped itself around me. I stopped climbing only when I felt as if my arms and legs were being torn off. I looked down. Where was I? My head reeled. I closed my eyes and wound my arms tight around the tree. The gentle warmth of urine flowed down my legs. Pressing my face into the moss-covered bark, I became yet another shadow amongst the dim branches. I stayed there like a lizard that had forgotten to move. Even when everything had become silent and quiet below, I did not move. After a long time I took hold of a branch and straddled it. In the evening, it rained. Even after the rain stopped, the leaves dripped on me all night long.

In the morning, I limped, shivering, to the river. I saw no one. Only Pattelar lay there. I crossed the river, walked up to his body and looked at his face wonderingly: this was Bhaskara Pattelar who lay on the grass by the river! The body had begun to smell. I held my nose with one hand and asked, 'Yejamanare, in this really you?' Pattelar lay cold on the grass with his eyes closed. Bhaskara Pattelar was dead! Bhaskara Pattelar, who had bought me mundus, who had found me a job, who had loved my wife, was dead! I squatted there and wept. Forgive me, master, for having once betrayed you! I looked at his swollen, discoloured face and wept again.

I opened his dead fingers and took the gun from his hand. For a moment, I held his wrist. I said, 'Get up, yejamanare. Sarojakka might be waiting for us.'

I covered Pattelar with grass and twigs. Then I took his gun, walked along the bank of the river, climbed on a rock and threw the gun into the rainbows that fluttered in the waterfall beneath me. I felt a kind of relief. And also, a kind of courage. Crossing the river, I ran to Ichilampadi to tell Omana that Pattelar was dead.

[*Translated by Gita Krishnankutty*]

The Scooter

Skuuttar

Sarah Joseph

The start of the journey was, naturally, very enjoyable. They were filled with expectations about the extremely beautiful part of the world they were going to. But scooters cannot be relied upon for long journeys to distant places. Before they had gone very far, a screw came loose and the scooter stopped on the highway!

The woman and child who were on the scooter got down first, then the man. He pushed the vehicle until it was in the shade. He examined it—leaning down, bending to one side, straightening himself, standing up. A scooter that has a screw that has become loose puts human beings in a quandary.

The rider could not identify which screw it was that had come loose, as a mechanic would have done. He wasted a lot of time knocking on the vehicle, tapping it all over. As for the woman, she stood leaning against a tree, pursing her lips tighter and tighter as her displeasure grew. The child lay asleep on her shoulder. As she shifted the one-and-a-half-year-old burden back and forth from her left shoulder to her right and then back again to the left, her hands began to ache.

'Please carry him!' she appealed to the man who was lost in the complicated nerve formations of the scooter. Exhausted with his efforts to find the spot where a screw had come loose, he turned round and glared at her.

Their eyes met and blazed in the hot noonday sun!

She shifted the child again from one shoulder to the other and ground her teeth.

Perspiration poured down his forehead and neck and dripped on his collar. As he worked hard, his face grew distorted. He was very selfish. He would distort his face like this even at the climax of the sexual act. She turned away in disgust.

The disgusting memory of her rough buttocks came to his mind as he tapped the engine cover of the scooter lying on its side. Thin, with protruding cheekbones and backbone, worn-out nails and cracked heels . . . she was growing less and less worthy these days to lie on a beautiful mattress! He wiped the grease on his lip with the back of his hand and spat out noisily. What could he share with her? Except turn her this way and that and enjoy her physically as if she were a scooter like this one, with a loose screw . . .

He lit a cigarette. He stood on the scooter's belly and gazed at the woman like a villain.

She moved. Cramps had begun to creep up her legs because of the child's weight.

'You too could carry him for a while,' she said, her voice full of dislike. Disgustedly, she cursed the crores and crores of seeds he had planted in her at a moment when she had not wanted him.

Their eyes met and blazed in the hot noonday sun!

A red Maruti car braked to a stop near the overturned scooter. The driver's puffy-cheeked friends put their heads out of the car and hooted. They slammed the doors and came out. Roaring like the evil spirits in sorcerers' stories, they circled the scooter. Two minutes later, she heard the scooter start up, turned and saw them shake the dust off their hands and get into the car while he straddled the scooter victoriously.

The scooter sped over a road shimmering in the noonday sun. As they flew, raising the dust over paths filled with black sand and crumbled horse dung, a vision of blue hills, green lakes and soft, cold mists descended into the travellers' hearts. Loosening their taut nerves, hope flew before them like a swarm of yellow dragonflies. The child dozed on the woman's lap, lulled to sleep by the sunshine, the gentle hum of the vehicle and the wind that blew against it. Thinking of the beautiful spot they were bound for, she raised her hand in a moment of tenderness and laid it seductively on his shoulder as if they had just begun the journey. He turned his head and rubbed his chin gently against her palm as if he too was within a dream of blue hills into which the mists melted.

But scooters cannot be relied upon for long journeys to distant places.

As they roared through sugar-cane groves, cemeteries and villages and reached a steep slope, a screw came loose and fell out. The scooter swayed and zigzagged. Hugging the child to her breast, the woman jumped off at a moment when it seemed safe. After spinning the man round for quite a while, the vehicle crashed against a tamarind tree on the roadside and hung down from it precariously.

The woman and the man looked at each other, their faces dark with anger. After grunting meaningfully as if to suggest that she was the reason for everything going wrong, he began to search for the spot where the screw had come loose. She struggled, perched on the uncomfortable surface of the slope with the crying child in her arms, unable to maintain her balance in any position. She shifted the child from one shoulder to another many times, but he had still not found the spot where the screw had come undone.

'Please hold the child!'

Pulling the child away from her shoulder resentfully, she held it out to him.

'And then? Will you repair this?' he asked, hitting the back seat of the scooter with his knotted fist. She curled her lips in deep contempt and laughed. Then she said, 'Yes, better than you're doing it!'

He stared at her, a spanner in his hand. He calculated: he could hit the right side of her forehead with just one throw. Or her protruding left cheekbone. Aiming a blow at the engine cover with the spanner, he overcame this thought.

Then he began to push the scooter up slowly. He found it difficult because the slope was really steep.

Deep satisfaction filled her as she stood watching him push the vehicle up, panting like a dog. This was the punishment for the dexterity with which he could do a variety of tasks on ordinary days. A revenge for the long hours of monotony when they had to stand or sit or lie down face to face in the closed flat, in the restricted space between the bits of wooden furniture, with nothing to say to each other. She could not contain her laughter and happiness when she realized this was an escape from the absolute boredom of having to see his face no matter where she turned. She suddenly burst out laughing.

He turned round as he pushed the vehicle up, finding it difficult even to breathe, and saw her break out over and over again into laughter, her head thrown back, pointing him out to the child as if he was a clown. The child too was pointing its little index finger at him. He shuddered, aware that all the suppressed cruelty in her had been unleashed.

He recalled that she smiled cheerfully only when he took home things he had bought on instalment schemes. He wanted to laugh too, in the pleasure of his secret: that it was to erase the unpleasantness of looking at her that he used to join instalment schemes, that he found more pleasure now in paying an instalment than in making love to her. And when he thought of how he had registered each of the things he now possessed through instalment schemes—the scooter, the TV, the fridge, the almirah, the cot, the mattress—in his own name and put away the documents secretly, without her knowing, at the bottom of his box, he burst into mocking laughter. Pointing his finger at her and the child, he laughed aloud. Outwardly, they seemed a happy family rolling over with laughter so delightedly in the middle of the road that their mouths were full of mud, but the precariousness of the steep slope made them lose their balance. The scooter slipped from his grip and overturned and the child fell from her hands! The two of them looked angrily at each other.

Their eyes met and blazed in the hot noonday sun!

The child wailed loudly. Neither he nor she paid any

attention. He was trying to lift the scooter with difficulty.

It was really hard to do so on that steep slope. She walked up to him with an arrogance that befitted the occasion, lifted up the carrier and managed to stand the vehicle upright by herself. Then, her face twisted in a mocking laugh, she made an effort to push the vehicle up, doggedly trying to cope with the lack of balance on the slope.

Even her partial victory over the scooter maddened him. Pointing to the crying child stumbling behind her, he shouted, 'Carry the child, woman!'

She looked round arrogantly. The child was clinging to his leg, crying. Turning her head away sharply, she tried with even more obstinacy and force to push the vehicle to the top.

He suddenly pushed the child out of the way and obstructed her with all the strength he had.

The scooter grated on the tarred road, unable to go even an inch backward or forward, caught between them as they exerted their strength in opposing directions, facing each other disgustedly.

A crazy Bullet that was tearing down the slope at a thousand horsepower speed braked suddenly beside them. It was a priest wearing gumboots, faded jeans and a torn cassock. He had dark glasses and his hair and beard were windblown. He stared at them in astonishment for a couple of minutes. Then he leaned the Bullet against a tamarind tree, took the crying child and put it in its mother's arms without saying a word, picked up the scooter as if it were a flower and put it on top of the steep slope. In two minutes, he tightened the loose screw, got on to his crazy bike and roared away at a thousand horsepower speed!

The scooter tore over the level road. Although sunlight, dust and wind attacked them all the time, the hair that blew against her in the breeze, the crackle of her saree, the wild forest scent of the nape of his neck kept arousing her. While flying through the crowded streets of the city, she raised her arms and put them around his neck so that the girls would feel jealous. The expectation of the limpid lakes they were going to reach seemed to him to waft mist into the blazing sunshine. He turned his head and rubbed his rough chin against her hands.

But scooters cannot be depended upon for long journeys to distant places!

Before their hopes could be realized, there was a severe petrol leak in the scooter. Dripping a trail of evil-smelling petrol behind them, the vehicle began to shake and sway. It was she who became aware of it first. She writhed with shame, seeing passers-by cover their noses, shudder and back away, while a pack of dogs, sniffing the dripping petrol, gathered behind them. The child began to retch, unable to bear the stench. She thought she would soon start throwing up as well. His condition was no different. His head was spinning with the odour.

'Which cursed pump did you buy the petrol from?' she shouted loud enough to pierce his ears.

The odour of the petrol unnerved him. He thought of the smiling face of the boy in the pump where he always bought petrol. He must remember to ask him whether petrol or oil ever had the smell of a dead rat's rotting carcass. He decided to stop under the shade of a tree on the roadside and examine the vehicle. Covering her nose with the end of her saree, she jumped off with the child.

He tied his handkerchief over his nose, lay prone on the ground and began his examination. An unbearable disgust and self-loathing took hold of him. The rotten, ulcerating womb of the scooter kept oozing fluid. Wherever he touched it, its limbs turned soft and the decayed skin kept crumbling in his hands. He nervously gripped its bent handlebar tight. It fell into his hand like a broken arm. Pale with fear, he flung it away. The dogs gathered in a circle around him and the scooter and howled.

She moved quite a distance away from him and sat on a culvert on the roadside. The child lay asleep on her lap. She thought of the dogs, of him, of the horrible odour as evil experiences in a bad dream.

Green lakes, blue hills, mist and the cold: these were the truth. She longed to snuggle into the green blanket that crept down the hills, enveloping them. She gazed steadily at the vehicles speeding towards them, raising dust. She was like a leaf spinning in a whirlwind of hopes.

She wished she could ask the young man tearing along on a gleaming Hero Honda to give her a lift to the land of the lakes. She thought, if he stopped his vehicle, she would put her hand round the Hero Honda fellow's shoulder in full view of her husband and fly joyfully away.

The scooter lay on the road like a rotten, stinking bandicoot. Catching sight of his frightening face in its shaky mirror, he shuddered and moved back. Walking backwards until he was quite far away from her, he sat on the roots of a tree, his head in his hands. The dogs began to lick the scooter and pull it apart with their teeth. Now and then they looked up at the sky and howled mournfully.

People came out inquiringly from the houses and tea shops in the vicinity, their noses covered. Once they discovered that the rotten, decayed smell came from this bandicoot, they began to protest.

'Hey! You have to take this thing away!' they called out to him. He did not raise his head. He wondered how he had become the owner of this thing. The number of people increased. And they began to get very angry.

'It's not mine,' he muttered.

'Nor mine either,' she said, turning her face away in disgust.

'Then d'you mean it's ours?' The people were furious. They pushed the two of them towards the scooter. They lifted the decaying corpse of the scooter whose limbs were coming apart and heaved it on to their heads before either of them could escape.

Their faces grew dirty with the stinking fluid that dripped from the scooter's rotting flesh. They began to weep and retch. Their eyes protruded from their sockets in fear. The dogs circled them, howling. The people laughed in satisfaction as they watched the man, woman and child turn and go away, crying and retching.

[*Translated by Gita Krishnankutty*]

Fear of Pulayas[1]

Pulappeedi

N.S. Madhavan

That Devi who manifests in all living beings as liberation . . .

It was not possible to see the compound from the room the
women used, the one situated above the western chamber.
Savitri therefore generally marked the passage of days and nights
through the opening in the nadumuttam, the courtyard of the
nalukettu, which could be seen from the door.

When Amma opened the granary downstairs, a miniature
whirlwind rose up, bearing the scent of new paddy. Just for a
minute—barely a minute—passion awoke in Savitri, like the
hiss of a thought. Startled, she scrambled up from the cow-
dung-smeared floor and went down the stairs to the veranda
surrounding the nadumuttam. Dusk had fallen. It was the hour
when the Pulayas started to hoot.

The Pulayas were just beginning to return from the fields to
their huts, hooting to warn passers-by on the road not to pollute
themselves. The first hoot was loud and strong. As her thoughts
slipped from the reddish throat from which it had emerged to
the Pulaya's black-skinned chest below, Savitri quickly walked
to the bathing tank near the kitchen, feeling confused. Parvathi

---

[1] Pulappeedi is the name of a custom that is said to have been prevalent in
parts of Kerala until the seventeenth century. Once a year, on a particular
day, lower caste men were allowed to touch upper caste women. The
women so touched had to accompany the men who touched them and
were no longer accepted in their own homes.

was seated on the steps of the tank, cleaning vessels with ashes and tamarind.

'Why so many kindis and lamps, Parvathi?'

'What do you mean? The veli, the annual funeral rites, is tomorrow. Don't you know?'

'I've no idea what's happening any more. I wonder whether Parameswaran's arrived from Madras.'

'Yes, he came yesterday, the junior Namboodiri.'

'This is the fifteenth year we're doing the rituals.'

'Umm . . .'

'How many more will there be, Parvathi?'

'What are you talking about?'

'After he died, I spent some time looking after Parameswaran. The child was only two years old when I was brought here as a bride. He's grown up now, ready to become a householder.'

When Savitri got back to the house, she saw her father-in-law, Puthinapilly Achan, looking at the things that had been made ready for the funeral rites: the karuka grass, the tortoise-shaped low stool, the bar of sandalwood. Standing there wearing only a konakam, he looked so old it saddened her.

As she climbed the stairs, the scent of new paddy wafted out again from the open door of the granary. The first time she had smelled it was on the night she first slept with her husband. The gurunathan had led Vasudevan and Savitri to their bedroom and withdrawn. All there had been in the bare room were a huge circle drawn with new paddy and a blanket in the middle of it.

'You're still a child, aren't you, Savitri? Haven't overcome your childishness in the least!' said Vasudevan. Savitri bit her lips and fought down laughter. That morning, according to tradition, Vasudevan had had a bath, wound jasmine flowers in her hair and begun to rub chandu on the front of her body. Every time Vasudevan touched her body, Savitri had giggled, not able to endure the ticklish sensation. Taken aback, he had quickly applied a spot of chandu on her neck and ended the ritual.

It was with some trepidation, therefore, that Vasudevan placed his hand on the right of her stomach, under the navel. When his fingers began to move, Savitri closed her eyes and started to pick out the scents in the room. The scent of new paddy, of the rasnadi powder that had been rubbed into his tuft, of the chandu that had been smeared on her own body that morning, of the old cow dung that had been smeared on the floor—she lay there drinking in the scents, separately and together. The next day, when she lowered her hand along with Vasudevan into the copper pot filled with water to catch the manathukanni fish inside it, for the first time she felt shy to be touched.

She heard voices downstairs, of those who had come to perform the veli rites. She took her upper cloth off the bamboo clothesline, put it on and went down. Amma asked when she saw her, 'What's the matter, Tatri, you've been going up and down endlessly? As the time for the rites draws near, your mind is crowded with thoughts, isn't it?'

Amma hurried into the kitchen, came back and said, 'Look, have you seen this? It's the first time I've seen one. Parameswaran brought it from Madras. It's an apple. What's that verse Vasudevan taught you, Tatri?'

'I don't remember, Amme.'

'A for Apple. You wouldn't have forgotten, Ittitatri . . .'

After Vasudevan died, Savitri began to sleep in the women's room above the western chamber. One day, when she appeared at the foot of the stairs with the first-level English reader Vasudevan had ordered from London, Amma stopped her, 'Stand where you are, you inauspicious Mars-in-the-seventh-house woman! Wasn't it you who killed my Vasudevan?'

'What are you saying, Amma?'

'You entered this house and snatched away my Kuttan.'

'Was it my fault I was married into this house?'

'Ah, listen to her baby talk, the little infant! You began to entice my boy the moment you set foot here. Weren't you with Vasudevan all the time, learning Ingirees, having him read to you . . . He was lost to this illam from then.'

'Amme!'

'You evil one! Sitting there upstairs, doing nothing at all. Give that to me!'

She snatched the book from Savitri's hand and murmured as she tore it, 'Learn Ingirees, sprout a little tail like those subcollector sahebs have and walk around, you nasty woman!' The pictures of the apple Savitri had never seen in her life, of the instrument called the xylophone she'd never heard lay scattered over the nadumuttam.

The next day, when the rites were over and everyone had left, Savitri went back to her room, wanting to be alone once more. It was during her two-day period of solitude that Amma had stopped her raving.

Savitri had her period around the day of the Karthika star. And Amma about ten days later. One day, while she sat by herself in the windowless room in the western wing where the women had to spend their time when they had their period, Amma came up. 'Oh God, I have to sit with this sinful creature for two days!'

They managed to get through the daytime in silence. Savitri was too afraid even to sob. Suddenly, Amma came up to her, caught her hand and lifted it. 'When I see this hand, shorn of bangles, sorrow thuds, dup-dup, through my heart, just like grains of rice-malar popping in the fire.'

Amma made Savitri turn round and started to run her fingers through her hair.

'Tatri, remember, I'm like you too. Rituals of collective prayer and temple festivals are all my husband wants. He has no enthusiasm at all for the affairs of the household. I can wear brass bangles on both my hands, that is all.'

Savitri went down the stairs; it was a bad habit with her. She walked to the pounding shed in search of Parvathi, but she was not there. Going back, she ignored the scent of new paddy. Thoughts kept repeating themselves endlessly in her mind—the only thing was, they whirled round and round like the pebbles in a rattle, making all kinds of sounds. Her knowledge was so limited. She had to face this solitude with nothing for company except a single book, the Adhyatma Ramayanam.

Which is why, parrot, teller of the Ramayanam,[2] you've been telling me the story of the Ramayanam all this while. Now I'll tell you my story. There's no one but you, my baby parrot, in my cage. All I see is the sky that is visible from the compound. Beyond the compound, I see only the ground. And the touch-me-not plants on the way to the temple. Grains of gravel and sometimes hairy blades of karuka grass. All I hear is—but I never sharpen my ears to listen. The rare occasions when I do is when the wind wafts towards me the sounds of the rites of exorcism performed on the unmarried girls in the Nair quarter. (Why exorcize these evil spirits, parrot? Isn't it a good thing for one body to hold two people?) I also sharpen my ears when I hear a woman's hoot among the Pulayas' hoots. Scents: they are with me all the time. My own, when I wake up, before I have a bath, of vaka and inja after my bath, when I have a period—I repeat myself through scents. Then, touch: no one touches me, except my clothes. Sometimes, when the washerwoman puts too much starch in them, there is an added roughness when they rub against me. My journeys: when sin stabs my thoughts, I climb up and down the stairs.

'This is my story, my story . . .' Savitri pressed her face into her mat and wept. Then it struck her for the first time that she was making no effort at all to control herself; she decided to weep loudly, as if it was a rite.

'Oppol, elder sister,' Parameswaran called from the other side of the door.

Savitri sat up with her head bent. Parameswaran asked, 'Why are you crying, Oppol?'

'There's a pain in my stomach.'

'Does it hurt badly?'

'Mm . . .'

'On the right side?' asked Parameswaran.

'Mm . . .'

---

[2] Thunchath Ezhuthachan, author of the *Adhyatma Ramayanam* in Malayalam, uses a parrot to narrate the story.

'Below the navel?'

'Mm . . .'

'A throbbing pain?'

'Yes.'

'A swelling?'

'I don't know,' said Savitri.

'None of the symptoms look good. Might have to take you to the hospital in a palanquin. I'll examine you.'

'No, don't. I was telling lies. Besides, young Namboodiri boys who have finished their samavarthanam cannot enter this room.'

'What are you talking about, Oppol? There was not even the grain of a lie in that weeping. I'm studying medicine in Madras, don't you know? In two years, I'll be Dr Puthinapilly.'

'You can lie down, Oppol,' said Parameswaran as he came in. Although she saw Parameswaran as a shadow because of the great square of light in the door, Savitri burrowed out of that shadow the child she used to send out to play after oiling his body, giving him a bath, touching his eyes with collyrium, fastening on him a konakam made from the spathe of an areca-nut leaf . . .

Parameswaran sat on the ground and ran his hands over the right side of her stomach, under the navel, to find out if there was a swelling. After a while, his hands stopped moving. Then Savitri felt his fingers starting to move gently. An indistinct throbbing, like the fluttering of a dragonfly's wings—she thought it was only her fancy. At the first tangible movement, she sprang up.

When Parameswaran got up, Savitri cried, 'Get out of my sight!'

'Oppol . . .' Savitri thought that Parameswaran lunged forward. She pulled back the wooden container holding holy ash that hung in a rope basket from the rafters and swung it at Parameswaran's face. Blood spurted from his forehead. Parameswaran turned and ran. And then there was the thudding of footsteps down the stairs.

'What's that? What's that wound on your forehead?'

'It doesn't matter.'

'Tell me, Parameswara. Shiva, Shiva! The blood is running into your eye!' Amma began to weep.

'Oppol sent for me saying she had a stomach ache. When I went there, she looked strange. She smiled and signalled to me to go into the room. I turned and ran and hit my head against the stair rail.' Parameswaran walked to the well to wash his face.

Moments later, they heard his father, the senior-most male member of the Puthinapilly family, shout from the veranda, 'Get out at once, out of the gate! This is no place for people like you. Get out, will you, you despicable creature!'

Dusk had deepened by the time Savitri walked out of the gate in the fence at the back of the house, into the path to the river. A dusk filled with the hoots of the Pulayas was being gradually taken over by the birds and cicadas. Chathan, the last Pulaya to remain in the compound, scraped the earth off his spade, hoisted it on his shoulder and began to walk home. When he reached the crossroads at the spot where the path from the Namboodiri illam led to the river, Chathan hooted. He saw an unusual sight: an antharjanam, a Namboodiri woman, draped from head to foot in white cloth, was coming that way, carrying the umbrella these women used to cover their faces. He crept behind a jackfruit tree whose trunk was covered with white blotches.

Savitri went round the tree and asked, 'What's your name?'

'Thampuratti, mistress!'

'What's your name?'

'Chathan.'

'Will you come with me as far as the river, Chathan?'

'No. The men in the house will kill me tomorrow.' Chathan took a step forward, intending to run away, but Savitri caught his hand to hold him back.

Savitri started to walk with Chathan to the river. As soon as darkness fell, fireflies began to flicker in the thickets. The hollow beat of a mizhavu could be heard from the temple in the distance.

Chathan stood on the river bank leaning against a pooparuthi tree that hung low over the river. Savitri squatted on the ground and let her umbrella float on the water. Then she stood up and let the upper cloth that covered her slip into the water. A full square, it floated away like a carpet.

Lifting up her eyelashes with difficulty, as if they were an imponderable weight, Savitri surveyed the world from her height. Through eyes dazzled by the novelty of vision, she saw the flaming palm-leaf torches moving across the opposite shore as red patches of colour. For the first time in her life, she squared her shoulders daringly and the deer-faces on her still-young breasts turned away from each other, pointing left and right. Standing close to Chathan so that their bodies touched, Savitri bent forward and hooted loudly.

Acknowledgement
It was Muthirangot Bhavathrathan Namboodiripad's short story 'The Fate of Widow' which inspired me to write this story. I have also used a quotation from it.—N.S. Madhavan

[Translated by Gita Krishnankutty]

Note on Contributors

V. Abdulla was born in 1921 in Tikkodi near Kozhikode. After graduating MA and BL, Abdulla joined Orient Longman, from where he retired as divisional director in charge of publication. He published many books of translations from Malayalam into English, mainly in the area of prose fiction and including novels and stories by M.T. Vasudevan Nair, S.K. Pottekkat, Malayattoor Ramakrishnan, N.P. Mohamed and Vaikom Muhammad Basheer. In 1998 he received the Yatra Award.

Anand, the pen name of P. Sachidanandan, who has brought out several novels since his first one, *Aalkuuttam* (The crowd), appeared in 1970, is also a distinguished short story writer. In addition he has published plays and collections of essays. He won the Kerala Sahitya Akademi award for the short story in 1981 and for the novel in 1985. Among his other awards is the Kendra Malayala Sahitya Akademi Award (1997).

Lalithambika Antherjanam wrote many collections of short stories and one novel, *Agnisaakshi*, which won the Kerala Sahitya Akademi Award and the Vayalar Ramavarmma Award. Most of her stories reveal the little-known world inhabited by Namboodiri women of her time and the agonizing experiences they endured because of the severe social restrictions they had to live with.

R.E. Asher is Professor Emeritus of Linguistics at the University of Edinburgh. His publications include translations of five Malayalam novels, grammars of Tamil and Malayalam, and books on the literature of the French Renaissance, on the history of linguistics and on contemporary Malayalam literature. In 1983 he was elected Fellow of the Kerala Sahitya Akademi.

Vaikom Muhammad Basheer, one of Kerala's finest writers, wrote several books in Malayalam, of which the best known is 'Ntuppuppaakkoraaneendaarnnu!' (*Me Grandad 'ad an Elephant*). Basheer revolutionized the art of storytelling in Malayalam using lively, colloquial idiom to describe everyday matters. He was awarded the Sahitya Akademi Fellowship in 1970 and the Padma Shri in 1982.

Kamala Das was born in March 1932 in Punnayoorkulam in the Malabar district of Kerala. She is the daughter of V.M. Nair and the well-known Malayalam poet Nalapat Balamani Amma. A prolific and bilingual writer, with innumerable poems, short stories and novels in English and Malayalam to her credit, she writes as Madhavikutty in Malayalam and as Kamala Das in English. She won the Kerala Sahitya Akademi Award in 1968 for *Thanuppu*.

An American in love with Kerala, Donald R. Davis, Jr teaches at Bucknell University, Pennsylvania. He speaks Malayalam fluently. He has translated and edited a collection of short stories by M. Mukundan to be published shortly by Michigan University Press.

Sarah Joseph is a professor of Malayalam and feminist activist. Her published collections include *Paapathara* (The ground of sin), *Kaadinte sangiitam* (The music of the woods) and a collection of novellas, *Nanma tinmakalude vriksham* (The tree of good and evil).

Gita Krishnankutty has translated many short stories and novels from Malayalam into English. She has translated M.T. Vasudevan Nair's *Kaalam*, N.P. Mohamed's *The Eye of God* and Kamala Das's *Childhood in Malabar*. She has also published a selection of the writings of Lalithambika Antherjanam, which includes short stories and extracts from her autobiography.

N.S. Madhavan joined the Indian Administrative Service and has worked in Bihar, Kerala and Delhi. He has published two collections of short stories, *Choolaimeettile savangal* (The corpses of Choolaimedu) and *Higvitta*. He won the Kerala Sahitya Akademi Award in 1995 for *Higvitta*.

N.P. Mohamed has won the Kerala Sahitya Akademi Award and the Sahitya Akademi Award. His books include *Thoppiyum thattavum* (The cap and the veil), *Prasidantinte aadyaathe maranam* (The president's first death) and the novel *Daivattinte kannu* (The eye of god).

M. Mukundan was born in Mahé (Mayyazhi), then a French enclave in Kerala. He has written twenty-seven books in Malayalam including a selection of essays and a play. He won the Sahitya Akademi Award in 1993 and his novel *Mayyazhippuzhayude tiirangalil* translated as *On the Banks of the Mayyazhi* won the Crossword Award for Indian language fiction in English translation (1998). The second Mayyazhi novel, *Daivattinte vikritikal*, which won the Kendra Malayala Sahitya Akademi Award in 1992, was published as *God's Mischief* by Penguin Books India in 2002.

M.T. Vasudevan Nair, one of the most versatile writers in Malayalam today, has published short stories, novels, screenplays and articles on the state of literature and cinema in India. Awards he has won include the Kerala Sahitya Akademi (1959 and 1978) and Central Sahitya Akademi (1970) awards, and the Jnanpith Award (1996). His screenplays too have won many awards.

T. Padmanabhan has published twelve collections of short stories including *Makhansinghinte maranam* (The death of Makhan Singh), *Saakshi* (The witness), *Kaalabhairavan* and *Patmaanabhante kathakal* (Padmanabhan's short stories). His autobiographical work *Ente katha, ente jiivitam* (My story, my life) was published to much acclaim. In 1973 he won the Kerala Sahitya Akademi Award for *Saakshi* but he declined it.

Karoor Neelakanta Pillai became a teacher after clearing the seventh standard from a vernacular school. Founder leader of the Writers' Co-operative in Kottayam, he published thirty-seven books, most of them short story collections. He won the Kerala Sahitya Akademi Award.

Thakazhi Sivasankaran Pillai wrote more than twenty-five novels. *Thoottiyude makan* (The scavenger's son, 1947) was the first work to win him acclaim. *Chemmiin* (Shrimps), *Randitangazhi* (Two measures of rice) and *Kayar* (Coir) are some of his well-known novels. He won the Kerala Sahitya Akademi Award in 1965 for *Eenippadikal*. He was awarded the Jnanpith Award in 1965, the Padma Bhushan in 1985 and the Sahitya Akademi Fellowship in 1989.

S.K. Pottekkat won the Kendra Malayala Sahitya Akademi Award and the Jnanpith Award for the novel *Oru deesathinte katha* (The story of a nation). He was president of the Writers' Co-operative and executive member of the Sahitya Akademi.

C.V. Sreeraman's published collections include *Vaasthuhaaraa* (Dispossessed), which won the Kerala Sahitya Akademi Award in 1983, and *Sriiraamante kathakal* (Sreeraman's stories), which won the Kendra Malayala Sahitya Akademi Award in 1999.

A.J. Thomas is the assistant editor of *Indian Literature*, the journal of the Sahitya Akademi. He has translated the work of Paul Zacharia, among others.

O.V. Vijayan broke new ground in Malayalam literature with his novel *Khasaakkinte itihaasam* (The legends of Khasak, 1969). Since then he has published several novels, short stories and essays. His third novel, *Gurusaagaram* (The infinity of grace, 1987), won the Kendra Malayala Sahitya Akademi Award, the Kerala Sahitya Akademi Award and the Vayalar Ramavarmma Award. Vijayan is also an accomplished political cartoonist and his works have appeared in the *Hindu*, *Statesman*, *Mathrubhumi* and *Far Eastern Economic Review*.

Paul Zacharia is one of Kerala's best-selling writers. Collections of his stories available in English translation are *Bhaskara Pattelar and Other Stories*, *Reflections of a Hen in Her Last Hour* and *Praise the Lord: What News, Pilate?*